PART 1

THE RULE OF THREES

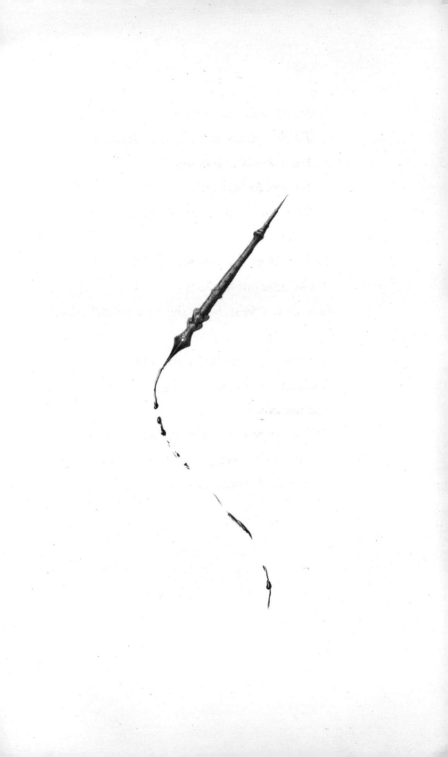

B efore the two School Masters named Rhian and Rafal, there was another.

A young lad with dark red curls and a smattering of freckles, who'd presented himself to the Storian, like all School Masters who sought to rule.

The Pen assessed the boy, long and steel, sharp at both ends, its tip like an eye.

Then it spoke.

> *In exchange for immortality*
> *In exchange for eternal youth*
> *I choose you.*
> *A soul that is as Good as it is Evil.*
> *But every School Master faces a test.*
> *Yours is balance.*
> *Between the Goodness of your soul*
> *And the Evil of its shadow.*

Neither side must win out.
Tip the balance and the test is failed.
You will wither and die.
You will be replaced.
Raise your hand to seal this oath.

The boy does, his vow sealed with blood.

But he does not last long.

Less than a year later, the new School Masters find him.

A trembling voice in the shadows.

A withered old man.

The test failed.

"What happened?" they ask before he dies.

But it is the wrong question.

They should have asked who he is.

FALL

OF THE

SCHOOL

FOR

GOOD AND EVIL

FALL
OF THE
SCHOOL
FOR
GOOD AND EVIL

ALSO BY SOMAN CHAINANI

"I said you were real . . . ," Arabella breathed. "I told them . . ."

Rafal slid off the bed. "Sometimes it's hard to tell Good from Evil. Lately, I've made mistakes. First with a student. Then with my brother. But do you know how I could tell you were special? I saw you reading a storybook. My favorite of all the Storian's tales. About an entitled little girl who tries to sweet-talk a bear and he eats her in the end. Most people find it a horrible story. Not you. You knew it was the girl who was the villain and the bear the hero. You knew Good was Evil and Evil was Good. That's what I need in a student. Someone who won't be fooled. But before I take you, I need you to make me a promise."

The girl stared at him, his eyes like green pools, so deep, so clear that she seemed lost in a trance.

"Will you do anything I tell you to?" Rafal asked. "Protect me? Obey me? *Fight* for me? And in return, I'll open the gates to a fairy-tale world. My faithful soldier . . ."

He waited for her to come to him, his back to the door, the girl hovering in the corner beneath a painting of a red fox.

When Arabella spoke, her voice was a ghostly rasp. "You didn't believe me."

The School Master looked at her strangely, not understanding.

Then he realized she wasn't looking at him. She was looking *behind* him.

Rafal whirled around—

A broom handle came down, smashing him in the head.

3.

Far, far away, in the middle of the Savage Sea, Aladdin was trying not to get slaughtered by vampires.

"Hephaestus, help!" he yelled, slashing at two Night Crawlers with a sword he'd grabbed from the armory below decks. But like everything on the *Buccaneer*, it was old and dull and rusty, and wouldn't hold off the pale-faced bloodsuckers much longer. He needed to use his spells, his fingerglow that had been unlocked at school, but it was still new to him and under stress, he couldn't perform, the light on his fingertip smoking uselessly. The nighttime ambush by the black-veiled bloodsuckers had come so suddenly, so violently, that his legs and mind were still wobbly; he couldn't focus his emotions or summon his magic. Hephaestus was clearly having the same problem because he was without a weapon and down to his fists, battering his own batch of Night Crawlers, the strapping, bald-headed lad kicking and punching them overboard before they could sink teeth into their intended target: not Aladdin or Hephaestus, but young James Hook, cowering behind a mast.

THE RULE OF THREES

"You are a *pirate*, Hook! To sit there like a lump while we fight for you takes some kind of pride!" Hephaestus lashed, snatching a Crawler and heaving him over the rail. "Or lack thereof."

Normally, James would have been incited by another boy shaming him, but when it came to Night Crawlers, he'd sacrifice his dignity. For one thing, he'd already spent ten days in their clutches, sucked of so much blood he'd almost perished, after Rafal had bartered Hook's distinctive blue blood to them. For another, they no doubt remembered Hook's blood and still had a taste for it, because they were coming straight for him, all five, gnashing sharp teeth and flaring raw eyes, as if they intended to devour more than just his blood this time. Thankfully, Hephaestus and Aladdin were holding them at bay—until James heard screeching and turned to see ten more Crawlers leaping onto deck from their ship, the *Inagrotten*, which they'd pulled right up against the *Buccaneer*. James scrambled backwards, looking for a weapon to defend himself and finding only a rancid-smelling mop.

"Use Rhian's magic!" Aladdin shouted.

"It's gone!" Hook shouted back, for the Good School Master's magic, the piece of sorcerer's soul that Rhian had breathed into his body, seemed to have vanished from inside of him.

Had he used it all up when he'd stolen the best Evers and Nevers from the School for Good and Evil? Had Rhian a way to reclaim it, even from far off? No time to consider such things. The Crawlers were flooding past the Everboys' defense, Aladdin and Hephaestus thrown aside, a score of vampires storming straight at James—

BOOM!

The impact of a cannon rattled the ship like an earthquake and James turned to see an iron ball fired off the *Buccaneer* blast at the *Inagrotten* . . .

. . . and miss.

He leaned over the rail to see Princess Kyma working the cannon, shoving another ball into the bore.

"We can't attack until you hit!" a deep voice berated her, and Kyma looked up to see the Pirate Captain of Blackpool hanging off a rope from the sails, along with nine sword-armed Nevers from the School for Evil, all suspended off their own ropes, ready to leap the distance between ships and invade the *Inagrotten* once they had the Crawlers on their heels.

BOOM!

Another miss.

"It won't shoot straight!" Kyma carped, wrestling the rusted, squeaking iron.

THE RULE OF THREES

"Crikey, we need a new ship," the Captain murmured, tilting up his wide black hat. "Never mind. *Charge!*"

The Pirate Captain and his Nevers dove off their ropes, landing on the Night Crawlers' vessel, the Captain swinging two swords and scattering the vampires, while hulking, one-eyed Timon and the squadron of Evil students unleashed their villain talents, dispatching Crawlers with fire, ice, and whatever their wicked souls could produce until soon, the vampire ship was contained.

That didn't solve the problem of the Crawlers left on the *Buccaneer*, though, and they came hurtling at Hook now with added vengeance—

Kyma landed in front of James, spewing spells from her fingerglow, stunning Night Crawlers who dropped face-first to deck. She turned and gave Hook a stone-cold look—a look that reminded him that she and her friends had trusted him as their *leader* and that is why they were here in the first place and if he did not start fighting, then he wasn't their leader after all. It was the girl's glare that finally sprung James to action, bashing heads with the end of his mop to make up for his cowardice before. Only he was too late, a Night Crawler racing up behind him, none of his friends' cries of warning sounding in time. The vampire seized James and sank teeth into his shoulder, spraying bright blue blood before Kyma felled the Crawler with a spell. Hook collapsed to his knees, clutching the gash, but more vampires were coming, pinning him to the floor and plunging teeth in, like a fawn to panthers, the Crawlers' teeth stained blue as they reared their heads, until James realized he was going to die like this, to these demons, to these perversions of nature, and suddenly his heart burned like an acid bomb, a rage he'd never known, his hand stabbing up in their faces like a claw out of a grave—

Glow exploded from his palm, a golden wall that engulfed the vampires and ignited them all to flame.

Shrieking in horror, they leapt overboard, back onto their ship, drowning it in fire, before it dove underwater in retreat, the Pirate Captain and his Nevers rope-flying back onto the *Buccaneer* just in time.

Everyone stared at James, shellshocked, the Pirate Captain included, but Hook was panting in a crouch, blue blood soaking his shirt.

"Still there . . ." he gasped. "Rhian's magic . . . still there . . ."

"That's a good thing," the Pirate Captain assured, kneeling at his side.

But Hook shook his head as if to say that it wasn't.

4.

A short while later, they sat for dinner: the Pirate Captain, Hook, Aladdin, Hephaestus, and Kyma.

It was three days into the journey from school and it had become routine—this group eating food from the larders and sitting in the dusty dining room, adorned with the portraits of past Pirate Captains who had served as Blackpool headmasters, while the Nevers preferred to eat alone in their cabins or angle for fish up on deck and split the spoils amongst themselves. Even away from school, it was Evers with Evers and Nevers with Nevers.

"Didn't plan on a vampire ambush," Aladdin grumbled. "One of them bit me in the bum!"

"We won, didn't we?" said Kyma. "Whole point of why we came. To make it to Neverland and fight for Good, instead of staying at school where Good was cheating to win."

"I blame our School Master. All went wrong at the Circus because of him," Aladdin carped. "First Evers to lose to Evil in ages. So embarrassing. At least as pirates we can be *real* heroes."

"And we'll all be heroes when we land in Neverland tomorrow and dethrone a rotten king," Hook said, folding back his fresh white sleeves so they wouldn't dip in his clam soup. A futile bit of fussiness, given his shoulder wound was spotting blue blood on his shirt through its bandage. "We'll anchor near the east beach, away from Pan's lair, but it won't be long before he's alerted to our presence. He has fairies, cannibals, Lost Boys on his side, plus all his minions."

"Who do we have on ours?" Aladdin asked.

James slurped at his soup.

"Your sister? Your mum?" Kyma pressed. "Anyone?"

"Both escaped to Ooty after Dad died," James muttered. "No one else worth their salt. No one like that boy Fala, who beat all of you at the Circus. Wanted him on my crew over anyone else. But by the time I went to find him, he was gone."

"So it's us against the world, then. A pirate's life, indeed," the Pirate Captain sighed. He leaned back in the lamplight, revealing steely green eyes and dark, rumpled locks under his hat. "It's also no secret we need a new ship if we're to have any chance against Panny Boy. This ship can't even shoot straight. Which begs the question . . . Where is the *Jolly Roger*, James? Where is your famed family vessel that you promised us passage on?"

James didn't look up. "We have to get it back first."

"From who?" said Aladdin.

THE RULE OF THREES

"From *Panny Boy*," James gritted.

"Ha!" The Pirate Captain chuckled. "A family that can't even hold on to its ship. Now I see why no Hook has killed a Pan before."

"No Hook has had as talented a crew as this one," James snapped at him. "Mark my words: We will kill Pan. We will free Neverland from that tyrant. We will take back my ship. And Neverland will have a new king: Captain James Hook."

"I'm afraid the only captain on this ship is *me*," the Pirate Captain pointed out. "And King does sound better than Blackpool headmaster. Who's to say I won't challenge you for the throne?"

"Neverland is a land of youth. You are eighteen years old. In Neverland that makes you an old man and no one in Neverland listens to old men," James barbed back. His voice turned colder as if he took the Captain's threat seriously. "Besides, you left Blackpool full of students expecting you to bring back Pan's head and here you are talking about *deserting* your post—"

"Hold on," Kyma cut in, blinking so fast her pink eyeshadow strobed. "No one said anything about *killing* Pan. You told us you needed us to save Neverland from a wicked king. That's why we came with you on this mission. To free Neverland's people and remove the king from power. I wouldn't be on this ship if I'd known you were hunting down a child."

"He isn't a child. He's a filthy little dictator who many in Neverland would kill if only they knew how," James scorched. "What do you expect us to do, princess? Gently coax him off the throne with cookies and hugs? There's no way to free Neverland without erasing Pan off this earth. Until then, we're all at his mercy."

"We're Evers. We're *Good*. We're not killing anyone. And if that's the plan, then kindly take us back to school," Kyma retorted, nodding at Aladdin and Hephaestus for support.

Neither boy offered it.

Aladdin peeked at Hephaestus. "I mean, if Pan is that bad . . . isn't getting rid of him the Good thing to do? Heph and I came on this ship to be heroes. To go questing for glory faster than we would have at school. And killing a villainous king? Sounds like glory to me."

Kyma glowered at her boyfriend. "Evers only kill their Nemesis. We don't go around to foreign lands delivering vigilante justice."

"Trust me, princess," Hook growled. "Once you know this Pan, your tune will change."

"But you said no one can kill him . . . ?" Aladdin asked.

"I said no one knows *how*," James explained. "Each Pan is

given a hundred years, frozen in age when he reaches the prime of youth. This one is named Peter. But you can kill a Pan if you drain him of his youth. Youth kept in his shadow. Kill Peter Pan's shadow and you kill Peter Pan."

"A shadow?" Aladdin said. "How do you kill a shadow?"

Kyma suddenly looked curious herself.

The Pirate Captain answered: "The same way a shadow attaches to a soul. By *magic*. No Hook has ever found sorcery strong enough to do the job. But James and I have. Why do you think James and I conspired to steal Rhian's powers? Pan's shadow is no match for a School Master's magic."

He turned to James, expecting his former student to mirror his smile, but Hook was quiet, brows creased, eyes furtive.

"I can't find it," he said, almost to himself. "Rhian's magic. I can't find it inside me the way I could Rafal's. When Rafal breathed his soul into mine, it was always there like a glow, guiding me. But his brother's . . . it hides. And when it came out up there, it was rageful, like dragon fire, like it would level everything in its path. Only now it's all gone again."

"Precisely what one would expect from a Good School Master's soul," the Pirate Captain heartened. "It saved your life and will be there whenever you need it. What else could you want?"

James nodded, bowing his head. But inside, he was thinking

how terrible Rhian's magic felt, how terrible it had always felt, even when it was saving his life. The question hung in the air: What else could you want? Hook wished his answer silently.

I want it out of me.

5.

Rafal stirred to the sharp reminder that he was now mortal.

Blood dripped down his head, pain ricocheting in his skull. Decades of eternal life had left him coddled. He'd forgotten blood and pain were possible.

"Who are you?" a hard voice clipped.

Rafal opened his eyes and found himself flat against a window, tied to Arabella's bedpost, three old men watching him.

They wore long gray cloaks and tall black hats, each with a stark white beard, and Rafal sensed from their sneering looks and the sagebrush dangling from their necklaces that these men thought they were holy.

"He's the devil!" a woman's voice hissed, and Rafal spotted Arabella's mother near the door, clutching her daughter and pointing at him. "Come to kidnap her to his wicked school! Evil incarnate, he is."

Rafal's eyes locked on Arabella. Here he thought she'd be

his loyal soldier and instead she'd betrayed him to Mummy. Yet another mistake in telling Good from Evil, his compass thoroughly broken. Worse still, his plan to protect against his twin had foolishly backfired. He was captive in mortal danger now, while Rhian was probably strolling town, eating pastries.

"We long suspected the presence of magic in Gavaldon," the man with the longest beard spoke. "We, the Elders of Gavaldon and all the Elders before us, entrusted with protecting this village. Light magic or Dark magic, though, we couldn't tell. The storybooks that mysteriously appear in our bookshops . . . the forest that no matter where you enter, leads straight back into town . . . the talking fairy caught by a child . . ."

He reached into his pocket and pulled out a small jar.

The School Master's eyes grew.

Inside the jar was a green-faced fairy with black wings and sharp teeth bared at Rafal, shouting curses, as if she blamed him for this predicament.

"Marialena?" he rasped.

"Ah, so you know this magic," the second Elder said, with the second-longest beard. "And given you planned to kidnap young Arabella here, we have our answer to whether this magic is Light or Dark."

Rafal stared intently at Marialena, his former student and

seer who he'd turned into a fairy as punishment and who he'd now reward if she could use her foresight to extricate them from this cursed village. But from the way she was frantically buzzing in the jar, it was clear she either didn't know what their future held or she didn't like what she'd seen.

"Do you know what becomes of Dark magic in our world?" the first Elder asked, drawing towards Rafal. "We bring it to the Light for everyone to see. And there is no better Light than the holy flame."

"It's what we do to witches who practice Dark magic in our village," said the second Elder, looming over the bed. "Burn them at the pyre and scatter their ashes in the forest."

Do I even have my magic anymore? Rafal thought. He glanced at the unhealed gash on his arm. If his immortality was compromised, would his sorcerer powers be too? His eyes roamed the room. Only one way to find out.

"But you'll enjoy a good burning, won't you?" said the last Elder, reaching for him. "A devil returned to hellfire . . ."

Rafal smiled at him. "I'll enjoy this more." He kicked backwards and smashed the window with his boot, raining glass inside. Elders shielded themselves; Rafal caught a shard and sliced through his binds, launching off the bed. He snatched the fairy jar from the old men, sprang through the broken window, and soared out into swollen gray clouds, away from Gavaldon, arms wide, like a high-flying hawk.

Relief washed over him. His magic was still intact.

He tried to fly faster, with his usual speed and aggression . . . but where there once was power, there was weakness instead— the void of something missing.

Now he understood. The magic was fading. Just like his healing.

The Storian was warning him.

Him and Rhian.

Either they repaired things between them fast or their test would be failed.

Their lives and powers cut short.

Rafal's heart kickstarted. Forget this Reader nonsense. Forget the prophecy. Forget protecting himself against Rhian and suspecting his twin of future crimes. They needed to love each other again. The way they used to. That was the path to happiness. For *both* of them.

He held up the jar and looked at Marialena. "I've never been so relieved to get back to schoo—"

CRACK! He slammed into an invisible barrier, dropping out of the sky and skidding down the cold, rubbery shield before landing face-first on the ground. Somewhere in his fall, he'd lost hold on the fairy jar and seconds later, it came shattering into grass, Marialena ejected.

"My leg . . . I think it's broken . . ." the School Master moaned, waiting in vain for it to heal.

He tried to crawl forward, to will himself to flee, but he was beaten not just by the fall, but also by the shield, still there in front of him, walling off Gavaldon from the Woods, like a pane of glass.

Then he saw Marialena on the *other* side of it.

"What's happening?" Rafal croaked. "The shield let Rhian and I through to get into Gavaldon. Why is it back—"

"*Balance,*" Marialena hissed.

Rafal's eyes widened.

Balance, which had let him and his twin into this town to take two Readers, one for Good and one for Evil.

Balance that must have been broken for the shield to re-appear.

Which meant . . .

Rhian.

He'd done something.

The musk of smoke cut through his thoughts.

Slowly Rafal raised his eyes.

They were coming for him, their torches spitting fire.

Not just the Elders.

The whole town, too.

He had nowhere to fly.

No immortal healing to protect him.

Not even healthy legs to run.

Panicked, he whirled back to the fairy . . . the fairy who could see what he should do next . . .

But he didn't have her either.

Marialena was gone.

6.

A short while earlier, Rhian was tramping through Gavaldon, armed with a chocolate croissant.

He was back to his humdrum disguise, wellies, trench coat, and wizened old beard, and trying to waste away time until his brother was done kidnapping a child. Rafal had insisted Rhian do the same—find a young soul who could replace the Evers he'd lost—but the Good School Master had no intention of stripping a child away from its rightful home. That sounded Evil, *very* Evil, and given how badly he was trying to be Good right now, better if he just wandered this strange, unmagical little town and stayed out of his brother's schemes.

He wished he could just abandon Rafal and return to school . . . but there was that business of the shield and only Rafal could fly him back, since human flight was dark magic and restricted to Nevers. He could mogrify into a bird, but he hadn't paid attention on the route, too racked with guilt over enabling Hook to rob his and his brother's students, which is why he'd let Rafal bring him beyond the Woods to find replacements. He didn't even know which direction Gavaldon was from school, north, south, east, or west.

Rhian dithered and poked around a few shops, hunting a gift for Rafal, a scarf or suit or something to alleviate his guilt over the stolen students. But everything was so grubby and cheap in this town that Rhian gave up and bought himself the croissant, only to find it dry and treacly, nothing like the cloud-soft pastries the enchanted pots made at school.

No wonder they love our fairy tales, he sighed, observing child after child immersed in one of the Storian's books, perched on a drab bench or lounging by a stunted tree or waiting in line at that pitiful bakery. These Readers knew their world lacked something. Something they couldn't quite name or grasp, but an absence that draped a dull veil over their lives. That's why they believed in fairy tales. That's why they invested themselves in the heroes and villains of another world. Because deep down, they could feel the absence of magic in their own.

The thought sparked Rhian's curiosity. *Imagine if one of these Readers came to my school.* They wouldn't be like the rest of his Evers, who'd lived in a world of magic all their lives. Magic that had become mundane to them. No wonder they'd failed so badly at the Circus and incited this whole mess—they were lazy, spoiled, *bored.* But a Reader wouldn't be bored. Everything would be new to them. Exciting. Magical. Fresh. Rafal was right. A Reader would be a shock wave of ambition and energy, a surprise rival to jolt new life into his students. Maybe it would jolt some new life into *him* too. Suddenly Rhian wanted one . . .

An alarm went off inside.

No. No. No.

No kidnapping.

Nothing that might even remotely be considered Evil.

Not after everything he'd done . . . not after he'd come so perilously close to the murder of a student . . .

He'd lost his head in the moments after the Circus, undone by the arrival of that new Neverboy Fala, who seemed poised to reverse Good's winning streak and turn his school into losers. The idea of Rafal gloating victory, believing himself superior to Rhian, the way Rhian had always believed he was superior to Rafal . . . It had sent Rhian into a spiral. There were two

School Masters, yes, but only one was a winner. And now this Fala had threatened to make that one winner Rafal. All it had taken was for Hook to suggest the crime . . . disappearing Fala forever . . . and Rhian had been swept along. How easily he was swayed. Was it Hook's plan from the beginning to push Rhian into murder? Or had he sensed a crack in Rhian's soul? The Good School Master chilled. One more mistake like that, where he was Evil instead of Good, and the Storian might consider it a breach of his oath to protect the school. To keep the balance between Good and Evil. To always be loyal to his brother. Break the oath and the Pen would punish him.

A memory came back now.

A dying old man, crouched in terror.

The previous School Master who the Pen had robbed of eternal life.

What happened? they'd asked.

"I failed," the dying man answered.

Rhian brushed crumbs from his hands. He needed to get away from Gabblegook, or whatever this place was called, as far from people and temptation as possible.

Gray skies reflected off a lake beneath a hill that led up to a graveyard. Rhian roamed around the lake, with a view to the men working at a distant mill. How quiet everything was here.

THE RULE OF THREES

He kicked off his shoes and dipped his toes in the water.

Who does Rafal have his eye on? He grazed his foot against the rocky lakebed. *A girl? A boy?*

Not that it mattered. One unskilled, ordinary Reader couldn't possibly make up for the ten best Nevers that Rafal had lost to Hook. Regardless of who Rafal found, Evil would go back to being the loser. Especially once Rhian found three new Evers to replace those who'd deserted Good to join Hook in Neverland. As soon as he and his brother were back to the Woods, Rhian would go to the King of Foxwood and ask for his three best—

His foot slipped on a rock, firing a sting of pain.

Blood curled through the water in ribbons.

Clumsy fool, he sighed, waiting for the break in his skin to instantly heal like it always did, the Storian's immortal magic.

Blood kept dripping.

The Good School Master drew his foot out and inspected the wound, only slightly closed up. Had dressing as a bumbling villager confused his soul for a mortal's?

Quickly, he reverted to his young, magical self, glimpsing his wild hair in the water's mirror . . . a reflection broken by more blood rippling off his foot . . .

It wasn't healing.

Rhian's heart seized. If it wouldn't heal . . . he was no longer immortal . . . and if he was no longer immortal, then the Storian was already punish—

"Who are you?" a voice asked.

Rhian turned and for a moment saw no one.

Then he spotted the lad, swimming in shadow at the edge of the lake, snug under the high, grassy bank like it was his own private cove. He had broad shoulders and smooth brown skin, the color of terra-cotta, and his hair was the same hue, highlighted with gold and curled in ringlets that spilled to his shoulders. His eyes were gray and for a moment, Rhian thought he was a faun or a fairy, before he remembered this town was devoid of enchanted pleasures.

"Well?" the boy said.

"Rhian's my name," the Good School Master replied. "And yours?"

"Never seen you about," the boy came back. "Never heard of a Rhian, either."

"I'm not from here," Rhian answered.

"Wherever you're from, you should get back to it before my dad or the Elders find you," the lad warned. "Elders believe in witches and devils and dark magic. Anyone suspicious they burn alive for all to see. And nothing more suspicious in this town than a stranger—"

Rhian was already kneeling at the bank, his face not far from the boy's.

He looked Rhian's age. Sixteen or seventeen perhaps. He was too handsome for this village, Rhian thought. Too intelligent and aware. No wonder he was swimming alone.

"Tell me, Nameless Boy. Do you read the storybooks that come to your bookshop?"

The boy studied him, cocking his head. "Wait . . . are *you* the one who brings them? Miss Harissa claims they just appear. Elders have been trying to find out who leaves them—" He froze. "You look like him. The School Master. The Good one. I read about him in one of the books. It had paintings that looked just like you. The tale of Aladdin brought to a school . . . but that *can't* be you . . . can it?"

Rhian blushed. It was strange to think the boy knew him as a character. That he had opinions and thoughts about him brewing behind that handsome facade. "And what do you think of me and my school?"

The lad's eyes widened. "It's *real*? The School for Good and Evil?"

The School Master smiled. "As real as you, Nameless Boy."

"Then that means . . . It's true? The Evers, the Nevers . . .

All of it?" The boy's voice shivered slightly. "That means you can see if I'm Good or Evil?"

The School Master's fingertip glowed, spinning a silver mist. "How about you come see for yourself?"

The boy looked up at the mist. At first, he didn't understand. Then he felt the spell's effects, his muscles slacking. "No!" he cried.

Moments later, the oversized dwarf with wellies stomped into the forest, carrying the sleeping boy in his arms. He'd used a basic stun spell, strong enough to keep the boy in slumber until his brother could fly them back to sch—

BLAM!

Rhian slammed into an invisible barrier and stumbled back and dropped the boy, who rolled into the grass and stayed asleep.

The Good School Master poked at the unseen wall. He tried to find the edge of it, but it went up and down and left and right without any sign of ending.

Rafal had explained the shield before . . . something about balance between Good and Evil it was meant to enforce . . . that neither School Master could kidnap a child without the other taking one too . . .

Suddenly Rhian caught a glint of light in the surface. A reflection of orange and gold, growing larger and larger, filling up the shield.

He turned.

Fires raged from the center of Gavaldon.

A crowd's chant rose: *"Witch . . . Witch . . . Witch!"*

The boy had warned him.

Nothing more suspicious in this town than a stranger.

And Rafal was certainly that.

Rhian left the boy behind and started running towards the flames.

7.

The *Buccaneer* neared the coast of Neverland not long after the sun rose, which made Aladdin nervous, since surely Pan would spot their ship.

Hook chuckled when he pointed this out. "Peter and his Lost Boys sleep half the morning away. Lazy little buggers," James said, standing at the prow, squinting into the fog that cloaked the island. "Night is when you really have to watch out for them."

The plan, then, was for Hook and Aladdin to venture into the forest while the boys were still sleeping, find Peter's lair—for Pan changed it often, both to evade pirates and because he trusted no one—and determine how well-defended it was. From there, Hook and Aladdin could regroup with the rest of the crew and figure out the best way to kill Pan.

"There will be no killing!" Kyma rehashed angrily, gnawing on stale toast with Aladdin as they sat near James. "And if you so much as nick a hair on that boy's head, Aladdin, I will fight to defend him, which means fighting *you*."

"Can't fight your own boyfriend, princess," Hook mocked, rubbing his bandaged shoulder. "That'd be poor form."

"Especially since we came here to fight Evil," Aladdin said, mouth full. "We're all on the same side, Kyma. If Pan's as wicked as they say, then Good *has* to act. And *we're* Good."

"*If* he's as wicked, and I don't trust you and James to make that assessment," Kyma returned. "Which means I'm coming with you two."

Hook moaned, "Two works well. A third adds complications. The Rule of Threes."

"Never heard of that rule. For all we know, you just made it up," Kyma snipped.

"Eyes peeled for Mermaid Point!" the Pirate Captain called down from the helm.

Aladdin looked up to see the mist break, revealing a surf shimmering with violet sparkles, running up to a beach of purple sand so smooth and shiny that at first he confused it for marble. The beach broke into a series of lagoons, the water bubbling fiery colors, blue, green, orange, pink, that mirrored the hills of the island, rising and falling in the most unlikely hues and bathed in phosphorescent glow, as if an aurora borealis had fallen and stained the earth. Everything was in a haphazard shape, the lagoons, the land, all strange angles and curves, like they were drawn by a child. The sky had an odd tint too, like lavender gauze stretched over a dark shadow, at once beautiful and dangerous.

"Mermaids only come up at night, so we're safe for now as long as we don't disturb any of the lagoons," said Hook, lacing up his boots and pulling on his cloak. "Pirate Captain, any sign of beasties?"

Up one level at the wheel, the Captain peered through his telescope. "All quiet in the north hills."

Aladdin scanned the fluorescing pools. "There's mermaids in there?"

"Mermaids are sensible creatures," Kyma ventured. "Surely they wouldn't protect an Evil king."

James threw Aladdin a smirk. "She thinks the rules of Good and Evil apply here." His eyes flicked back to Kyma. "As long as Pan is king, this is Pan's world. An island that shifts and changes to reflect the deepest parts of him. Neverland's a mirror of his own chaotic soul. Everyone and everything here is spawned from his imagination. That's why it's so dangerous. And why we have to set it free."

The ship drew close to the beach and Hephaestus hustled out on to deck from the galley, sweat-stained and covered in polish, which he'd used to clean the three swords he was carrying.

"Don't do anything daft," he said, handing the blades to

Hook, Aladdin, Kyma, before eyeing Aladdin. "You especially. Pirate Captain and I will man the ship with the Nevers in case we get attacked. Find Peter's lair, map out the defenses, and get back to the ship. Quickly."

Aladdin frowned. "Hook said Peter and the Lost Boys are sleeping. And that mermaids only come out at night. Who else would attack us?"

A shrieking, beastly roar pierced the silence, echoing far over the north hills.

"That," said the Pirate Captain, dropping anchor.

Moments later, Hook was bounding across the narrow paths between lagoons, Aladdin and Kyma struggling to keep up.

"It's why I needed a formidable crew. Peter is only one threat on this island," James called. "We need to move quickly. Peter will stay asleep for a while, but he'll have booby traps, boys on guard, and a hundred ways to foil us. Sooner we scope out his defenses and get back to the *Buccaneer,* sooner we can hide the ship offshore and figure out a plan of attack."

The path grew so tight that they had to go single file, Aladdin falling behind Kyma, who hurried forward and tapped Hook on the shoulder.

"What makes Peter Pan so terrible that we have to kill him?"

Hook tramped faster. "You know, I was sure about everyone

else we took from that school except you. Too self-righteous and goody-goody for a pirate ship, to be honest. But Aladdin wouldn't come without you, so . . ."

Kyma flinched. "It was a simple question—"

"Why is he so terrible? Because Peter actually thinks he's a good king! He's convinced everyone that I'm the villain and he's the hero. That's why."

"And what if he is?" Kyma challenged. "No offense, James, but the more insistent you are on killing your nemesis, the more you sound like a villain yourself."

Hook whirled around and glowered at her. Kyma stood her ground.

Oblivious, Aladdin knocked into her, tripping straight for a mermaid pool—

James lunged and caught him in his arms, just above the water. "Don't go disturbing mermaids, Laddy. They've longed for a boy to come into their clutches. You don't want to be the first."

Aladdin blinked at Hook, then sprung back to his feet, dusting himself off and clearing his throat. "Thanks. Um, you said Pan's only one threat on the island. What are the others?"

"Besides your own threat to yourself?" James quipped.

Aladdin tried to kick him, but James dodged his foot and

danced ahead. "Cannibals in the east, beasts in the north, and . . ."

But Aladdin and Kyma couldn't hear the rest because a lagoon spouted a jet of pink steam, soaking them both. Ahead, Hook bounded past the last of the pools, disappearing down a valley path. Aladdin hustled to follow.

"You sure we can trust him?" Kyma said.

"James? Didn't you just see him save me?" Aladdin scoffed. "I trust him as much as I trust you. Whole reason we're here. To fight for Hook."

Kyma grimaced. She'd left school and come on this ship with her boyfriend to fight for Good, but now his loyalty had reoriented towards a pirate. *Typical*, she thought. From having grown up around her brothers, she knew how quickly the bonds between boys could form and how ironclad they could be. So where did that leave her?

The Rule of Threes, Hook had warned.

"Also, just so you know, trying to be a hero defeats the point," Kyma groused at Aladdin.

"What?"

"You said you and Heph came on this mission to be heroes. But being Good just to win glory isn't all that Good. It's selfish. Reminds me of the boys in Maidenvale who want to marry me just to be a prince. They don't really care about me. They want to be famous."

"Wanting your name known doesn't make you Evil. It means you want a legacy. A life that lasts longer than the one you get. That doesn't sound so bad to me."

"Just like a Pan who thinks he's a hero doesn't sound so bad to me," said Kyma.

But Aladdin wasn't looking at her.

The landscape of Neverland stretched out before them, hills and streams and lakes and forests, the same bold, spectral colors that they'd seen on the coasts. Only there was something different here . . . The signs.

On the hills:

PAN'S PEAK
MOUNT PETER
PETER'S KNOLL

In the streams:

CREEK O' PETE
PANNY BROOK

THE RULE OF THREES

Near the lake:

PETEY'S SHORE
LAKE PAN

And so on, labeling every piece of land and water the eye could see, including PETER WOOD at the edge of the forest, the whole of Neverland claimed for the boy, but even this wasn't enough, for at the center of it all was a massive topiary statue of the feather-capped Pan, fifty feet tall, arms crossed, a smirk on his face, as he towered over the horizon, naturally topped off with a sign:

KING PETE

"Obsessed with himself, isn't he?" Aladdin cracked.

"Only thing he can't claim is the Mermaid Lagoons," Hook said, further down the slope, gazing up at the statue. "Mermaids stay out of Neverland politics and Peter doesn't dare cross them." James turned to Kyma. "Still think he's just an innocuous little boy?"

Kyma shrugged. "So he wants to stamp his name on things. No different than you wanting to be king or Aladdin wanting to be a hero."

"She really doesn't get it," Hook griped to Aladdin.

"You can address me directly instead of looking to my boyfriend like he's my warden," Kyma retorted.

Aladdin stayed out of it, surveying the silent land. "You said Neverland has a thousand children. Where is everyone?"

"At the Morning Report," said Hook, making for Pan's statue.

"The what?" said Aladdin.

James pushed his way into the hedges of Pan's legs and disappeared inside. He poked his head out. "Your princess needs more proof than the obvious. Follow me." Hook vanished back into the leaves.

"He helped us cheat at the Circus, you know," Kyma reminded Aladdin. "James and the School Master were a team, corrupting Good against Evil so we could win. How do we know he's not doing the same thing now? *Using* us?"

"He was searching for a good crew, that's all," Aladdin defended. "The best Evers to help him free Neverland. A real mission more important than school. Wouldn't you have done the same?"

Kyma didn't get a chance to answer—

Aladdin pulled her into Pan's statue and through the hedge, the leaves unusually soft and silky, a soothing rustle in their ears. Together, they moved into quiet darkness. Aladdin lit his glow and Hook was there, a finger to his lips. James was crouched in a corner, near the top of a long, winding staircase, built out of the hollow of a tree. Aladdin and Kyma kneeled beside him and peeked over the staircase to what lay down below.

Hundreds of boys were assembled on the floor, lit by hanging lanterns that had the shape of giant *P*s. The boys seemed to range in age from about seven or eight to thirteen or fourteen at most. All wore bright green uniforms: one-piece union suits combining long johns with a flap over the bottom, and full-sleeved, button-front shirts, the words "PETER BOY" stitched across each one's chest. Peter Boys were further divided into four groups, gathered under separate banners:

PETER FOOD
PETER DEN
PETER FIGHT
PETER FUN

Addressing all these Peter Boys was an older lad, fourteen or fifteen years in age, tanned and shirtless in a green sarong, with close-shaven black hair, violet eyes, and a thick necklace that had a silver star dangling at its end.

"Morning Report! Peter would like a breakfast of butter

pancakes with baby strawberry compote, mermaid pearl drizzle, and a side of puffer fish caviar, along with a milkshake made from the milk of the young mountain goat he saw roaming around in the east. For lunch, he would like an ostrich egg omelet dressed with forest moss foam and a soufflé of conch and tuna tartar. For dinner, he wants a barbecue roasted hog and yes, Peter is aware that the hogs have migrated to the cannibals' side of the island and he doesn't accept that as an excuse and he'd also like a chocolate cake made with month-aged butter and if you didn't start aging the butter a month ago, then you're behind and will be punished. For his den, he'd like a new blanket made out of *banaran* skin, a thorough cleaning of the den as usual, and a team of masseuses to rub his head and feet for most of the afternoon. For his fight, he'd like an army of thirty boys to attack him in Peter Valley at sundown and no one is to land a blow on him until he's beaten each of you to a pulp."

Aladdin heard one of the PETER FIGHT boys murmur: "Why'd I get fight today?"

To which one of the PETER FOOD boys who had his arm in a sling replied: "I was on fight yesterday and he threw all of us off a cliff!"

"And finally for his fun," the head boy went on, "Peter would like a full original production, titled *Peter Pan Superstar*, performed during his supper, complete with music and cho-reographed dancing. He is aware that this is a new musical commissioned under time constraints and that is no excuse for poor entertainment and anything other than a five-star produc-tion will be punished."

The PETER FUN boys shuddered.

The head boy concluded: "Today's punishment for poor per-formance will be flogging and a night in the stocks, slathered in honey, in the north hills between beast and cannibal lands."

Now *all* the boys shuddered.

Hook stared at Kyma. "Still think he's harmless?"

Kyma hesitated. "There are plenty of difficult leaders in the Endless Woods. We can't go around killing everyone whose management style we dislike—"

Suddenly the older, saronged boy paraded out a large, fluffy white animal, floppy-eared, pink-nosed, that looked like a cross between a dog and a bunny.

"What's that?" Kyma whispered.

"A *banaran*," James whispered back.

"For Peter's rug," the head boy ordered, thrusting the animal at PETER DEN.

Kyma gasped. "Let's kill him!"

But she'd spoken too loudly, for all the boys whipped their

heads to where Kyma and her mates were hiding.

Spotlights flooded onto them: the glow of a thousand fairies, leaping out of the lanterns, illuminating them like a prize.

"Mmm, pretty sure we're about to be killed first," Aladdin peeped.

8.

Good is supposed to do the rescuing, but that's not how things usually went between the twins.

Most of the time, Rhian plunged himself into some unnecessary trouble and Rafal would have to swoop in and save his brother. But now the situation was reversed, as Rhian charged back into Gavaldon from the forest, watching flames curl towards Rafal, who was lashed to a pile of birch. Disguised in his beard and wellies, Rhian barreled into the crowd, a thousand-person deep, gathered outside a church that looked like a haunted house, the mob chanting "*Witch! Witch! Witch!*" Rafal didn't appear calm and stoic, as he always did in situations of peril. Instead, his head was limp, his cheeks and eyes bruised, his body slack against his binds, like he'd been overpowered and beaten before they'd thrown him on the pyre.

Rhian's chest hollowed. He wasn't the only one with

diminished healing, then. Whatever was left of Rafal's immortal powers, it would be no match for the fires about to consume him. Rhian shoved aside more villagers, pushing towards his brother. And what of their sorcerer magic? Was that gone too?

Rhian thrust out a finger, bellowing a spell.

Nothing happened. Fire licked around Rafal's legs like a lasso.

Again Rhian yelled the spell, a cry of desperation—

This time rain exploded from the cloudless sky, sweeping down in angry sheets, extinguishing the pyre.

Slowly Rafal lifted his head, his bloodshot eyes slitting open, the bruises and welts glistening in the downpour, and when he saw Rhian's overgrown dwarf standing there, finger glowing, Rafal managed a brilliant smile of relief, as if his brother's act of Goodness meant more than Rhian could know. Rhian was relieved, too: yes, it was the simplest of weather spells, one a first-year could do, and it had come late and unsteady . . . but still, his magic was there.

Problem was the villagers also saw this magic, Rhian's lit finger pointed at the rain. The crowd parted, revealing three old men in gray cloaks and black hats, the oldest now raising his own finger at Rhian and hissing . . .

"*Witch!*"

Rhian scowled. "How original."

A thousand villagers dashed for him and Rhian fled in his wellies, realizing that there was no spell to run faster—

But then he heard the pyre collapse with a resounding *crack!* and he turned his head to see Rafal flying towards him before he snatched his twin in his arms and soared into the forest.

"Shall we make our exit?" Rafal asked, grinning.

"Never should have made our entrance!" Rhian said, reverting to his young self.

His Evil twin flew higher and Rhian felt his brother pull him closer, his grip softer, more loving than on the way here when he'd been cold and silently punishing. Something in Rafal had changed, Rhian thought. As if their old, balanced love had restored—

A rock skimmed through the sky, smashing into Rafal's ribs with enough force that he dropped his brother and then went plummeting too. Both brothers landed in a tree, their clothes torn open by branches as they crashed their way down, into a mound of dead leaves. Battered and bleeding, they raised their heads.

A curly-haired, dark lad about their age loomed over them, bare-chested and armed with a slingshot.

"Nameless Boy," Rhian croaked.

"The name's Midas," the boy retorted. "And no, you won't

be taking me to your cursed school."

Rafal looked between Rhian and Midas and in a flash, he understood.

This was the Reader his brother wanted to bring to the School for Good.

A Reader who with his strong presence and alluring gaze shared a lot in common with the strangers that Rhian tended to pick up whenever Rafal was away.

Vulcan.

Hook.

Now Midas.

But Vulcan was a School Master. Hook was a Dean.

Midas would be a . . . *student.*

Whatever hope that Rafal had that Rhian could be Good again . . . that he could commit to their brotherly bond . . . that they could be the way they were, loyal to each other above all . . .

It went up in flames.

Rafal glared daggers at Rhian and for a moment, Rhian's eyes flickered as if he read his brother's mind.

But now Midas was raising another rock into his slingshot, right at Rhian's head—

Rafal flew up in a single bound and slammed Midas by

the throat against the tree. He expected fear and submission from the boy, a boy he was punishing for his brother's sins, but instead Midas thrashed aggressively, his gray eyes dauntless, as if the harder Rafal squeezed, the more alive he became. Rafal peered curiously at the lad as he strangled him, suddenly enjoying this battle of wills. Mortals were scared of him. Not this one.

A serpentine thought curled through Rafal's head.

Imagine the boy's potential. Imagine what he could be, guided by the right hand—

"Rafal, watch out!" Rhian cried.

An arrow grazed Rafal, landing in the bark above Midas' head. Rafal threw the boy aside and spun to see the townsmen of Gavaldon rushing him and his twin, bows and spears in hand. Quickly, the Evil School Master lifted off the ground, grabbing Rhian into his arms and letting Midas escape, just as villagers flooded the forest—

Then Rafal thought better of it and flew back down.

"What are you doing!" Rhian cried out.

Rafal snatched Midas like a falcon picking off prey, clutching both his brother and the boy against his chest, dodging a hail of arrows as he soared them straight up.

As Midas writhed against him, Rafal heard his brother shout:

"Rafal, the shield! We won't get through with one Reader! The rules of balance! You need one for yourself too!"

But Rafal flew on and the shield never appeared.

Away from Woods Beyond they went, the Evil School Master grinning acidly to himself.

His twin was right.

They both did need a Reader to leave Gavaldon.

One for Rhian. One for Rafal.

But that was the thing about Midas.

Each School Master thought the boy was *his*.

And that in itself was a curious kind of balance.

9.

The purple-eyed head boy who delivered Neverland's Morning Report was named Botic.

Aladdin learned this because BOTIC was tattooed on the boy's back above the fold of his sarong and because the lads kept using the name while arguing which group should be the one to present Pan with the prisoners, who were now bound and gagged to a pole.

"We saw Hook first so we deserve the credit," a small boy in PETER FOOD insisted—the fairies who found the prisoners making a loud sputtering sound to dispute his claim—but the boy barreled on: "We'll lay a tablecloth on Hook's body and serve Peter's breakfast on him. Imagine how surprised Peter will be! Every other Pan took years to capture their Hook. And we got ours as soon as he's back from Blackpool!"

"Peter will appoint Botic to Grand Consort!" another PETER FOOD boy crowed. "And he'll give our whole group silver stars!" He clapped his hands, beaming at his fellow Food folk. "We'll be official Lost Boys like Botic, with names Pan knows, instead of no-name Peter Boys!"

"Only six Lost Boys, aren't there? Surely Pan needs some more!" a third PETER FOOD boy hoped.

Botic fingered his silver star necklace. "And why shouldn't I present the prisoners to Peter myself? And say *I* caught them?"

"Because *we* caught Hook!" a boy from PETER FOOD argued. "And if we tell Peter you're lying to gain his favor, what will he think?" Again the fairies sputtered, this time sprinkling rainbow dust into the boy's long johns so the underside magically flew upwards, wedging up his bottom. "Hey!" he yipped.

"Seems like the fairies want credit too," Botic muttered.

Hands cuffed to the pole, Aladdin lit his fingerglow, but the Good School Master had unlocked the Evers' magic only to cheat against the Nevers and hadn't taught them any useful spells. (Even the one Aladdin learned for the Circus, a hex to turn skin see-through, was pointless.) Still, if magic followed emotion, surely he could manifest something! He focused on his fear, his determination, his love for his princess . . . His finger flickered and dribbled blue mist. Kyma noticed and urgently shook her head. Aladdin's glow snuffed out.

"Our group should present the prisoner!" a PETER DEN boy proposed, not noticing the wisps of smoke. "Peter will be more surprised if we hide them in his new *banaran* rug and when we unroll the rug for Peter, there he is: James Hook and two extras just for fun. Won't Peter be happy with you, Botic? For such a grand gift?"

A PETER FIGHT spokesman cut in: "Or we could arm Hook with a butter knife and let Pan lead a whole army against him! That's what Peter would like best!"

"Peter will like our idea more!" PETER FOOD chorused.

"No, he'll like ours more!" piped PETER DEN.

Botic rubbed his chin as if the question of which idea Peter would like best was a serious question indeed. Then he noticed the flock of boys under the PETER FUN banner. "Well?"

The FUN boys peeked at each other, befuddled, until one reedy boy with a poof of red hair raised a nail-bitten finger and spoke in a voice that sounded like he'd swallowed a balloon:

"We could pin feathers on them and make them do a samba?"

Botic bolted straight. "Peter *loves* sambas!"

A short while later, Aladdin and James Hook waddled their behinds in nothing but headdresses and tiny shorts made of peacock feathers, Princess Kyma dancing next to them, her clothes hamstrung in feathered boas, the ends of which Botic held like reins, while the PETER FUN procession drummed bongos and hooted behind them, into the jungle of Neverland's forest, which turned new colors every few paces, green to pink to gold.

Kyma hissed at her friends. "How's that plan to kill Pan going?"

"About as well as James' tan," Aladdin cracked.

"I can always get darker. You can never get taller," James replied.

"Dagger to the heart," said Aladdin.

Only boys could be making jokes now, Kyma groaned to herself. But she could see the uncertainty in James' eyes: his sense of confidence shaken, as if he was waiting for something to save them and it hadn't appeared. *Rhian's magic,* she thought. It's why Hook had come to the School for Good and Evil in the first place. Not just to steal students, but also to acquire the sorcerer's magic that would kill Pan's shadow. Except that magic wasn't working now or operating at his control. Which meant they were on their way to certain death with no way out. She caught Hook glancing at her, as if he'd gleaned her thoughts.

The forest morphed into a palace of blue, gleaming fronds all around, shades of cobalt, periwinkle, navy, indigo, turquoise. It was so full and dense that they couldn't see sky or dirt, the air a wall of dew and sweat.

"You can't find Rhian's magic, can you?" Kyma whispered to James. "You said you need it to kill Pan's shadow. That's your whole plan. What are we supposed to do if—"

Hook snapped: "You stunned all those Night Crawlers, didn't you? Why don't you do it again! Why don't *you* save us?"

"It was a basic hex! Barely lasted a few seconds. Aladdin and I aren't trained in magic—"

"Then use that two-bit magic lamp. The one that made Laddy kiss Hephaestus!"

Aladdin gasped. "I did not *kiss* Hephaestus! Who told you that! Besides, that lamp's dead broken and last I heard, a Never found it at the Snow Ball and Humburg locked it in his office. We need the Nevers! They learned real spells!"

Hook scanned the path ahead, the foliage becoming bright green. "No way to call the Pirate Captain or get the Nevers' help—"

Botic kicked him in the rump and James shook his hips

harder, earning loud whistles from the boys behind him, giving Aladdin cover to lean in.

"Maybe Rhian's magic will be there when we need it. Like it was there with the Night Crawlers. We need to pin down Pan's shadow long enough for you to use it."

James quivered, the memory of Rhian's magic ripping through his body, alien, violent, unwelcome. But Aladdin was right. They needed it, no matter how terrible it felt inside him.

"How do you pin down a shadow?" Kyma wondered.

"A shadow's where you keep all your emotions, so we have to get Pan riled up somehow. Too much emotion and your shadow starts having a life of its own. Rile Pan up enough and his shadow will separate from him entirely. That's when you can attack it," said James.

"Happy to kick that animal-abusing creep in the pants," Kyma proposed. "That'll rile him up—"

Suddenly the bongos bashed louder, Peter's Boys erupting into song:

> *Good King Peter!*
> *Let us serve you well!*
> *Let us be your wards!*
> *Let us show our love!*
> *Bold King Peter!*

THE RULE OF THREES

Let us tout your brawn!
Let us be your flock!
Let us kiss your feet!

Kyma frowned. This is what happened with too many boys in one place.

She glimpsed fronds rustling ahead like a curtain about to open, the lads chanting:

Peter the Wise!
Peter the Strong!
Peter the Great!
Long Live the King!

The fronds parted and there, framed by flowering vines on all sides, was a throne made of skeletons, faced away from the procession, two Lost Boys in green sarongs with names tattooed on their backs and silver star necklaces fanning the throne's occupant. A tanned arm rose from the chair, fingers swaying with the chants, as if conducting the arriving parade: *"Peter the Wise! Peter the Strong! Peter the Great! Long Live the—"*

He drew his fingers together sharply and the chants stopped.

The shadow of these fingers rose into a viper's mouth, a shadow with a life of its own.

A lilting voice filled the silence.

"Every hundred years, the North Star descends to earth, sneaks into the graveyards, and searches for all the boys that never grew up. She picks the best one, the one most destined for greatness before his life was cut short, the one who deserves a hundred years in the prime of youth to make up for what he lost. A second chance at life for a child so perfect and rare that Heaven herself comes down to find him. And she picked me. Not any of you. *Me*. Every day, you worship and flatter me, hoping I'll learn your names and give you a silver star, but the game is getting old. There's no challenge. No tension. I was chosen to be the Pan, while you were chosen to be what? Lemmings? Honeybees? At least with Hook there's the fun of a madman who thinks he can beat me. But he's off at Blackpool, so now I'm bored. Bored by you, bored by this island, bored of waiting for Hook, bored, bored, bored. Which is why the time has come for me to—"

He swiveled in his throne.

Green eyes found Hook, flaring with surprise.

"Hold that thought," said Peter Pan.

He had a cupid's mop of curls, sun-dyed blond on top, fading darker and darker brown to the roots. His eyes were slim and far apart, his ears big and floppy, his nose a tight little button. His forehead stretched high and the bottom of his jaw jutted out, flashing pearly sharp teeth. He was thin and tan, dressed in a skintight suit of green vines, his face a child's but laced with restless mischief, so he looked older than his thirteen years.

"Hello, James. Impeccable timing, as always," said Peter, his shadow peeling off his body and circling Hook's feathered form. "You came to dance for me?"

Hook bared his teeth. "I came to kill you. And to get my ship."

"The first will be a challenge since you have no weapons or defenses, two friends who look even less capable than you do, and no Hook has come close to killing a Pan before," Peter replied. "As for your ship, well . . . it's *busy* at the moment."

He put two fingers in his mouth and wolf-whistled, and on cue, the flower vines fell, like drapes come down, revealing the *Jolly Roger* wedged between rosewood trees, Hook's famous ship, rakish and sleek and shaped like a dragon's tail, with a black hull that raised steeply and seven bloodred sails, flying skulls and bones.

Or at least it once had these things.

Because up in the trees, two sandy-haired, light-eyed teenage boys were hard at work remodeling it, one older, one younger,

in orange sarongs and necklaces with golden suns that spangled twice as bright as the Lost Boys' silver stars. A few other Lost Boys joined them on deck, repainting the ship green, raising new green sails with silhouettes of Peter's head, and hanging a shining bronze bust of Peter off the prow.

Hook clutched his chest as if he'd been stabbed.

"I'm going on a trip," Pan explained. "So there will be no time for a fight, James."

Botic frowned. So did his Lost Boys. Clearly this was the first they'd heard of this. "A *trip*? But . . . this is *Hook*! Delivered to you like a Christmas Pig!" Botic said incredulously. "What *kind* of trip?"

"Top secret, of course," Peter crowed, winking at his two golden boys on the ship, who gave him subtle nods in return. Botic opened his mouth to protest, but Peter was already up from his throne. "And I'll kill Hook another day, if and when I return—"

"*If?*" Botic yelped.

"—and then there can be the same old battle, a Hook versus a Pan, like it's been done for a thousand years, with the same old result," said Peter, climbing up the tree. "Until then, put Hook and his friends in Cannibal Cave and tell Luoto Bakhti they're not to be killed until I order it. Though if they lose a finger or foot in the meantime . . . Oh, and I'm guessing they didn't swim here, so send a fairy scout to find where Hook's new boat is hiding and put the crew in Cannibal Cave too. And wipe that look off your face, Botic, or I'll throw you in with them."

Peter hoisted himself through branches and onto the ship, as one of the boys aboard repainted the JOLLY ROGER to say . . .

THE MIGHTY PAN

Aladdin and Kyma peeked at Hook, who'd bleached a new shade of pale, before boys descended to cuff them to a rope. There would be no riling up of Pans, no slaying of shadows, no triumph for a team that had come to find glory far from school. As Botic and the Lost Boys led the three prisoners away, back into the jungle, Hook turned to see a cloud of fairies arrive, sprinkling the old *Jolly Roger* with glittering fairy dust, which made it rise into the air and fly towards the sea, his father's ship and his father's before him now under the control of Pan. Hot shame blotched James' cheeks, his long-sought revenge curdled to humiliation.

And yet, that's not what disturbed Hook the most, nor the fact that he and his friends were on the march to their doom.

No, what frightened Hook the most were those two boys with the golden suns.

Two boys he knew.

Brothers that he'd met in Monrovia Prison.

Sader brothers.

A pair of seers, who once saved Hook from the bottom of the sea and had now sailed off with his mortal enemy.

Why had they come *here*?

What had they seen that made them switch sides against Hook?

And what future had they shared with Peter Pan?

For if that future was worth more to Pan than killing his eternal nemesis . . .

Hook's gut twisted.

Then it was a very grim future indeed.

10.

One School Master instead of two.

That was what the Saders foretold.

That a brother would die.

Rhian or Rafal.

It's not going to be me, Rafal thought, standing at the window of the School Masters' tower, looking out at the School for Good and Evil, shadowed beneath a half-moon.

He couldn't trust his brother anymore. That much was clear. What happened with Vulcan and Hook had spooked Rafal— his brother allying with strangers over him, so easily giving away his loyalty to replace his blood and family. It wasn't such a leap to consider that Rhian might go further and get rid of Rafal completely. The prophecy made true, and not in Rhian's favor. It's why Rafal had wanted a Reader: to protect himself . . . to have his own ally that his twin couldn't corrupt . . . to shield against the prophecy with his own faithful soldier. But his error with Arabella had made him wary. Better to abandon the plan and recommit to his brother, regardless of the risks. Forget the prophecy. Kill him with kindness and devotion instead. Surely fate's course could be corrected by love. In this world, love always won the day.

But that's how the Good think, Rafal realized now.

And Rhian *wasn't* Good. No matter how much he played the part.

Which is why just as Rafal was abandoning the plan to steal a Reader, Rhian had found one for himself.

Midas.

Rhian wanted the boy as an Ever. For what purpose, Rafal

wasn't sure. But judging from what happened with Vulcan and Hook . . . it would be a nefarious one indeed.

Except there was a twist.

Like his brother, Rafal had also seen into the boy's soul. That moment when he'd held him against the tree, the boy glaring back into his eyes. Where Rhian had seen confidence and charm, Rafal had seen something else. Something that made Rafal want him too.

Both School Masters, then, had chosen the same Reader.

Rhian didn't know that, of course.

For now, Rafal had let him have the boy.

Footsteps pattered up the stairs—

"I had the enchanted pot make you your favorites," said Rhian, carrying a mug of sandalwood tea and a plate of sandwiches. "Cucumber and herb butter."

"That's your favorite," Rafal replied, from the window.

"It isn't yours too?"

"No, watercress and egg is mine. So preoccupied with your charming new Reader that you've forgotten everything about me."

Rhian stiffened. "That's not true—"

"How is Midas?" Rafal asked. He was lying about the sandwiches. Cucumber and herb butter was his favorite. But it was time to repay his brother's games with some of his own.

"It's been five days and the rest of the Evers seem to be warming up to him," said the Good School Master, quickly putting the plate and mug down. "At first they taunted him about being from an unmagical land; you know, the usual snipes that he'd end up a newt or an artichoke. But then he started beating them in challenges. He might even end up being our best student. Your Dean Humburg doesn't approve, by the way. He wrote me a stern note, suggesting an unmagical Reader at school is pure abomination and he'd make sure you'd hear of it. I wrote back that it was *your* idea."

Rafal didn't take the bait. "And Midas is happy? He isn't trying to run away?"

"He tried the first night, until he realized there's things in the Woods that will eat him, and either he does well in his classes or his life will be cut short here too. And I've been reassuring him that he belongs. You know, finding time to talk to him, one on one."

I bet you have, Rafal thought. He limped to his desk and sat on its edge. He'd tried a spell to fix his leg, the one broken when he'd crashed into Gavaldon's shield, but it hadn't worked, his magic as vulnerable as his mortality. He could ask Humburg to mend the bone with his own spell . . . but given the Dean's dubious loyalties, the less Humburg knew about his predicament, the better.

He caught Rhian watching him, his brother's eyes darting between Rafal's wounded leg and the unhealed gash on his arm.

He knows, Rafal thought.

Rhian gestured at the Pen, writing in an open book. "It's started a new tale, I see."

"Some odd story about three children who go exploring an enchanted island and are caught and marched to cannibals. Nothing to do with us," Rafal dismissed. "I've been thinking about what to do with Hook's bridge." He nodded out the window at the stone passage between Evil's black castle and Good's glass towers. "Well, we shouldn't call it Hook's bridge, even if Hook mysteriously conjured it in the dead of night and used it to steal our children. No use memorializing a thief and a cad."

"I thought we were destroying it," said Rhian.

"Do you ever wonder what magic he used?" Rafal asked, gazing right at his brother. "Hook has no enchanted lineage. No magical skills. Someone would have had to help him. Someone with a sorcerer's power. Maybe we should ask a seer . . ."

"Let's demolish it this afternoon," the Good School Master pushed. "We can make a show of it for the students. You know how much the Nevers like to see things destroyed."

"But why destroy it at all? You seem intent on getting rid of it, as if the mere sight of it disturbs you," Rafal needled. "I'm thinking practically as a School Master *should*. You and I need an easier way to get between schools, especially since you can't fly. Faculty too. And we'll add an enchanted shield halfway down the bridge to prevent students from trespassing between schools. That's a name, isn't it? Halfway Bridge . . . Unless we name it after you, of course."

"Me?" said Rhian.

"If it wasn't for you cozying up to Hook, that bridge wouldn't exist in the first place," said Rafal.

Rhian raised his brows. He paused a moment, letting the silence thicken. Then he sat in the windowsill and set eyes on his brother. "Speaking of shields, I've been wondering why the wall in Gavaldon let us through with only one Reader. That doesn't trouble you? That it let us through unbalanced? Perhaps we should ask a seer about that too."

Rafal didn't flinch, though inside, his heart thumped faster. The old Rhian would have been flushed with shame by now, trying to appease him and make things better. This one had a different look in his eye.

"There's another thing I've been meaning to tell you," said

the Good School Master calmly. He slipped out of his shoe and held up a bare foot, a jagged cut along the sole. "It won't heal, just like your leg won't heal."

"My leg?"

"The one you're limping on." Rhian leaned back into shadow. "Is there something you've been keeping from me? Something I should . . . *know*?"

Rafal made his move. "What are you suggesting, Rhian? That suddenly, after a hundred years, we're . . . *mortal*? If so, that would mean the Storian questions our love for the first time. That one of us failed the test. That one of us has *violated* our bond."

Rhian stared at him, thrown. He fumbled for a response, but Rafal was already standing and prowling towards him. "I have no limp. I heal by magic. I am an *immortal* sorcerer. In fact, our bond feels stronger to me than ever. I forgave you for what happened with Hook. I helped you find a Reader to replace your stolen Evers. I rescued your precious Midas to this school. I've shown my loyalty to you again and again and again. And yet here you are, suggesting our love is *broken*? I'd think twice about that. Because if one of us has broken the bond, if one of us has failed the test, if one of us isn't fit to be School Master, I assure you . . . it's not *me*."

The brothers faced off. Darkness clouded the Good School

Master's eyes.

Then, like the clearing after a storm, the darkness receded. "You know, now that I'm looking at it, the wound is healing fine. Just like your leg," Rhian said lightly, slipping his foot back into his shoe. "Everything between us is as it should be. Never better, as you say. But I best be going. My dear students await . . . It's too bad you didn't get a Reader for yourself. Midas is the perfect pet. Nothing like Hook or Vulcan, who had minds of their own. He'll be the jewel in my crown. The Everboy tight under my wing. All thanks to you, of course." Rhian's blue eyes cut into Rafal's. Then he walked towards the stairs, before having one last smile at his brother. "I could have sworn you loved those sandwiches."

He descended, soon out of sight, the snap of the tower door echoing up the stairs.

Rafal sat there alone, his muscles clenched.

Masks were falling, little by little.

Good become Evil, Evil become Good.

There was danger in baiting a villain, Rafal thought. For at this very moment, both brothers were mortal. The wound on Rhian's foot had proved it. The Sader prophecy was in play. A School Master could die at any second. Two could become one.

Rafal had to make sure that it was the *right* one. That *he* would come out of this alive.

But first, he had to wait.

Midas was the key.

From what he'd seen in the lad's eyes, he too had a mind of his own, no matter what his brother thought.

It was only a matter of time.

Before the Everboy under Rhian's wing took flight.

Before Good's pet became Evil's secret weapon.

Patience, Rafal told himself.

Soon the Reader would come to him.

11.

Princess Kyma had a habit of letting boys overshadow her.

She'd grown up with three older brothers, all of whom would become King of Maidenvale before she could ever take the throne. When she protested to her father about this injustice, the king suggested she focus on finding a prince from a desirable kingdom to marry. "That's how a girl like you becomes Queen," he winked.

She was eleven years old.

But then Kyma's time came: she was chosen for the School for Good over her brothers. She would have the chance to earn her name in a fairy tale known by all the Woods . . . to be remembered not as a queen, but as a legend . . .

Things had started well. The Storian had included her in its tale of Aladdin and his lamp of bad magic. True, she'd been reduced to the role of girlfriend, the Pen focused on a cast of brashly behaved boys, but the fact she'd been mentioned at all must mean she was on a Good path.

So how then, by following this path, had she ended up a thousand miles from Good's school with even more brashly behaved boys, on her way to a cannibal?

Pan's henchmen marched them up a hill, cuffed to a rope, the sun whittling to a red orb. In front of her, Kyma noticed Hook and Aladdin whispering to each other, the two boys still in peacock feathers, Hook burnt a bright shade of pink from his samba in the sun. Meanwhile, Botic and the other two Lost Boys were huddled in their own conversation. Kyma could only catch sullen mumbles—"what trip . . . caught Hook . . . no reward . . ."—but it gave her cover to poke her nose between her friends.

"We're about to be *eaten*. We have to do something!"

The boys didn't answer. She kicked Aladdin in the behind.

Hook glared back. "Getting eaten is the least of our problems, princess. Look." She followed his eyes out into the sunset, where the *Jolly Roger* was flying south, a mere speck against the horizon. "Peter Pan is on that ship. *My* ship. Pan, who we came to kill!"

"And now he's gone and we're going to be dinner!" Kyma hissed. "We need to escape to our boat, to the Captain and Hephaestus and the Neve—"

BOOM!

Explosions rocked in the distance, a burst of fire and smoke, and the entire group spun to the west, where a flaming ship drifted out of mist, sinking into the Savage Sea.

Kyma clasped her chest.

The *Buccaneer.*

On the shore, a mob of Peter Boys raised their weapons and cheered.

Aladdin's eyes sprung with tears. *"Hephaestus."*

He looked at Kyma, then the pair of them looked at Hook, whose eyes roved the sinking ship, searching the smoke and wreckage for life . . .

Botic shoved them forward, forcing the prisoners to march on, the two boys side by side in feathers, Princess Kyma chained behind them.

Night settled over Neverland, an inky darkness, wet with mist, and against this darkness glowed the hills that the prisoners climbed, spatters of fluorescent color that had no sense or pattern. A few miles away, a hole in a cliff spewed fiery smoke, as red as molten lava.

Kyma didn't need a map to know that this was Cannibal Cave.

Botic grinned back at Hook. "Luoto Bakhti."

Kyma saw James stifle a shudder, as if the name itself had power.

But where the prospect of death should have fired Hook up, instead he was slouched and deflated, glancing back not at the lost *Buccaneer* but at his family's ship, trailing away. He has Rhian's magic, Kyma thought. Why isn't he using it to fight back? Yes, he said he couldn't control it, but at least try! Meanwhile, Aladdin was pale and morose, bereft over Hephaestus. The same Hephaestus who had been Kyma's first suitor at school. But Kyma couldn't let her mind go to grief—she had to save herself and her friends, because one boy was mourning a boat and the other a boy and clearly they weren't up to the task. If she could make a dash for it and get Peter's goons to chase her, it would create enough diversion for Hook and Aladdin to flee. She was lightning fast; she could outrun them all. She just had to communicate her plan. But this was the problem with these boys. With all boys. Communication. And as usual, Aladdin and Hook were ignoring her, no matter how much she glared and grunted behind them.

But now Peter's lads seemed to be slowing, the hills eerily quiet, their captors peeking and pussyfooting around, as if anticipating something they couldn't see.

"Any sign of her?" Botic whispered.

"She knows our voices," another boy said. "Knows we don't have anything to offer her."

"Who?" Aladdin said, suddenly alert. "Who knows your voices?"

Botic spun, purple eyes wide, finger to lips—

"AAAAYAAAAIIIIIII!"

A scream shattered the earth. Hands flew to ears, just before the ground caved in, opening a chasm under Kyma. Her legs crumpled, her body sucked down whole, before Aladdin lunged with cuffed hands, catching her wrist, his girlfriend dangling over the jaws of a pink beast with slimy, salmon-colored skin, too large and covered in dust to make head or tail of it. A long, ribbon-like tongue flicked for Kyma, the princess just out of reach. Kyma gripped Aladdin harder to yank herself up.

"Don't let go!" she pleaded.

"Never," Aladdin vowed.

But the monster's breath was hot and wet, soaking them like

rancid dew, and Kyma's hand slipped in Aladdin's grasp. Aladdin redoubled his hold, but the effort caved more ground around him and he pitched forward, about to fall with his love—

From behind, Hook snatched Aladdin's waist, towing him up, but Aladdin clung tighter to Kyma, gritting his teeth so hard the veins in his face throbbed, his force dragging Hook towards the pit. Peter's boys rushed to save Hook, not wanting to lose Pan's precious prisoner. They grabbed James, who grabbed Aladdin, who lurched back and lost grip on his princess.

"NO!" Aladdin cried.

Kyma gaped in shock as she fell, watching Hook pull Aladdin into his chest, while her body plunged, down, down, down . . .

. . . into a web of warm, thick goo that trapped her in place. She peeled ooze out of her eyes, only to find a wall of dark in every direction. A big, black hole. But then the darkness contorted and quaked, and she realized the beast was on the move, burrowing deeper, the sounds of crumbling dirt echoing like an avalanche. Around Kyma, sour-smelling air shallowed in rapid puffs, as if she was in the creature's lungs. Then for an instant, it all stopped: the moving, the breathing, the beast as still as its prey dangling in slime . . .

A blast of air and noise came from beneath, a guttural sneeze, ejecting Kyma straight through a veil of mucus, like water from a spout. Out the monster's nostril she went, Kyma flailing with a shout, until she landed in a soft, wet patch, the world pitch black around her.

"Aladdin?" she whispered. "Are you there?"

Light sparked from every direction, bursts of orange glow, fireflies abuzz in a cavern hollowed out of dirt.

Slowly Kyma's eyes raised to the beast, holding Kyma up in its soggy, slimy palm, a gargantuan pink mass crowned with blinking black eyes, an elephantine nose, sharp gray teeth, and wispy coils of white hair. It had a fat belly; bony limbs wrapped in loose tangles of skin; dark, hairy armpits that attracted the flies; and the long, limp tongue that lolled out its mouth.

A troll, Kyma thought, recognizing the creature from her schoolwork. But not just any troll . . .

"An Ingertroll!" she blurted.

The troll dropped Kyma in surprise. Kyma flipped over to see the creature's nose to hers. "You knowwww what I *am!*" the Ingertroll squawked, a voice so high and shrieky that it made Kyma jump.

"A female troll found in any kingdom with a preponderance of males," Kyma prattled, trying to extend the conversation before the troll ingested her again. "You roam in search of handsome young men to steal from their beloveds. But I am not a man, which means I am no use to you and you should set me free—"

"He is your beloved, isn't he! The one whose voice I did not know!" the Ingertroll screeched. "He must not love you much if he dropped you. I don't want a boy like that! You can keep him! Hee haw!"

Snot flew out of the troll's nostrils and Kyma dodged it. "Well, if you don't want Aladdin and you don't want me, then kindly let me g—"

"Your Aladdin seemed much more interested in the other boy with him. The skinny, handsome one! So cute in their feathers!" the Ingertroll squealed, wagging her bottom.

"No, that's not it," Kyma said, irritated. "James and Aladdin . . . they're like brothers . . ."

"So Aladdin saved his brother over his beloved and left you to die! Sounds about right! He's like all the boys in Neverland. More interested in the boys than the girls! That's why you're down here in the dumps with me! Hee haw!"

Kyma stood up. "You have the story all wrong. Listen, Miss . . . Troll. Please let me go. My friends are in danger. Our ship's gone, we have no way home, and they're about to die. I need to get back to—"

"—a boy who doesn't want you?" The Ingertroll scratched

her armpits, dislodging more flies. "Is that why you come to an island where girls are worth nothing? Because you think *you* are worth nothing?"

Kyma's face went hot. "You don't know me or Aladdin at all."

"Stay down here with me!" the Ingertroll squawked, giving Kyma a pat-pat on the head. "You'll be happier than with that awful boy. You and me, in our own little world. No boys allowed!"

"Think I'll take my chances up there," Kyma snapped, and moved back, her ears ringing from the troll's awful shrieks. But then she saw the Ingertroll's face: mournful, hurt, as if Kyma's rejection had struck a nerve. Kyma shook her head. "Why are you in Neverland, if girls are worth nothing? Why stay where no one wants you?"

The Ingertroll glanced off. This time her voice was somber and soft, the shrieks and artifice gone. "I could ask the same of you. Those boys left you. So why are *you* here?"

To do Good, Kyma thought instantly. *To save Neverland. To dethrone an Evil tyrant.*

But none of these are what she answered. Instead, she felt something else tug at her heart, as if deep in the earth with no one to hear except a troll, she could finally speak the truth.

"To be with him," she breathed.

After Good had lost the Circus, Aladdin had been the one to jump at Hook's offer to escape school and sail to Neverland. He'd volunteered her too, even though both Hook and the Pirate Captain were reluctant to bring a girl along. Aladdin convinced them. She'd never spoken for herself or considered another option. The School for Good had seemed so unsettled after the Circus, its School Master questionable in her eyes . . . A boyfriend felt like a safe harbor. Staying with Aladdin would lead her to Goodness. To happiness. To Ever After. Isn't that how the best tales ended? A princess with her prince?

And yet, with each new day on this trip, she'd questioned that path.

As if in following a boy, she'd gotten further and further from herself.

Kyma looked up at the troll, who was smiling sadly.

"Told you we had a lot in common," the Ingertroll said. "We sacrifice ourselves for the boys we love. Yet here we are on this island. Alone."

"You love a boy here?" Kyma asked. "I thought Ingertrolls despise love. And boys."

"This one is different." The Ingertroll slouched into dirt. "The only boy in this place worth loving."

"Let me guess. Peter Pan," Kyma groused.

"Peter Pan! Hee haw!" The troll burst into shrieks and Kyma spun away, plugging her ears. "A heart that beats for Luoto Bakhti could never beat for Peter Pan!"

Slowly Kyma turned. "Luoto Bakhti. The *cannibal*. He's your true love?"

"Once a gentle, sweet, humble soul, who only had eyes for me. Until restlessness gave him a taste for something more. Now he doesn't want me and I don't know what to do," the Ingertroll admitted, sobering. "Don't you see? You and I are strong. But boys come first in this world. They make us doubt ourselves. They decide our fates and we go along. You brought here. Me abandoned. And yet, we're both lost now. Because a boy wrote each of our endings. And we let them, like every other girl. Boys have the last word in our stories. And no matter how strong we are . . . we're not strong enough to change that."

Kyma felt the sting of truth.

Her father. Aladdin. Hook. All the boys at school.

They'd seen her only as a girl. As a princess instead of a person.

Anger and purpose burned inside her like twin flames.

"We are strong enough," she said, looking up. "We *are*."

The troll blinked at her, surprised.

"What if boys don't have the last word in our stories? What if I could help you get the ending *you* want?" Kyma asked. "Would you help me in return?"

The Ingertroll drew a breath. She bent down, dwarfing the young girl in her shadow. "Yes."

Kyma's eyes twinkled like the fireflies lighting the dark. "Then it's time we paid a visit to Cannibal Cave."

12.

The problem with Midas was that he looked like an Ever with his gooey eyes and angelic curls, but he had a Never's heart.

It's why he'd tried to flee the first night after he arrived at the School for Good. Not just because he objected to being kid-napped from home or because he missed his life in Gavaldon: skipping school to swim at the cove . . . playing with his pet snake Bongo . . . picking pockets in town and using the money to buy expensive boots . . .

No, the biggest reason Midas fled the School for Good is because it was hell.

For one thing, he didn't like girls *at all* and this school was full of them in their ruffly dresses and fruity perfumes and rosy dabs of rouge that made them look like creepy dolls. For another, these girls kept smiling at him because he was handsome and looked like a sweet, loving boy and he was neither of these things and he'd be happy if all the girls here magically disappeared. The boys were no better. After the School Master introduced him to the class as their first "Reader," a student from a newly found realm beyond the Woods, the Everboys taunted him for being a "phony" and a "freak." But Midas glared back at them with ice-cold eyes as if they were nothing, and there is little that impresses a boy more than another boy who sees right through him. By lunch, the taunts had stopped. But then there were all the other offenses: the horrible glass castle with too much sunlight, the snooty teachers, the poofy uniforms that made him feel like a cream puff, the endless tones of "Good morning!" and "How are you?" and small talk in the name of politeness when the polite thing to do would be to leave a newly kidnapped stranger alone.

He willed himself to survive his first day, and the instant the sky went dark, he'd fled the castle, hightailing it into the Woods, looking for a path back to Gavaldon . . . only to hear a burst of growls, red and yellow eyes blinking open and rushing towards him, his legs snagged in vines as he stumbled to run, before a centaur on guard named Maxime streaked in and brought him back to school. The next morning, the Good School Master—"Call me Rhian," he'd said, a bit too chummy—sat him down in an empty Dean's office and served him honeybush tea and candied plums and explained there was no way home through the Woods without death and that Midas would either excel at his new school or end up a tree or a rodent in the forest he'd just fled.

Death or being turned into a skunk. Both poor options.

So was staying in Goody-Goody Land, though.

So Midas started thinking about switching schools. At least until he had a better plan to get home.

As he walked the cloying, perfumed halls of Good between classes, he entertained thoughts of Evil's School Master—the one who'd pinned him against the tree in the Woods. Yes, he'd been aggressive, frightening . . . but there was something in his eyes . . . intelligence . . . intensity . . . as if he could see right into Midas' soul . . .

"Good morning! How are you!" the most annoying boy in the world chimed, breaking his concentration.

The oaf's name was Rupert or Rufus or something, a hectic, overemotional type with ill-fitting glasses who kept trying to be his friend. Apparently his last few friends had made off to Neverland with the former Dean of Good, and Midas wondered whether getting away from this one had been part of their motivation.

He swiveled to the boy: "What's the School for Evil like?

Better than here?"

The boy looked shocked. "No! *Never*! School Master there is named Rafal and he makes his students sleep in burnt rooms and soggy beds and wear itchy black sacks and they're punished in the Doom Room by his great big man-wolf and beaten and tortured and ten of his best students ran away because they hate him and his school!"

No to switching, Midas decided.

What to do then?

His mind drifted back to the Good School Master. The one who seemed overly attentive . . . as if he was a bit too keen to win him over . . .

Ah, there's a plan, Midas thought. Do well in the School for Good, make the School Master think he was his perfect little pet . . . then manipulate him to get what he wanted.

As to how to do well, that was easy enough.

He did what any Evil student would do in a Good school.

Cheat.

In History of Heroes, he cheated on the Woods geography exam by pretending he had a hurt wrist and drawing the map of the Woods into the loose edge of the bandage, which he subtly lifted as he hovered over his booklet. In Forest Groups, he cheated in Animal Communication—a challenge to calm a tempestuous horse—by soaking the back of his neck with cashew butter, which made the horse lather him with kisses. In Dueling, he used so many dirty tricks and low blows that he beat every single Ever-boy, none of whom reported him, for fear of appearing weak. After each class, right on cue, the Good School Master seemed to magically appear, all smiles and buddy-buddy, congratulating him for his victories or pulling him aside to ask how he was doing, as if the very soul that had kidnapped him and forbidden him to go home now cared about his well-being. All was going to plan, Midas thought. By the end of the week, he was #1 in Good's rankings, which cued the School Master to appear once more.

"Class Captain Midas! And to think you wanted to go home!" Rhian mused, sidling up to him in the hall. Dozens of other Evers passed by, greeting the School Master, but Rhian didn't acknowledge a single one, his eyes fixed on the boy.

Midas could feel the heat off his stare. Now was the moment to find out what the School Master wanted from him and take full advantage.

"Just wondering, sir. Is there a reason I'm older than all the other students?" Midas asked innocently. "I look more like a School Master than a first-year. Ha ha."

"Clever fellow. I was hoping you wouldn't notice," Rhian chuckled. "Truth is . . . Let's talk over here, actually." Rhian gently guided the boy off the hall onto a secluded balcony, half-shadowed. "It's been strange times here of late. I've lost two Deans and a few of my best Evers in recent months. Not through any fault of my own, of course. The students and faculty . . . they're not what they used to be. There's a spark missing. The thrill is gone. I need something more from Good and I've been looking for it a long time. Something fresh and exciting that gives me those butterflies in the stomach. Something like . . . you."

Midas studied him. He had tousled, shiny waves of hair that caught the sun like precious metal and ocean-blue eyes with an almost reptilian glow. Immortal beauty, yes, but there was something distinctly young about him: a wild, hungry gaze, as if he'd been asleep for a hundred years and the deepest part of him had just woken up. Chills prickled up Midas' spine, his instincts sending a clear message. *Don't trust him.*

"You see, Midas, I don't have a Dean of Good anymore," the School Master went on. "I don't have a right-hand man or the kind of bond I need. Not that we have a bond yet, but . . . At the rate you're learning, you could be fit to be my Dean within a few years. Don't you think?"

Midas' stomach turned. "Dean? Me? That's very flattering, sir."

"Rhian. Call me Rhian," the School Master insisted.

Midas pretended to fuss with ruffles on his uniform and took a step back into shadow. "What happened to your last Dean, by the way? The one who ran off to Neverland . . . ?"

"Oh, you heard about that?" Rhian suddenly looked unsteady. "He wasn't right for the position. He was my brother's friend first."

"I can see that. Being your brother's friend first." Midas paused. "He's quite memorable, your brother."

Rhian hardened, pink slashing each cheek like he'd been slapped. "What do you mean by that?"

"Hmm?" Midas said, guileless.

"You don't *know* my brother." Rhian was stammering now, words rushing out of him. "Everyone k-k-knows I'm the better twin. Rafal fears that I could do just as well without him. Which is why he doesn't want me to get close to anyone or have someone to confide in. He's possessive of me. Jealous. He'd disapprove of us having this conversation if he knew. Probably even send you home to get you away from me. There's something amiss between Rafal and me. Something that's been lost. That's why I chose you. That's why I brought you here. I need someone on my side to be my other half. Someone who won't betray me. I need a . . . what's the word . . . a . . ."

"Friend?" said Midas.

Rhian exhaled in relief. "Yes. A friend."

Their eyes met. Silence lingered.

"Um, I have class . . . ," the boy said.

"Oh. Yes, of course," Rhian mumbled, moving aside, and Midas hustled past him, the School Master looking fraught.

That's when Midas stopped down the hall and, with the grandest of moves, he spun around and gave Rhian a warm, friendly wave.

The School Master burst into a bright smile and waved back heartily.

Midas stifled a laugh.

Getting home would be easier than he thought.

That evening, he smiled and nodded through a torturous dinner with Rufius in the Evers' dining hall, keenly aware that the Good School Master had his eye on him from the faculty table. Midas chose a seat by the window and acted like he enjoyed the broccoli-rutabaga roulade (fish and chips, anyone?!) and that he was immersed in Rufius' conversation (the boy spouted recipes they should bake together while Midas wished they could bake Rufius instead). All along, he kept his focus out the window, studying the bridge to Evil, assessing its stone and shadows and how to cross it undetected . . .

But then in the window glass, he caught Rhian glaring at him.

Quickly Midas' gaze flew back to Rufius and he nodded along to the idiocy the boy was rambling. Over Rufius' shoulder, Midas peeked at the faculty table, but the Good School Master was laughing with his colleagues, as if whatever Midas had seen in the glass had been a mirage.

That night, Midas waited in bed until his roommates fell asleep (he hadn't bothered to learn names beyond "Snorer" and "Teeth Grinder"). Soon snores were snuffling and teeth were clacking and Midas slipped out of the room, down the stairwell, and out the side door of the castle onto the bridge between schools. His Everboy pajamas flapped in the breeze, the moon a crescent spotlight as he hurried towards Evil, the black towers gleaming like open jaws—

BAM!

He smashed into something and careened to the ground.

Boggled, he looked up and saw his own reflection grinning down at him, wearing the same blue pajamas.

> *"Good with Good,*
> *Evil with Evil.*
> *Back to your tower*
> *Before there's upheaval!"*

Midas lurched to his feet and plowed forward, only to slam again into the invisible barrier, his reflection nestled within it.

"Remove yourself from Halfway Bridge," his reflection ordered.

"I need to see the Evil School Master," Midas demanded, tapping at the shield in every direction, hunting a way around it.

"Brainless fool," his reflection sniped. "Evers can't see the Evil School Master."

"I'm not an Ever," Midas insisted. "And I need his help."

"Go to your own School Master, then."

"That's the problem. I need to speak to the Evil School Master about his brother."

The reflection stiffened, his smile vanishing. "What about his brother?"

Midas stared hard at his own face. "I don't feel safe with him."

The phantom's eyes glowed green, like a spell unlocked. "School Master Rafal will be waiting for you in Malice Tower, Room 66."

The reflection disappeared. Midas reached out his hand and it passed straight through, the barrier gone. With a gasp of relief, he ran as fast as he could, his heart swelling with hope for home.

He didn't know someone was watching him.

Deep in the shadows, on the other end of Halfway Bridge.

A figure, whose gnashed teeth and gem-cut eyes gleamed through the darkness.

There, on Good's side the figure waited, until Midas was safely in Evil's castle, before they stepped into the moonlight and stalked across the bridge to follow him.

13.

Aladdin dabbed at his eyes with his cuffed hands. First his best friend, Hephaestus. Then his girlfriend. Both dead in the span of minutes.

The rope chaining him to Hook yanked them forward, night wind ruffling their feathered shorts, two prisoners dragged up a rocky path towards Cannibal Cave.

Aladdin's nose dripped, his sobs trapped in his chest. *Don't let me go,* she'd pleaded. He'd promised to save her. He'd tried to hold on with every ounce of his strength, until James ripped him away. Now he'd have to live with the memory: his true love falling into a monster's jaws, staring up at him in shock for breaking his vow. His whimpers grew louder, but Botic and the other two Lost Boys didn't chastise him, his captors' faces soft with sympathy, as if they only liked to play at violence and Kyma's death had affected them too. All the while, Aladdin ignored James' glances and huddled into himself, a pitiful shadow under the night sky. Once upon a time, he'd been a loner in Shazabah, hunting glory instead of friendships. Now he understood why. When he gave his heart, he gave it too deeply. He'd never make that mistake again.

Meanwhile, James had his own point of view about all this. *What the hell.*

He'd saved Aladdin from a monster. And not even a word of gratitude? Here he thought Laddy might be his first genuine friend! Aladdin had once confessed to him that he'd struggled to win mates in his desert kingdom, too busy trying to make his name in the Woods. James had related; he had no friends at Blackpool, his focus solely on overcoming a legacy of failed Hooks. Naturally, then, he thought the boys' loyalty was to him over that girl he'd picked up at school. Especially after he'd wrested him from the jaws of death! He glared at Aladdin, but Aladdin kept on mewling as if James shouldn't have saved him at all. Hook yanked angrily at the feathers wedged up his behind. This is why he didn't get close to boys or girls. They didn't give him the respect he deserved. No use making friends, he'd reasoned. They'll always disappoint you. Better to use people to suit your purposes. The way a captain uses a crew. The way Rafal once used him. He should have learned then . . . Aladdin sniveled loudly. James whirled—

"A simple 'thank you' would suffice!" Hook hissed.

"For what!" Aladdin hissed back. "You couldn't use Rhian's magic? You couldn't use a *sorcerer's* power to save her?"

"I told you: I don't know how to control it!"

"I'd rather have died than be here without her!"

"Well, you'll get your chance to die again soon!" James spat.

Aladdin tracked his glare to the cave up ahead, spewing smoke the color of blood. Fear cut through his grief.

"What would Kyma want? What would Hephaestus want?" James asked quietly, so Peter's boys wouldn't hear. "Would they tell you to wallow and surrender? Or would they tell you to fight?"

Aladdin rubbed his eyes. He drew a deep breath. "How do we fight a cannibal?"

"By being smart and finding his weakness," James whispered. "Not that I have a clue what that is. Anytime the Pan captured Dad's pirates, he sent them to Luoto Bakhti and no one ever saw 'em again. When I asked my dad about him, all he'd say is 'Man with a face like that can't be spoken of.' If I could just summon Rhian's magic—"

"Quiet, you!" Botic lashed, kicking Hook's behind.

The sympathy was at an end.

Cannibal Cave loomed in the highest cliff over the Savage

Sea at the furthest edge of Neverland. Above the entrance to the cave hung a garland of human skulls. Upside-down torches made from banded twigs raged on either side, big bushes of flame lighting the path into Luoto Bakhti's lair.

Botic drew a knife and cut the prisoners off the rope.

"He's waiting for you," said Pan's lieutenant, with a sly grin.

Aladdin peered into the red, smoky passage . . . bloodstains on the wall . . . scattered bones everywhere . . .

He twirled to flee—

The three Lost Boys blocked the mouth of the cave, knives drawn.

"We'll be here 'til Luoto's well done with you," said Botic.

"Get it?" one of his boys sneered at Aladdin. "*Well done . . .*"

"No wonder none of you can find a girlfriend," Aladdin clapped back.

Hook grabbed Aladdin's hand, James' eyes fixed ahead. "Come on."

James led him forward, Aladdin's heart rattling. In Shazabah, the scariest things were sand cobras or the occasional rogue falcon. Even in the worst Never kingdoms, he'd heard nothing of cannibals. Man-eating people were the lore of old wives' tales, told to scare children onto a path. But now he was walking the path straight into a real cannibal's clutches. Aladdin pictured an eight-foot-tall giant with a bone through his nose and jagged teeth. How do you beat someone like that?

They were so deep in the cave now that they couldn't see or hear the Lost Boys behind them. A giant black rat skittered by, Aladdin nearly jumping into James' arms at the sight. Soon, the red glow deepened, the air muggy and salty, the path pulling downwards towards crooked, spiraling stairs. Slowly, the pair descended, unable to see what lay below, the steps hugging a hollow darkness, until finally, they came out the bottom.

Two pools of water seeped red mist on either side of a stone flat, like a stage. Behind the pools rose a vast grotto, the rock in the shape of a skull that seemed to be watching them. On cue, the pools began to bubble and churn. Aladdin's eyes widened as a thousand fish rose to the surface of each, small and shiny and glimmery gold, bobbing fleshy little lips.

Wish Fish? he thought—

All at once, they shot open jaws of serrated teeth, chomping with furious shrieks.

This time it was James who nearly jumped into Aladdin's arms.

Then out of the mouth of the grotto's skull, onto the flat between pools, strolled . . .

. . . a very handsome man.

He was tall and broad-shouldered, with golden skin, strawberry hair pulled back in a wave, slim blue eyes, a rugged nose, and a stubbly beard. He wore white gloves and a red tunic.

James shook his head, dazed. "You're *him*?"

The man smiled . . . and peeled off his own face.

He tugged at the edges and slipped it right off, revealing another face under it.

The face of an old pirate with a glass eye, bushy beard, and a crossbones tattoo on his cheek.

Aladdin jolted, gripping Hook's arm, but before they could make sense of what was happening, the man pulled off that face too, a rosy teenage boy beneath, who yanked off his face to become an even younger boy who whisked off that face, revealing a skinny, nut-brown man with slicked black hair, narrow eyes, a crinkled forehead, and upturned lips. He kicked his heels and did a dance, crooning a spindly voice.

> *Luoto Bakhti, if you please!*
> *Forever hungry, my disease!*
> *Each boy in my cave, I ingest,*
> *But not the face, that part's the best!*

Luoto Bakhti is the name,
Never satisfied or tamed,
But it's all so I can take your face
I'm you, I'm me, a man erased!

Luoto Bakhti, made of thirst,
Escape and you'd be the first!
Too late now, you're my next catch,
A pinch of pepper and down the hatch!

He did a pirouette and skipped closer, inspecting the boys in their feathers.

"Two little peacocks," he cooed. "Dinner is served."

Aladdin lit his fingerglow and held it out like a wand. "Don't take another step, you . . . you . . . *freak.*"

"Oh, an Everboy. *La di da!*" Luoto Bakhti piped, a few feet from the pair. "A first-year, I presume from how your finger is quivering. Go ahead. Do your worst."

Aladdin stabbed his finger at the face-swapping cannibal, praying for a spell, any spell—

The glow brightened . . . and petered out.

"My hero," James growled at him. He turned sharply to their captor.

"You're not to touch us," Hook demanded. "Peter Pan's orders."

"Too bad Peter isn't here," Luoto Bakhti replied, circling James. "But someone you knew was . . ." He ripped off his face, revealing a dark-haired man's with steely blue eyes, thick eyebrows, and a mustache that connected to a long, pointy beard.

From the way Hook's face blanched, Aladdin knew the face could belong to only one person.

"I didn't eat your father, to be fair," Luoto Bakhti assured, retaining his old weaselly voice. "The last Pan speared him in battle and gave me his face as a gift. The new Pan does it too. Sends me fresh meat and in return, I don't eat him or his naughty boys. Because I could, you know. I'm forever hungry is the problem. Once upon a time, I was content with a different life. But then I got restless . . . a taste for something more . . . Now, nothing of my old self satisfies me." He spotted a black rat passing and kicked it into one of the bubbling pools. The murderous fish leapt up and caught it, dragging it under with a flood of screams, and a moment later, they spat out a perfectly diced filet that landed in Luoto Bakhti's open palm. He admired it and shook his head: "I scarcely remember what I was."

Hook turned a sick shade of green. This dirty, evil *perversion* . . . wearing the face of his father . . . his father who believed in rules and principles and good form . . .

Luoto Bakhti tossed the rat back to the fish. "My precious little poopsies. They give me the best parts and keep the rest for themselves. You should see the pies and stews and fricassees they make of boys like you. Though I suppose you won't see anything, since you'll be *in* the stew." He grinned at Hook, wearing another Hook's face. "You first? Or your friend?"

Then his smile evaporated. He sniffed at the air suspiciously, before yanking off the elder Hook's face, revealing a scrawny boy's underneath with a precipitously long nose and enlarged nostrils, sniffing harder, all around.

"Something is here," Luoto Bakhti said. He tore off that face to an older boy's with an even longer nose, hunting around the grotto. "Something here that wasn't here before . . ."

Aladdin flared his eyes at James. This was their chance to run. But Hook wasn't looking at him, distracted by a strange sensation . . . the awakening of Rhian's magic inside him. The more Luoto Bakhti sniffed at the air, the more Rhian's soul throbbed in Hook's chest—a strange, formless hunger, as if the Good School Master and cannibal were connected. James pulsed with hope, expecting Rhian's magic to finally show itself, to help him like it had once before . . . but as quickly as it came, it went dormant again, the glow inside him gone cold. James ached with confusion and turned to Aladdin.

But the young thief's eyes were on one of the pools of fish. Because while Luoto Bakhti was still sniffing about, unbeknownst to him his precious poopsies were vanishing beneath the water. Aladdin's heart quickened as the pool emptied out, growing clearer and clearer, revealing the source of the fish's demise—

"I'll go first," Aladdin blurted.

The cannibal spun to him, but the boy had already taken a running start, surged past him onto the stone flat, and dived straight into the pool.

Hook let out a wail of surprise, his friend vanishing into bubbly foam. Meanwhile, Luoto Bakhti clapped his hands with glee and peered into the smoking pool, waiting for Aladdin to be served up, *à la francaise*, *à la orange*, or *à la mode*, along with a new face to wear as the cherry on top. And indeed, on cue, a body ejected from the pool, straight at the cannibal, landing shiny and wet on the stone flat in front of him.

Only it wasn't Aladdin a la anything.

It was Princess Kyma.

James blinked, quite sure he was dead and dreaming. The girl he'd seen eaten by a monster was now dressed in a toga of palm fronds, holding a stack of skeleton leaves, her hair curled in ringlets and sugared with neon-pink dew.

Luoto Bakhti pulled off his face, revealing a fearsome pirate's with scarred cheeks, scraggly beard, and bloodshot eyes. He snarled: "Who are *you*?"

"Who do you think?" Kyma answered, with a little waggle. "I'm a Fairy Princess come to answer your wishes. This *is* a wishing well, isn't it?"

"It is most certainly not—" the cannibal scoffed.

"And yet you wished for true love," Kyma went on.

"*Me?*" Luoto Bakhti snorted, mucus flying out his bulbous nose. "You're mistaken, useless girl. Now leave or—"

"Says it right here," Kyma replied, rifling through her stack of leaves until she found the one she wanted. "Luoto Bakhti. Made an oath of love and broke it. He hungered for more. More life, more power. No matter how many men he had to consume. Now his soul finds no peace and he hides his true face under a thousand others . . . when what he truly wishes for is the one who once loved him for who he was. That's you, isn't it?"

The cannibal's face reddened.

Inside Hook, Rhian's soul stirred anew.

"No," Luoto Bakhti spat at Kyma, baring blackened teeth. "*No!*" He lunged for the princess—

From one of the pools came an explosion of pink slimy flesh, launching out of the water, giant jaws open, spewing a thousand hungry fish at the cannibal. The fish devoured Luoto Bakhti's face, then the next face, then the next as he flailed at them, bashing them away with horrified shouts, until at last, all his faces were gone and all the fish dead, leaving a haggard, horned troll, hunched on the floor of the grotto.

Slowly he looked up at a pink Ingertroll, climbing out of the pool.

"Iga?" the troll whispered.

"Sixty years I waited for you, Luoto," said Iga softly. "All alone and underground, like I was in my grave. Waiting for you to come for me."

Luoto shook his head, shamefaced. "I was so hungry for something more. But it never satisfied me. No matter how many I had . . ." He looked up, his face leathered and desiccated. "With you, I never felt hungry or empty. I never should have strayed. Please have me back, Iga. We can be the way we once were."

Iga gazed at him, her body tense, as if everything within was pulling her towards him. But then a sweet peace filled her eye.

"No," was all she said.

Her beloved was stunned. "But . . . but nothing's changed between us!"

Iga smiled sadly at him. "*I've* changed."

Her eyes went to Kyma and the princess smiled back, something in her own heart roused.

Hook snatched Kyma's hand. "Let's go!" he whispered, tugging her back towards the steps.

"Wait! Where's Aladdin?" she asked. "I hid him in—"

Iga's jaws pried open from the inside, Aladdin crawling out, feathers coated in slime, the boy panting and looking like death. "James . . . you know the difference between . . . us and Kyma? She not only survived being in there . . . and came up with a plan to save us . . . but she still smells like flowers . . ." He collapsed in a puddle of ooze.

Kyma shot James a salty grin.

Moments later, they bounded back towards the mouth of the cave, Hook holding his nose from how badly Aladdin smelled, while Aladdin squeezed Kyma's hand so tightly she could feel her knuckles turning white.

"Never letting you go again," Aladdin promised her.

Kyma thought of the trolls they left behind. "Think we all need a fresh start," she mulled, almost to herself.

Aladdin slowed, letting go of her hand. "What does that mean?"

"It means we get back to school, beg the Good School Master to let us rejoin, and go from there," Kyma said briskly, speeding up. "But first we gotta get off this island, even if we have to swim to the next one."

"We're not going anywhere until we find where Pan's taking my *ship*!" James barked.

"No one cares about your ship! We need to stay alive!" Kyma shot back.

Aladdin accosted Kyma. "You're not saying you want to break up, are you—"

James stopped short, Aladdin and Kyma slamming into him.

"One teeny-weeny thing we forgot . . ." Hook breathed, staring into the shadows.

At the mouth of the cave, Botic and two Lost Boys were playing marbles on a rock, blocking the exit. Slowly the boys looked up, silver stars dangling around their necks, Botic's purple glare piercing the dark.

"Ain't they supposed to be food?" one of the boys asked.

"Can't keep a Good man down," Aladdin snapped back. "Get it? Keep . . . food . . . *down* . . ."

Instantly, the Lost Boys rocketed to their feet, drawing daggers from belts. They surged through the cave, James, Kyma, and Aladdin too stunned to move, a slew of knives about to tear into them—

Vines lashed out from behind, snagging the Lost Boys by the

feet, ripping them to the floor. Before Peter's boys could fight, they were yanked backwards, chests scraping the rocky path, before they were dragged out the mouth of the cave and flung off the side of the cliff into the sea, with seven horrible yowls.

Hook and his two friends blinked at the cave entrance.

A silhouette rose in the darkness, tall, booted, with a wide-brimmed hat.

"Ready to get your ship, James?" a familiar voice spoke.

The Pirate Captain stepped into the torchlight.

Hephaestus and nine Nevers flanked him, vine ropes coiled at their waists.

At the sight of Hephaestus, Aladdin clutched his heart as if this was too much happiness to bear. But James was still shaking his head.

"My ship? *How?*"

"Same way we escaped a burning *Buccaneer*," the Pirate Captain replied. "Peter made the mistake of sending a fairy scout . . ."

He held up a small burlap sack, the size of a shoe, the outline of something teeny inside trapped and thrashing around with high, twinkly squeals. The Captain gave the bag a spank and the squeals loudened, puffs of rainbow dust spilling through burlap pores and drifting towards Hook.

James thrust out his chest as the dust hit him, glitter coating his pale skin. Little by little, his feet began to hover off the ground, his arms spreading like wings, higher, higher, until his head bumped the top of the cave.

Hook looked down at Aladdin and Kyma, gaping up at him.

He flashed a pirate's grin.

"Let's *fly*."

14.

Malice, Room 66.

That was the appointed place for his meeting with Rafal.

Midas found the staircase to the tower with little trouble, the spiral banister with the letters M-A-L-I-C-E, carved with monsters, spotlit by moonlight through a small window, while the steps to MISCHIEF and VICE stayed hidden in the shadows of Evil's entrance.

That the School for Evil was facilitating his meeting with its School Master was obvious—the doors to the castle magically opened off the bridge; the ogre guards fell asleep the instant they saw him; at every fork in a hall, a shiny line of roaches formed an arrow, leading him right or left. It all gave him a stark sense of déjà vu, until he remembered the tale of Aladdin, that storybook he read back in Gavaldon, about the Everboy lured into the School for Evil to serve its School Master's own designs. Rafal was clearly helping him the same way.

Midas would have to be wary, then. He needed the Evil School Master to send him home. But no doubt, Rafal would expect something in return.

As Midas hurried up the steps to the sixth floor, he took in the cobwebbed ceilings, the gargoyles dribbling water like drool, the damp, rancid smell that stung his nostrils . . . Rufius was right. He wouldn't have fared well here. He might be Evil through and through, but he liked warmth and comfort and expensive things, and the sooner he got back to Gavaldon, the sooner he'd be back to his normal life—

Midas froze.

A step out of sync.

As if someone had been following him, steps invisibly matched, until one missed and instead of Midas' boot hitting crisply, it split in two, a dull stutter—

He whirled around.

No one was there.

Midas' breath caught in his chest.

If someone was following him, the sooner he was in the safe presence of the School Master the better.

He scuttled ahead, Room 62, Room 64 . . . And there it was at the end of the hall, Room 66, with names on the door—Fodor,

Gryff, Asrael—all crossed out, no doubt three of the ten Nevers that Rufius said had fled from this school.

He raised his fist to knock, but the door opened on its own.

"Come in," said a cool voice.

Midas entered and quickly closed the door, bolting both locks.

He raised his eyes to a dark dormitory room with burnt walls, a dusty stone floor, a spidery chandelier, and metal beds and furniture that seemed fitting for a dungeon. The only source of light came from the window, shaped like a circle, and the long, pale silhouette curled up in it, like a crescent moon.

"I hear my brother is giving you trouble."

Rafal's green eyes lanced the dark and the chandelier sparked to life with a dozen flames.

He was wearing a red jacket over a lace-up black shirt, his pants a tight-fitting black leather, his hair shinier and spikier than when they'd met in the forest in Gavaldon. The Evil School Master peered at Midas, his lips curled into the same twisted grin he had when he'd held the boy against a tree by the throat—a frosty calm so different from his brother Rhian's hot, hungry gaze. Rafal was the Evil one, but Midas felt drawn to him, the way he wasn't drawn to his twin.

Midas stepped into the light. "There is a feeling of . . ."

"Suspicion and distrust," Rafal preempted. "He says one thing and means another."

"Yes, that's right," said the boy, surprised.

"What does he want from you?"

"He says he's lost his Dean and his best students and that he needs someone he can confide in. That I might be his new Dean one day soon. His friend and right-hand man."

"Did he say anything about me?" Rafal asked.

"That you are possessive and jealous and can't be trusted," Midas replied.

"Remarkable how honest my brother is with strangers. Concerning on the one hand. But also useful." The Evil School Master slid down from the window and landed on his feet. He took a step towards the boy, the full light of the chandelier hitting Rafal's marble-white skin. "And yet you are not dissuaded by his opinion, otherwise you wouldn't be here. You come to me why? Because you want to switch to my school?"

Midas stood straighter. "I want to go home."

A long silence passed. Rafal's eyes lifted to a black moth flitting between flames of the chandelier, striving not to get burnt.

"We've never sent a student home," the Evil School Master said, his focus back to the boy. "And yet, the circumstances you describe are unusual. A School Master kidnapping a student for the wrong reasons and giving them no say in their fate. As School Masters, we take an oath to the Storian to *protect* our students. To keep that oath, I must return you to Gavaldon."

Midas flushed with relief.

"On the condition you do me a favor first," said Rafal.

The boy stiffened. *The price,* he thought.

The Evil School Master assessed the boy a moment, as if debating whether to go on. His fist curled and uncurled at his side. When he continued, his voice was harsher. "Just as my brother doesn't trust me, I do not trust him. My brother is never without a plan. And I suspect he is brewing one now. You are to return to school and spy on him for me."

"Spy on . . . a *School Master*?" Midas said, astonished.

"Keep your eye on his every move," Rafal ordered. "Become his confidante. His friend and right-hand man, just as he asks. He is already honest with you. More honest than he is with anyone else. Your job is to find out what his plans are. For me. For the school. For the Storian. All of it. Each night, just before midnight, leave a letter with a report in your window for me to retrieve. If you are loyal to me and do well, I will send you home and kidnap no further students from your village. If you fail, well, then . . . you are here forever in my brother's hands. Understood?"

Midas struggled to hold in his shock. But he had no choice as to how to respond.

"Yes, sir," he said quietly.

Rafal finished: "Let no one know of our arrangements or my brother won't be the only School Master giving you trouble. Now go."

Midas unlocked and hurried out the door, which slammed behind him with a gust, snuffing out the flames of the chandelier.

Rafal remained in the dark, thinking.

Things were happening quickly.

The Reader moved to his side, just as he'd planned.

Midas would do as he was told.

That he was sure about.

And yet something was still bothering him . . .

A needling feeling that things had already gone astray . . . a bug crept into the plot . . .

Rafal shook off his doubts.

He was safe from his brother for now.

As long as Midas played his part, Rafal would stay one step ahead.

15.

Midas scurried back down the Malice staircase, his legs wobbly, sweat streaking from his curls. At the bottom, he veered for the castle doors—

"Midas?" a voice spoke from above.

Slowly the boy looked up the hollow of the stairwell at Rafal, gazing down at him from the sixth floor.

"A change in plans," the Evil School Master said. "Leave your report for me by eleven instead of midnight. This way I have time to review it before my brother returns."

Midas nodded. "Yes, sir."

"Now go," Rafal commanded, and the boy did, scampering out of sight, back towards the bridge.

Rafal stood quietly a moment before he heard the door to Room 66 open down the hall, someone coming out of it—

Quickly he pulled behind a wall and began to shrink, little by little, to the size of a dog, then a bird, then a frog, then to a tiny black moth that flitted down the stairs, turning onto one of the floors and hiding in shadow, near an open window.

There the black moth began to grow in size again, reversing the spell, not into Rafal . . .

. . . but into *Rhian*.

He took a deep breath, then glimpsed Dean Humburg approaching—

Quickly he put a glowing finger to his temple and his face melted back into his Evil twin's, just in time for Humburg to spot him.

"Up late, School Master Rafal?" Humburg said.

"A student having nightmares," he replied.

"As he should!" Humburg huffed. "I wanted to talk to you about this new Reader—"

"Not now," the School Master snapped.

"Yes, Master Rafal," the Dean mumbled, moving on.

In shadows, Rhian's face reverted to his own. It was the same disguise spell he'd used in Gavaldon to mimic that oversized dwarf, but transforming into his Evil twin required extra focus to get every last detail right, and his magic was so weakened that he couldn't sustain the spell for more than a minute or two. The moth, then, had been helpful, not only in breaching Evil undetected, but also for slipping into Room 66 and eavesdropping on Rafal's conversation with Midas from the perch of that chandelier, his traitorous Reader now allied with his even more treacherous twin. Rhian had sensed Midas might betray him from the way the boy had gazed intently at Evil's castle during supper, which is why the Good School Master had followed the boy here and caught him in the act. But it wasn't Midas' disloyalty that stabbed Rhian through. It was his twin's.

"Just as my brother doesn't trust me, I do not trust him."

Spying on his own brother? Was this the true reason why Rafal wanted a Reader? To betray his own blood? Rhian's face coated with sweat. First Rafal hides the fact that their immortality and magic are compromised. Now he enlists one of Rhian's own students against him? In his own *school*? Yes, Rafal was Evil, but this was more than Evil. This was unhinged.

Why? Rhian asked himself. Why was Rafal spying on him? Why was he keeping secrets about their mortality? Why was he acting as if his own twin was the enemy?

Rhian heard footsteps coming and morphed his face back into Rafal's. Three Neverboys snuck by, out of their rooms and surely up to no good. They didn't notice him, frozen in the shadows. But it was too dangerous to stay here any longer. He needed to get to the bridge unseen and return to Good's castle—

A gob of green light scudded through the window, ricocheted against the wall, and socked him in the eye. He rubbed his face in shock, his lids prying open to a hazy vision of a green-faced, black-winged fairy, clinging to his hand.

"Rafal!" Marialena hissed. "Something's happened!"

Rhian focused on the disguise spell, struggling to keep Rafal's face as long as he could. But Marialena was a seer. Surely she'd see through him . . .

"My sight is failing me," the fairy said, breathless. "Ever since I left Gavaldon. The One who will rule is no longer clear. The future is uncertain now—"

"Slow down," said Rhian. "What are you talking about?"

Marialena stared impatiently. "The prophecy that a School Master will rise and the other will fall. The prophecy my family first told you. That you or your brother will die and the One who survives will rule for centuries to come. The One who will lift my family to glory. I thought one of you would kill the other to fulfill the prophecy. But I'm not sure anymore . . ."

"Ah," said Rhian, his brother's behavior honing into focus. He paused, careful not to misstep. "You see something else, then."

"There is a third between you now," the fairy replied. "An ally or a threat or possibly the One themselves . . . I cannot tell."

Midas, Rhian thought.

The fairy lifted off his hand, black wings beating. "I'll go to my family. Perhaps they can see what I can't. Until then . . . be careful, Rafal. Remember the Rule of Three. Alliances matter with a third in the fray. Who you choose to trust will either be your savior or your doom."

Rhian nodded, watching her go, his grip on his brother's form expiring. By the time the fairy had flown out the window, Rhian had become himself again.

He lingered by the window, moonlight lobbing cool, white light on his wild waves of hair.

Now it is all clear, he thought.

One would rise and the other would fall.

A prophecy his twin had long known.

That's why Rafal was spying.

That's why he was keeping secrets.

Rafal was making moves to ensure that he won this death match.

That in the end, he would be the One.

But Good always wins, Rhian told himself.

His blood simmered, color flooding his cheeks.

Midas and Rafal had allied against him.

A team of pure Evil.

They knew the Rule of Threes better than he.

And yet, they'd forgotten the first rule of fairy tales.

Evil attacks. Good defends.

They'd attacked him, School Master and student.

Now he would defend.

He would be the One.

And if Rafal and Midas both perished to a prophecy, as a result . . . ?

Rhian's blue eyes glittered in the dark.

So be it.

16.

To catch a pirate ship at night requires both skill and speed, two qualities elusive to first-time flyers.

"H-h-how do you make it s-s-stable?" Aladdin sputtered, careening up and down, torn between marvel at floating a thousand feet in the air and the turbulence of his flight. "Do you swim with the legs or kick with the arms?"

"Neither!" Hephaestus barked back. "Keep your emotions steady and you'll coast on the wind!"

Aladdin lagged behind his friend and the nine Nevers orbiting the Pirate Captain, all of them skimming over low-flying clouds towards the *Jolly Roger*, a good two leagues ahead and flying south, silhouetted beneath the moon. Hephaestus and the Nevers were already expert flyers, having deployed the dust of a stolen fairy to escape the burning *Buccaneer* with the Pirate

Captain and reunite with Aladdin, James, and Kyma. The fairy dust had looked sparkly and inviting, but it had stung Aladdin the second it hit him, like he was allergic to it—he the only one to scratch and itch and bobble and teeter as they lifted out of Cannibal Cave, while Kyma glided with the ease of a salmon swimming the sea. He'd tried to give her space after she'd implied she wanted a break from him. She couldn't possibly mean it. They were soulmates. Best friends. They'd be together forever. He just needed to play it cool. Better for him to ignore her completely . . . Aladdin whipped around to see where she was, but it veered him off-course, sending him somersaulting into a gust of wind. He girded himself straight and vowed not to think of her. "Emotions steady, emotions steady—" He plummeted into clouds with a yowl.

Far ahead, at the fore of the pack, James Hook glanced back and saw Aladdin fall.

Must be obsessing over the girl, he thought.

Fairy dust didn't much work on boys in love—it stung and rashed their skin. There was good reason: fairies in Neverland were all loyal to Pan and Pan forbid boys on the island from growing up. And what better symptom of growing up than falling in love?

James set his eyes ahead, his arms spread wide, pushing

himself to a faster pace. The *Roger* tilted on its side, sails inflating with wind, moonlight finding the hull and its horrible shade of green, the bust of Peter on the prow casting glimmers in the night like a North Star. Hook chased the ship south, his mind empty of thoughts, his blood at a boil, James focused only on recovering what was his. But killing Pan wouldn't be easy. They'd have to separate him from his shadow before the Good School Master's magic finished the job. Hook waited for Rhian's spirit to glow inside him, to give him certainty it would slay Peter's shadow when the time came, but the more he looked for the Good School Master's powers, the colder and emptier his own soul seemed. At every step, Rhian's magic had been riddling and unpredictable, as if it cared nothing for James' needs. He thought about that vast, gnawing hunger that rose when the troll spoke of his own . . . hunger like an icy black hole, nothing like the cozy warmth of Rafal's magic . . . Hook broke into a sweat. What if the Good School Master's magic saw James as Evil? What if, unlike Rafal's power, Rhian's magic *wasn't* on his side? What if it had turned against him? What if it wanted him *dead*—

"These Evil kids are fast learners. We stole the best possible crew from that school," the Pirate Captain said, pulling alongside Hook. He held up the tiny satchel with the trapped fairy.

"I keep asking how long fairy dust lasts, but she won't answer. Won't stop biting me through the sack and nipping my fing— Ow!" He shook the bag, dislodging her off his thumb, but this time no more dust came out. "Either she's out of dust or she figured out how to keep it from us. What's the plan once we get to the *Roger*?"

"Shock and awe," Hook puffed, swallowing away his doubts. "Kill Pan, take the crew prisoner, reclaim my ship, and tow Peter's body back to Neverland and make it clear that either everyone on that island swears allegiance to me or they'll suffer the same fate."

"I see," said the Captain.

"You would do the same," Hook pointed out.

"Would I?" the Captain mused. "My mortal nemesis whose existence revolves around my death suddenly pays little notice after my capture and leaves me alive so he can abandon the island where he's king and jaunt off on a mysterious trip? If it was me . . . I'd want to see where he was *going*."

James stared at him.

"But *you're* the captain," quipped his former headmaster and he looped round and flew back to his Nevers.

Hook slowed his flight, lost in thought.

"Those two boys on the ship with Pan. Who were they?"

Princess Kyma asked, catching up to him. "Lost Boys have silver stars around their necks. Those two had gold suns. What's higher than a Lost Boy?"

"Nice trick with the trolls back there," Hook breezed, avoiding her question. "You might end up useful after all." He surged ahead.

Kyma kept up. "First compliment you've ever given me. Albeit a backhanded one."

"Not a bad flyer either, even though you're small as a fairy. Practically levitating already."

"What is it about me that threatens you so much, James?"

"It isn't personal, princess. Girls are a distraction."

"Why? Because I save you from danger? Because I challenge you on your nonsense? Because unlike the rest of you boys, clinging to crews and gangs, I'm perfectly fine on my *own*?"

Hook turned to her. "Because you're pretty."

He dove into clouds.

Kyma stalled midair, stunned. Then she shook her head, with a wry smile. Now he was just trolling her—

Aladdin crashed into Kyma from behind.

"Ow!" she growled.

"S-s-sorry, can't control myself!" he yelped, veering in the wind. "Listen, I've been thinking about it and we can't break up.

We're the perfect couple. First off, you're my princess. Second, you're the only girl I've ever wanted. And third, you make me feel good about myself in a way I've never felt before. Without you, I blow around in the wind. And look at me now. Just talking to you calms me down," Aladdin proclaimed, his flight finally steadying.

Kyma's gaze was even steadier. "All those reasons you listed for us staying together. Those are all about you, Aladdin. Not about *us*."

Aladdin lost his bearings again like a severed kite, while the rest of their team zipped by. Kyma flew up and caught him. "Let's talk about this when we're on solid ground."

Aladdin shook his head. "But . . ."

"Almost there!" Hook's voice cried out.

Aladdin and Kyma looked down through a hole in the cloud to see the crew circling James, catching up to the *Roger*.

"We'll dive on your order!" Hephaestus called.

Hook hesitated and met the Pirate Captain's eyes. "Not yet. Kyma, Aladdin—come with me!" Then he spotted Aladdin tossing in the wind like a tumbleweed. "On second thought, just Kyma. Rest of you hold for my signal!"

James plunged for his family ship and Kyma dove after him without hesitation, letting go of Aladdin, who reeled backwards into clouds with a shout.

From a bird's-eye view, Hook could see the deck of the *Roger* was empty and still, except for a lantern hanging off the bow, tiny shadows buzzing inside, like it was full of flies. With no one on guard, it gave James cover to land in shadows behind a heap of ropes, Kyma arriving a moment after and huddling next to him.

"What are we doing here?" she whispered.

"Finding out where Pan is taking this ship," Hook answered. "Let's split up and look for him."

"Split up? It's *your* boat, James. I don't have the faintest clue where I'm going—"

The door to the galley opened behind them and three Lost Boys trudged out, silver star necklaces shining, the lads munching on burnt chicken legs.

"Still no word where we're headed except due south," one growled, the name STILTON tattooed on his back.

"See anything at least?" asked another, with the tattoo RIMPY.

"Just a map of the Endless Woods spread out on the desk and that pair of strange boys with him. Definitely not from Neverland, those two. Peter says the ship's losing speed. Ordered us to get more dust."

"Fairies won't give us any, not after those *Buccaneer* pirates stole their fairy friend who Pan sent scouting," said the third, tattooed ABEL. "Little pests told me no more dust until we either give 'em back their friend, free 'em from the lantern, or Peter gives all of 'em kisses."

"First rule of negotiating with fairies," Stilton replied. "*Don't negotiate with fairies.*"

They headed for the lantern, hanging off the bow. As soon as they were gone, James grabbed Kyma's hand. "Come on." He pulled her across the deck and through the galley doors.

"If there's a map on the desk, they're meeting in the captain's office," Hook whispered, his eyes narrowing. "My *dad's* office."

Kyma followed James down a tight spiral staircase, the wooden banister knife-slashed with the letters *P.P.* again and again and again. Hook ran his fingers over the vandal's initials, his lips curled in a sneer. Soon, they heard voices from the room at the end of the hall. Hook slipped out of his boots, Kyma out of her shoes, and barefoot they padded off the staircase and crouched at the double doors, peering through the crack.

Peter Pan reclined in a dark leather chair, feet up on the desk, smoking a cigar out of an open case and blowing smoke in the shape of the letter *P*. Meanwhile, his shadow coughed and retched on the wall. "Is this what all the cursed Hooks do? Sit here, filling their lungs with this foulness, and plotting my demise?" He put out the cigar on the desk, next to a case of ornate daggers. His little green eyes lifted to the two boys sitting in front of him in orange sarongs, one older, one younger. Pan leaned back, thin, ropy arms stretched behind his head. "One more day south until we reach the castles. And your sight remains unchanged? You still see what you did before? That it will be me?"

"My sight only gets clearer and clearer," said the older boy, with sand-colored hair and big hazel eyes. "Luca sees the same, don't you, Luca?"

"Yes, Matias," said the skinny younger one, looking at Pan. "It will be you."

Peter pulled a dagger out of the case. "You claim the Saders are great seers in the Woods. It's why I let you into Neverland and gave you higher status than my Lost Boys. But if what you say is the future . . . wouldn't you age ten years for telling me the truth? Isn't that the rule for all seers?"

Matias and Luca Sader glanced at each other. "There are exceptions—" said Matias.

"—for Pans," Luca finished.

Matias squinted at his brother. Then he turned back to Pan. "Precisely."

A pinprick of red appeared in each of Pan's pupils. He lunged over the table and pointed the knife at them. "Swear it, then! Swear on your *lives* what you have told me is true. That I will be the One. That in a matter of days, I will become School Master of the Endless Woods. I will replace the brothers Rhian and Rafal as protector of the Storian, keeper of the tales, and be made immortal and invincible, not just for the hundred years of a Pan . . . but for *eternity*."

Kyma collapsed against Hook in shock, sending him falling forward—*"James!"* Kyma gasped—before Hook slammed head-first into the door with a violent thump.

Kyma grabbed him back, both their faces dead pale, but Pan had already let out a shout. *"A girl! I heard her voice!"* Boot-steps rushed towards them from inside, the gleam of a dagger through the doors, Hook and Kyma scrambling in retreat . . .

Suddenly, a terrible fire sparked in James' chest, Rhian's magic reappeared without warning. A sorcerer's spell lashed through him, flooding up his limbs and out his hands with a lightning *crack*!, a net of golden glow exploding, just as Pan threw open the doors, knife raised to kill—

But the hall was empty, save two pairs of shoes at the bottom of the stairs.

"Someone was here!" Peter cried. He whirled to the Saders. "You can see everything, can't you? Who was there? Who did you see?"

The two Sader boys stared right at Hook and Kyma, lying invisible on the floor in front of Peter, as if they saw exactly who was there.

Matias and Luca looked back at Peter.

"No one," they said together.

17.

The night after he'd made his deal with Midas, Rafal watched the boy's window from his perch in the School Masters' tower, waiting for a letter to appear in it.

When no letter came, long after the tasked hour of midnight, the Evil School Master sighed and paced the room, stopping after a few lengths to observe the Storian, which had quietly finished its latest tale. What had begun as a story of a few children caught on a jungle island and sent to a cannibal had evolved into the tale of two trolls, a boy and girl, once true loves, now grown apart. The boy troll hungered for something more than the girl's love, a hunger so all-consuming that it led him as far from love as one could get. By the time he'd learned the error of his ways, it was too late. The girl had realized she could do better on her own. THE END, the Storian wrote, beneath a portrait of the doomed boy troll.

So it wasn't the children who were the stars after all, Rafal realized, the Pen carving THE TWO TROLLS into the cover before the book magically whisked onto a nearby shelf. It was the pair of monsters, their bond of love shattered by one longing for more.

Something stirred inside him. A familiar theme. As if once again, the Storian was finding the tale of its School Masters in other people's stories.

All of a sudden, the Pen spun to him with its sharp steel tip, like a taunting eye. It moved towards Rafal, the edge pointed at him like a blade. The Evil School Master backed up in surprise. Closer and closer the Pen came, until he was pinned against the window, the lethal tip grazing his throat.

Rafal lifted his chin, faced with his own reflection in the Storian's steel.

The Pen pressed the tip deeper into his neck without drawing blood . . . a warning . . . a mercy . . .

Then, in the steel, the School Master glimpsed a new reflection—something from Good's castle—

He whipped his head, peering out the tower, and spotted a fold of white parchment tacked to the outside of Midas' window, lit by the moon like a beacon.

By the time Rafal turned back, the Storian was hanging peacefully over the table, completely still, as if he'd imagined the whole thing. The School Master shot it a glare, then dove out the window, soaring through the cool night, swinging over Good's half of the bridge, up to the castle. He grabbed Midas' letter off the glass before skimming back into the School Masters' tower, feet hitting stone, his hands reaching for the letter opener on his desk—

"Watercress and egg, just like you wanted," spoke a voice behind and he spun to see Rhian ascend the steps in a rich golden cloak, balancing a tray of sandwiches on his palm. "Strange, because I asked the pots if they've ever made them for you when you've come to Good for the Welcoming, and they insisted that you always request cucumber and herb butter, just like I thought . . ." Rhian raised his eyes to his brother, who was standing still, his hands frozen on Midas' unopened letter. "What's that?" Rhian asked.

The twins stared at each other. Tension brewed so thick it seemed to cast shadows around them.

That's when Rafal noticed the glint at the edge of his brother's coat.

A sword sheathed inside it.

Rafal pocketed the note. "Oh, just the Doom Room Master's report."

"Ah, of course," Rhian offered, putting the sandwiches

down. "Speaking of the Doom Room . . . Midas almost ended up there, so you know. But then he sewed this cloak for me. Pure gold thread. Somehow the boy found a way to spin straw into gold after I gave him the Rumpelstiltskin Challenge as a punishment for slipping out of his dormitory last night. Locked him in his room and ordered him to either make me a cloak out of gold or I'd bring him to your dungeon for a *real* punishment. In the end, he succeeded. He was mysterious as to his methods, but we both know he's a special one. Do you think that's why the shield let us through leaving Gavaldon? Because you wanted him too? Because we *both* chose him as our Reader?"

Rafal's eyes flickered, pink spotting his pale cheeks. "What are you talking about?"

"I suppose it's your revenge," Rhian said. "You take Midas from me like I took Hook."

Rafal leaned back against his desk. "You really have lost the plot," he said, his fingers inching behind him for the letter opener. "I don't even *know* Midas."

"Oh?" Rhian replied, with a puzzled look. "From what I hear, you asked him to write a letter to you each night. A letter like the one you just hid in your pocket. Go ahead. Open it. See what it says."

Rafal froze like a corpse. Sweat beaded on his face. His mouth went very dry.

Slowly, he reached into his pocket and drew out the folded letter, prying it open with the edge of his nails.

He unfurled the parchment, revealing a single black image on the page.

For a moment, Rafal didn't understand.

Then he remembered.

Room 66.

Chandelier.

Moth!

Instantly, he grabbed the letter opener like a knife—

Rhian had already pulled his sword.

They moved in a circle around the Storian, each pointing a weapon at the other, the Pen reflecting their twin faces.

"Using my own student to *spy* on me. Bonding with a stranger against your own blood. Hiding secrets because you think you can outlive me," Rhian hissed. "You really are Evil. If the prophecy is true, if one of us deserves to fall, then it is you, brother. Only you."

Rafal spat back: "Plotting to murder my students. Manipulating your own. Cheating every step of the way. You broke the bond. You made us mortal. You failed our test. You don't think the Storian knows what you've done? It's *you* who will fall."

"You forget something, brother." Rhian's face was cold as ice. "*Good* always wins."

They rushed each other, sword and knife out—

BOOM!

The entire tower quaked, sending both boys toppling to the ground.

BOOM!

Rafal stumbled to the window.

A ship descended out of the night towards the school, its cannon firing at their tower.

BOOM! BOOM! BOOM!

Craters blasted into the spire, threatening to bring it down. As stone tiles shattered around them, Rhian clung to Rafal's leg to pull himself up. They gaped at the flying ship with green sails, turning its cannon at their heads—

The brothers dove just in time, an iron ball smashing into their chambers.

"Protect the Storian!" Rafal cried at his twin, but the Pen was nowhere to be found.

THE RULE OF THREES

Then they saw it: hidden in a gap between fallen bookcases, peeling open a blank book and painting the tower under attack, the invading ship, and the words to begin a fresh tale:

> *A test had been failed.*
> *Two School Masters would be replaced.*
> *And now . . .*
> *The new one had come.*

Twin brothers locked eyes.
Together, they gripped their blades and ran.

PART 2

THE NAME OF THE ONE

1.

The ship landed on the pebbly shore of the lake between the two schools, directly in front of the School Masters' tower, which leaned and teetered precariously from all the holes in its stone.

Rafal flew Rhian from the base of the tower, the two School Masters locked in arms, before Rafal touched down at a safe distance from the ship and freed his twin, who instantly pointed his sword at the enemy vessel. A few seconds ago, they'd been on the precipice of murder. Now they were brothers once more. They peered up at the ship, sleek and shiny in the moonlight, and for a moment, all was deathly quiet.

"I know this ship . . . ," Rafal murmured.

"The *Jolly Roger*," said Rhian, his gold cloak rippling in the wind. "Shaped like a dragon's tail with seven sails . . . The greatest pirate ship of Neverland."

"And yet it has a different name," Rafal noted.

Rhian followed his eyes to the prow. "The *Mighty . . . Pan*?"

"But you can call me *Peter*," said a voice, and the School Masters whirled to see a plank slide from ship to shore and an elfish boy walk down it, tall, lanky, and dressed in green vines, followed by six barechested teenagers in green, wearing silver star necklaces, and two more, dressed in orange, one with a golden sun necklace, the other without.

Rafal bristled at the sight of this last pair, who stared right at him with their hazel-colored eyes. *Sader brothers,* he thought.

He glanced at Rhian, but his brother was squinting upwards at the schools, scores of students come out on the balconies, sleepy-eyed in their pajamas, including Midas, all of them woken by the cannon fire.

"Now, I don't want a fight," Peter Pan crowed, a dagger glinting on each side of his belt. "I've been well-informed your time is almost at an end. Soon the Storian will strip your powers, rob you of immortality, and name me its new guardian. *I* will be School Master, training your Evers and Nevers to be *my* soldiers, and molding the Endless Woods into a realm as peaceful and obedient as Neverland itself. A united world under Pan. Good and Evil both loyal to *me*."

A soft cry came from the ship, prompting the Lost Boys to turn their heads, but Pan stayed focused on his rivals.

"This is the future, whether you like it or not," said Peter, his green boot toeing the shore's sharp-cut pebbles. "You have two choices, then. You can accept what's coming and submit. Or you can risk death and fight. The latter will not end well, given we share eternal youth . . ." Peter grinned at the School Masters.

Then he noticed the hint of something unexpected in both their faces.

Fear.

"Or do we *not* share it any longer?" Pan probed, moving towards them. "Oh my. Has the Pen already left you behind? Let's test it—"

He kicked a storm of pebbles at them and Rhian shot a flimsy spell, forging a shield of glow, which ricocheted the stones back at Peter. But Pan was fast, already sliding under the rocks, before he sprinted up Rhian's shield like a launchpad, backflipped over the top, and drew twin daggers from his belt, one to each fist. Unsure who he was coming for, the brothers hesitated a moment too long, then tried to run—but Pan was landing between them, knives out, cutting a gash in each of their ankles, felling them to the ground.

Blood flowed freely, Rhian and Rafal writhing in pain,

clutching their legs, each unable to stand.

"Well, that answers that question," said Pan, snapping his fingers, and a moment later, the Lost Boys threw nets over the fallen School Masters and cuffed their hands in shackles before bagging them both up.

The last thing Rafal saw was the Sader brothers, arms folded by the lake, watching him and his twin dragged away towards Evil's castle.

Rhian, meanwhile, looked desperately to his and Rafal's students, gathered on the balconies of Good and Evil, an army of a hundred Evers and Nevers that could save them . . . that could overwhelm this intruder . . .

None of them moved.

Soon the brothers were towed inside the School for Evil and the doors locked behind them.

A few moments later, the *Mighty Pan* rose into the air with a last burst of fairy dust, depositing Peter Pan and the Sader brothers through the window of the School Masters' tower, before the ship floated down to the lake and dropped anchor.

Aboard the vessel, two sets of eyes peeped over the railing, checking to make sure Pan and the Saders were well inside the spire and that the students were back in their castles.

"Almost got us killed by yelping like a goat, princess," Hook accused Kyma. "Suppose they'd seen us?"

"Peter Pan just threatened to turn the whole Woods into his own personal dictatorship!" Kyma retorted. "We have to do something!"

Shadows rose over them and they looked up to see the Pirate Captain and nine Nevers descend in a cloud of fairy dust and touch on the empty deck, along with Aladdin, who crashed face-first into a sail before toppling between James and Kyma.

"Only one thing to do," the Pirate Captain declared. "We take back the *Jolly Roger*, fly to Neverland, and seize the island for ourselves. Bring in my Blackpool lads and turn all those Peter Boys into fresh crew under the pirate flag."

"And leave Pan in charge of the School for Good and Evil?" Kyma said, aghast. "He just attacked and captured our School Masters. You all can do whatever you like, but I'm staying here and fighting."

Aladdin bobbed up groggily. "Wherever Kyma goes, I go," he said, targeting Hephaestus, expecting his friend to agree.

But Hephaestus wasn't so sure. Nor were the nine Nevers, led by Timon. Like the rest of Good and Evil, who'd stood by as the School Masters were taken, their loyalties hung in doubt.

Instead, they turned to the only person who could decide their next move.

The one to whom they were all loyal.

The one to whom this ship belonged.

But James Hook was quiet, his eyes darting between the window of the School Masters' tower and the castles of Good and Evil.

He wasn't thinking about his ship or Pan or Neverland.

He was thinking about those two brothers. And the way the Saders had stared at him and Kyma earlier on the ship, seeing through their invisibility spell, before they had lied to Peter and said no one was there. They knew Hook had been hiding aboard. Surely they knew he was *still* hiding there, in the very spot he sat right now. He and Kyma and all the rest of them. Which meant the brothers *wanted* them here. As if Hook and his crew would play a key part in the story to come. As if perhaps the Saders' allegiance to Pan wasn't as clear as he thought . . .

In which case they couldn't leave yet.

They had to let the tale play out.

They had to find their place in it.

But how?

That's when Hook spotted it.

Right in front of him, hanging off the railing, as if it had been put there for him to see.

A necklace with a golden sun.

James's eyes twinkled, reflecting its light.

"Well?" the Pirate Captain pressed. "What's our move, Captain Hook?"

"There's only one move to make," James replied.

He plucked the necklace and held it up to his crew, the back of the sun carved with a message for them. Three crisp words that left no uncertainty as to what two seer brothers were telling them to do:

Go To School

2.

"Who are you?" growled the man-wolf.

He was standing outside the Doom Room dungeon, where he administered punishment to wayward Nevers, glaring down the sewers at a group of lads, dragging a net with two bodies.

"We're Peter Pan's boys. Pan's the new School Master," their leader announced, towing the bodies forward and kicking them into the light. "How much these two paying you?"

The man-wolf peered at the two School Master brothers in the net, hands cuffed, pants soaked with blood.

"Not enough," said the Doom Room Master.

A satchel of coins launched across the path and landed at his feet. "There's twenty gold coins to guard and torture these two at will," said the Lost Boys' leader. "They're mortal now. Ain't got much magic left either, from what we can tell. Go ahead, boys. Get yourself out of there."

Rhian and Rafal struggled against their cuffs. At full magic, they'd have already blasted free and obliterated their captors. But the lad was right. Something had changed. They summoned and chanted and flicked weak fingerglows . . . but no spell came.

"Like I said," the Lost Boy crowed, looking back at the man-wolf. "Twenty gold coins to put these two in their place and keep 'em there 'til they're bones and dust."

"Triple it," said the man-wolf.

Rafal lashed out: "You came here because you and your man-wolves wanted protection from Camelot as your price. From the king who was hunting your kind—"

"And what good are you at protecting us if you're mortal without good magic," the man-wolf snapped. "At least with gold my wolves and I can buy ourselves the loyalty of Never kingdoms to shield us."

Two more satchels of gold flew through the air and landed at his feet.

The man-wolf threw open the cell. "Bring 'em in."

By the time the Lost Boys had left the sewers, the man-wolf had cut the School Masters out of their net and chained their hands above their heads to the dungeon wall beneath dozens of torture instruments: whips, knives, racks, clubs, clamps, thumbscrews, and more.

"Told you those wolves would be trouble," Rhian browbeat his twin.

The man-wolf tapped his foot in front of their faces. "You two got yourself into a royal mess, haven't you? Title stripped, powers weakened, school turned over to a boy famous for being a twinkly little brat . . ."

"Whatever they're paying you, we'll double it," Rafal vowed.

"Triple it," said Rhian.

Rafal looked at him. "Don't be cheap," Rhian murmured.

"Funny, ain't it," the man-wolf continued, "that all this time you sent children here to be punished and now the children have sent *you* instead."

"Rafal sent children to you, not me—" Rhian started.

"No one respects you anymore," the man-wolf snarled. "The School for Good and Evil was once famed for its twin School Masters whose love for each other overruled their loyalty to their sides. But word has spread of a rift between them—a rift that has brought strangers and invaders to the school . . . a rift that threatens to rob the brothers of their powers. Little does the Woods know the threat has already come to pass."

Rafal surged towards the man-wolf, pale arms straining against his chains. "*Ten times* what they're offering you."

"*No.*" The man-wolf loomed over the twins. "Some things are priceless. Like punishing two selfish brothers who not only failed my kind but failed the whole of the world they were supposed to protect."

He reached up and grabbed a cudgel off the wall. "Never thought you'd get your turn in the Doom Room, did you. A good old taste of your own medicine." He raised the club over their backs. Rafal and Rhian braced—

"Perhaps you'll let *me* have the honor instead," said a voice.

Boys and man-wolf looked up.

A tall, dark lad with coppery curls, dressed in Ever clothes, stood in the open doorway of the cell.

"I believe I can meet your price," Midas told the man-wolf.

"And what price is that?" the man-wolf snorted.

Midas raised a finger and touched a gray brick on the wall.

The brick instantly turned metal.

Midas pulled it off the wall and tossed it at the man-wolf's feet, landing with a heavy, clanging thud.

The man-wolf gaped at the brick. So did Rhian and Rafal.

It was gold.

Pure, solid gold.

The boy turned another brick to gold, flinging it to the floor. Then another. Then he put his whole palm flat upon the wall and all the bricks in the dungeon turned to shining, flawless gold.

By then, the man-wolf was already scooping as many as he could in his big hairy arms, ten, twelve, fifteen, before dashing out of the cell and bounding away from the sewers.

Midas waited for the sounds of the creature to fade.

"So. You know that cloak you're wearing? The one you made me spin last night while I was locked in my room?" His gray eyes fixed on Rhian. "Turns out I learned a *lot* more than sewing."

3.

"Let me get this straight," said Aladdin, biting into a burnt turkey leg. "You want us to return to school, where Peter Pan claims to be the new School Master and . . . go to *class*?"

"I thought we came to kill Pan!" said one of the Nevers, waving his meat.

"Aye!" chorused the other Nevers.

"No way am I going to school," the Pirate Captain rejected, building a carefully cooked egg sandwich. "First of all, I'm the headmaster of my *own* school, and second, I look like a man, not a child like the rest of you, and third, we have no idea what cockamamie classes Pan is going to run or what he's going to do with this place. So how about I sail the *Jolly Roger* back to Blackpool and leave the rest of you to whatever pea-brained plan that James has cooked up."

"Fair points," said Hephaestus while he sharpened his sword, as if his time with the Pirate Captain escaping the *Buccaneer* had cemented them as a team.

Kyma cleared her throat. "Look, if James wants us to go to school, he must have good reason."

Aladdin frowned, mouth full. "Since when do you defend *James*?"

"Everyone shut up," James ordered.

They were in the forest outside school, seated around a fire, small enough to warm them without catching the eye of any guards who might be watching from castle belfries. They'd stolen provisions off the *Jolly Roger*—frozen turkey legs, a box of eggs, a few hunks of bread—and cooked their dinner over the flames. From their vantage point, they could see through trees and glimpse the bridge between schools, but no one had crossed from Good to Evil or Evil to Good since they'd settled here, the night beginning to fade towards dawn.

"Those two boys in orange on Pan's ship. They're seers," Hook explained. "Rafal and I met them when we went to Monrovia Prison to learn our futures. They left us this message, knowing we'd be here." He held up the sun necklace with the order to *GO TO SCHOOL* carved on the back. "Which means they see something in the future that we're a part of. Something that might bring Pan down."

"How do we know they're not on Pan's side?" Aladdin asked suspiciously.

"Because those two boys spotted me and Hook when they were *with* Peter Pan," Kyma said. "We snuck onto the *Roger* and they caught James and I together, but they didn't tell Pan."

"What they *did* tell Pan was that a new School Master would rise and it would be Pan himself," said Hook, looking at Kyma. "But it isn't clear they're telling him the truth."

"Especially since they lied about seeing us," Kyma affirmed.

Aladdin grumbled, as if the idea of Kyma spending time alone with his friend, let alone agreeing on something, was deeply offensive. "I'm sorry. Whole point of this journey is to kill Pan, get our name in the storybooks, and be famous in all the Woods. Not to go to class with Peter Pan as *School Master*."

Kyma shot back: "Whole point of this journey is to do what's right, which is protect our school. But if you'd rather go after glory, by all means, go chase it from here to the Murmuring Mountains without us."

This clammed Aladdin up.

But Hephaestus was still unconvinced. He peered at the Pirate Captain. "If you take the *Jolly Roger* and head out to sea, I'll be your first mate."

The Pirate Captain tapped his finger to his lips. He looked at James. "A new School Master will rise, eh? Peter Pan is obviously convinced that it's him. That the seers are telling him the truth. But what if the seers think it's one of *us*? Why else would they tell us to remain at this school unless one of us proves pivotal? So pivotal that *we* could be the master of the Storian ourselves?"

"We meaning *you*," said Aladdin.

"Just a thought," the Pirate Captain replied archly.

"You tried to steal the Storian before and look how that turned out," Kyma reminded him, but the Captain pretended to fuss with the last of his eggs as if he hadn't heard.

"Here's the plan," said James. "Pirate Captain and Hephaestus: you go find the two School Masters. Sooner you free them, sooner we have them on our side against Pan. Timon, you and the Nevers sneak back to your old dorm rooms in Evil before classes begin. Peter's never seen you before, so he won't know you're working for us. Pan's seen Aladdin, Kyma, and I, so we'll stay behind and find a way to disguise ourselves before we attend class too. We'll all meet back here tomorrow at midnight. Any questions?"

The Pirate Captain put his arm around Hephaestus, squiring him towards the school. "Keep that sword handy," he said, nodding at the blade on the boy's belt. "You're a pirate's henchman now."

Hephaestus wagged his brows. "You know what they say: those who can't do . . . *teach*."

Timon and the other eight Nevers hastened after them, pulling their black cloaks and hoods over their heads and vanishing into the night.

Which left James, Aladdin, and Kyma alone by the fire, the flames spitting and crackling as Aladdin tossed the scraps of everyone's dinner in.

"Shouldn't we have gone to find the School Masters ourselves?" Aladdin asked. "They might not trust the Pirate Captain."

"They'd trust me even less," Hook muttered. "Besides, not sure I'm ready to face Rafal again. Or Rhian for that matter.

Lots of history between the three of us."

"I'll say," Aladdin snorted. "Rafal blows his magic into you. Then he takes it back and leaves you to die. Then you take revenge by stealing his students and duping his twin to blow *his* magic into you. Magic you can't even control. No wonder you don't want to see them."

"Well, I hope the seers are wrong," said Kyma. "I hope that the old School Masters take back their place the way it's been for hundreds of years and everything returns to what it was. That we can start the whole story over. And do it right this time."

"Cheers to everything going back the way it was," Aladdin echoed, "when you *liked* being my girlfriend."

Kyma ignored him.

"Saders seemed to imply it was *one* School Master who would rise," Hook pointed out. "Maybe the Pirate Captain's right. Doesn't have to be Rhian or Rafal. Could be anyone. Could be one of us." He gazed into the flames, the heat beading him with sweat. "Truth is, it's not just about killing Pan anymore for me, or reclaiming my ship. It's about finding out why I'm on this mission in the first place. This whole adventure that took me away from Neverland, away from Blackpool, and keeps bringing me back to this school. As if I'm meant to be here . . ."

"As if *you* could be the One," Kyma said quietly.

Their eyes met.

"Seriously doubt that," Aladdin growled.

James snapped back to attention.

"We need to disguise ourselves," he refocused. "Enough that Pan and any of the other students can't recognize us, in case they give us away."

"How?" Aladdin said.

"Surely you both know some useful magic," Hook groused, unbuttoning his shirt, his face flushed from the fire. "You go to the School for Good and Evil, for god's sake."

"Other than a few lame defensive spells, all we have are the talents Rhian taught us for the Circus," said Kyma. "You were there, James. Mine was supposed to be turning the Nevers into mice. Didn't use it because our side was cheating. Not much good to us now either—only lasts a few seconds, which is why I didn't try it in Neverland."

Hook glanced at Aladdin. "And yours was lighting up our insides like a creepy taxidermist. Also useless."

Aladdin raised a glowing finger and pointed it at Hook, illuminating his organs and bones through his skin like he was a living skeleton. "I could move your bones and cartilage around to disguise what you look like, ha ha. Truth be told, I always wanted a smaller nose and a strong jaw like Hephaestus."

"I'll take four more inches in height, please," said Kyma.

"If it wouldn't kill us from pain in the process, some magical surgery to disguise us might actually be a good idea," James quipped.

"My parents always wished I was a doctor," Aladdin said with a yawn.

Suddenly, Hook's finger began to glow bright orange.

He shook it, confused, but the glow only beamed stronger.

"Who's doing that?" he said, holding it up to the firelight.

Then that familiar sensation brewed inside him, that violent warmth, roiling at his chest—"It's back!" he cried—before heat surged through his finger and a gray jet of smoke burst from its tip with a whipcrack, detonating into the sky and raining over them like ash, the three youths cowered to the ground, hands over their heads.

The forest was quiet, save an owl hooting somewhere far off.

Slowly they lifted their eyes.

Aladdin and Kyma stared at each other, James panting beside them.

For a moment, it seemed like nothing had happened.

"Was that the School Master's magic?" Aladdin asked, baffled. "What did it . . ."

He looked down suddenly. "Wait. I can't feel my legs."

"I can't feel my face," said Kyma.

"I can't feel anything at all," said Hook.

Kyma blinked. "Did Rhian's powers just make us . . . *numb*?"

Aladdin shook his head. "Why would it—" His eyes flared.

Hook burst out laughing. "Well, well, Doctor Aladdin. Your parents are about to be proud." James stripped off his shirt and lay flat on the ground, puny chest puffed, arms to his sides like a ready patient.

"Give me muscles," he said. "*Lots* of muscles."

4.

A night earlier, Midas had been trapped in his dormitory room, tasked with turning a bale of straw into a gold-thread cloak for a School Master who seemed onto him in more ways than one.

Firstly, that warm spark Rhian had in his eye anytime he'd set it upon Midas had gone cold, as if the Good School Master knew full well that the Everboy who'd acted like his friend had since betrayed him. Second, Rhian had somehow discovered that Midas had snuck out of his room the night before, which meant it was also possible that he knew Midas had gone to Rafal and asked the Evil School Master to send him home.

Propped up on blue silk pillows in a canopied bed, Midas

had looked out at his quiet room, furnished with walls the color of a robin's egg, bronze-finished chairs, white-wood floors, and that lump of dusty brown hay that taunted him with a horse manure smell.

He'd thought Rafal was on his side. The Evil School Master had been brisk in their meeting, but attentive and sincere . . . and yet, how else would Rhian know about Midas' actions the previous night unless his brother had told him?

Midas' skin had gone cold.

Were they in on it together?

Were both brothers teaching him a lesson?

Was there truly no way home and this school was his prison forever?

But these questions had no use for now, because either he found a way to spin this straw into gold by morning or he'd be sent to the Doom Room, and from what he'd heard about the man-wolf in the dungeon, that was an unendurable fate.

He knew the challenge that Rhian had left him. Back in Gavaldon, he'd read the tale of *Rumpelstiltskin*, about a maiden locked in a king's tower and commanded to spin straw into gold, and only by summoning the little devil with the strange name and promising him her firstborn could she get his help to complete the task. But as the story went, she'd killed the wicked imp to save her child, which meant Midas couldn't benefit from his skills, so here he was at a dead end once more.

Straw into gold, straw into gold, straw into gold, he'd pondered, scanning the room. How does one do that? What did the maiden do to call Rumple in the first place?

She'd cried and felt sorry for herself, Midas recalled.

Of course she did, he thought. That's what *all* Evergirls did when things got hard. Meanwhile, Midas didn't believe in crying, even in the worst situations, like the one he was in now—far away from home, trapped at this insidious school, captive to a School Master, maybe *two* . . . No matter how bad things got, emotions were wasted energy and never solved anything.

But *faking* emotions to get help?

That he could do, especially if it would save him from a Doom Room beating.

Midas threw himself onto his pillows, face down, bottom up, mewling like a princess: "Please . . . I'm scared . . . someone help me . . ."

No one came.

Midas cried harder, his crocodile tears spotting the silk, before forcing a concerted effort to raise his volume, in case his fairy godmother or guardian angel couldn't hear. "Poor little me . . . . I am but a wee child . . . hellllllpppp . . ."

Nope. Nothing.

Midas hurled the pillow against the wall and shouted, red-faced, like a gremlin: "How come a stupid girl cries and she gets help and I get—"

Something crashed through the ceiling.

A big, yelping body, which tore through the canopy of Midas' bed, bounced off the mattress, and landed in a heap on the floor.

Midas recoiled against his bedframe.

Rufius lifted his face from the floor, specked in plaster. "I asked School Master Rhian where you were and he said you were locked in your room and being punished so I used the air vents to break in!"

The pink, doughy boy had a knapsack fixed to his back and his hair was wet, either from sweat or a bath. Midas shot him a withering look: he'd asked the universe for a Rumple and gotten a Rufius instead. Midas' eyes went to the hole in the ceiling, big enough to fit through. Should he run? Where would he go? He'd tried fleeing this school through the Woods and nearly been killed for it. If he got caught escaping again, the Doom Room might be the least of his problems.

"What did you do to get punished?" Rufius pressed.

Midas screwed the boy with another glare. "Listen, I need to spin this straw into gold by morning or I have an appointment with the man-wolf. So unless you can help, please go skittering back to your—"

"I can turn it into bread!" Rufius piped.

"What?"

"Look!" said Rufius, yanking off his knapsack and drawing out a sealed vial filled with a thousand little bubbles, each sky-blue in color and the size of a beetle. "Wish Fish eggs. They helped me with my Circus talent! Been meaning to return them to the lake—there's a nest right by that ugly black-leafed tree near Evil. . . Oh, wait. You're a Reader, so you won't know what Wish Fish are. They tell you your soul's greatest desire. Mine is having my own bread bakery. Yours will be spinning this straw into gold! Eat a Wish Fish egg and you can bring a little piece of your wish to life!" He opened the vial and popped a tiny blue egg into his mouth and pursed his lips at the taste. Then he raised a glowing finger, touched one of Midas' strewn pillows, and turned it into . . . "Almond sourdough," he boasted, cracking open the rectangular loaf and revealing its fluffy, buttery center. "But you have to be careful: every time you eat a Wish Fish egg, something bad happens to you to balance it out. Everything at this school is about balance. Plus it means Wish Fish never go extinct, since no one's willing to try their luck or eat more than a couple; I ate one at the Circus to do my talent and the next day woke up with a blistering rash on my—"

Midas snatched the vial out of his hand and emptied all the Wish Fish eggs into his mouth, the salty, slimy baubles gushing down his throat.

"Noooooo!" Rufius cried. "Do you realize what you just . . ."

But Midas was already wiping his lips, his gray eyes locked on the bale of hay as he strode towards it, sweeping his finger across its surface.

A thousand pieces of straw fluttered to the ground, now golden strands of silk.

But that wasn't all.

Beneath the golden threads, any piece of the white wood floor that they touched also turned to solid gold.

"Oh my God," Rufius croaked.

Midas circled his finger over the thread, magically spooling it into shimmering fabric.

"Bad things . . ." Rufius breathed, watching his friend spin a collar, lapel, two sleeves. "You ate all of them . . . so many bad things coming . . ."

Sharp sounds flew from the door—

A key jamming into the lock.

Rufius dove under the bed and Midas threw sheets over the

golden planks in the floor, just as School Master Rhian strode through, expecting to deliver his Reader to punishment, but instead witnessing the boy sink to bended knee and deliver a cloak as pure and perfect as the sun.

"Which is how I'm standing here, with the power to free you or leave you both to rot," Midas said now, standing in the dungeon, his shadow cast over the School Master twins chained to the wall.

"I had the same power and chose to *help* you," Rafal shot back. "When you came to me, I promised to return you home."

"Before you tattled to him about it," Midas retorted, pointing at Rhian.

"No, I didn't," said Rafal. "He heard it himself."

For a moment, Midas didn't understand. Then he saw Rhian fidgeting with his nails.

"How?" Midas asked.

"That moth in the chandelier was my dear twin, eavesdropping on our conversation," said Rafal stonily. "We are potent sorcerers, after all. Or *were*, before my brother's treachery weakened us both—"

"Bygones. Let's make a deal," Rhian cut in, flashing a smile at Midas, as bright as it was forced. "Set me free and I'll whisk you back to Gavaldon, where you can resume your life in your charming little village and you'll never see me again. Plus, you'll have your gold touch, however long it lasts. You said you ate a lot of Wish Fish eggs, didn't you? Your powers will endure for years and years. Imagine that. Safe and rich until the end of your days."

Midas took this in. "And your brother? What do we do with him?"

Rhian ignored his twin's glare and kept his focus on Midas. "The prophecy says only one School Master will rise. It's why Peter Pan is here. To stake his claim as the One. But the Storian doesn't care about claim. It will choose a School Master when the time is right. The One who *proves* himself. And who is the School Master that most students respect? Who is the School Master whose side has won again and again for a hundred years? If there is a One, it's *me*. The *Good* one, who will do right by you. So leave Rafal here, Midas. Free me and you'll be back in Woods Beyond by sunset."

Rafal glowered harder at him. "Leave me here? How *Good* of you."

"At least until Midas is home safe and I've taken my place as the One," said Rhian, not looking at him. "Then we can deal with loose ends."

"Now I'm a loose end? You can't even *fly*!" Rafal spat. "How are you going to return him to Gavaldon?"

"We'll take a stymph," said Rhian, smiling at Midas.

"They're under *my* command," Rafal returned.

"Point being, Midas, that it was I who brought you here and yes we've had our ups and downs, but you can trust me to send you home," the Good School Master assured.

Midas turned to Rafal. "And you? What do you offer me?"

"Nothing," Rafal answered.

The Reader's eyes narrowed to slits.

Rafal continued: "The Storian will decide who is School Master. Not us. We don't know who it will choose, no matter what my brother says. What we *do* know is that the Pen is punishing Rhian and me. It has stripped us of our immortality and now apparently most of our powers too. I couldn't even fly you home if I tried. That is the truth. Maybe the Storian thinks Pan will be a better School Master. Maybe my brother is right and the Pen thinks Rhian is the One. Or maybe the Storian is challenging me and Rhian to prove we are up to the task and get rid of that maniacal elf-child together."

He looked at his twin, who averted his eyes.

"A task we will fail because I no longer trust Rhian and Rhian no longer trusts me," Rafal continued, turning back to Midas. "So you have to make a choice, Midas. Who do *you* trust to defeat Pan and win the Storian's faith as the one true School Master? Who do you trust to reclaim his magic and get you home?"

The only sound in the cell was the creak of the brothers' chains.

Midas' eyes shifted between twins.

A voice erupted behind him. "I saw the man-wolves fleeing. What's happened—"

Midas whirled to see a figure coming out of shadows: Dean Humburg, clutching a dagger. He spotted the bound School Masters . . . then Midas. "The Reader!" Humburg choked. He lunged at Midas, who did the first thing he could think of and slapped the Dean hard, leaving a handprint on his cheek. Humburg let out an indignant shout and raised his blade—then his eyes bulged and his muscles stiffened, like he'd been stabbed. All at once, his sallow color took on a metallic sheen, spreading from Midas' handprint, the large pores smoothing, the softness of tissue gilding hard as a rock, even the last rasps from his throat shrunk to a tinny, hollow sound, before he was nothing but silent, frozen ore, shining in the threshold of the cell.

Midas stumbled back, gaping at the Dean he'd just turned to gold. "Wait . . . that's not what I . . . I didn't mean . . ."

He spun to see the two School Masters recoiled against the

wall. It was the shock in their eyes that made Midas even more scared of what he'd done. He looked back at Humburg's statue, the golden face paralyzed with horror, as if he'd just witnessed the worst kind of monster . . .

Midas snatched the sword from the statue and dove at Rafal, slashing his chains and setting the Evil School Master free.

Rhian tightened the bind between his wrists, waiting for the Reader to free him too.

He didn't.

"Quickly," Rafal ordered Midas as the Evil School Master limped to his feet, past his cursed Dean, and out of the cell.

"What about me?" Rhian demanded.

Midas let the question dangle and hurried after Rafal, their footsteps rising and fading, leaving the Good School Master all alone.

Rhian's face gnarled, his blue eyes brimming with rage. He thrashed at his chains and screamed into the dark—

"WHAT ABOUT ME!"

5.

"Why won't it give me the oath?"

Pan's face reflected in the steel of the Pen, waiting for it to make a move.

But the Storian stayed still, lit by the moonlight of the window, frozen over the last words it had written.

And now . . .
The new one had come.

Peter spun to the Sader brothers, who were standing in shadows between cratered walls and two battered bookcases of fairy tales. "'The new one' it says. That's *me*. I'm the new School Master. So what's it waiting for?" Pan demanded. "I can't be immortal until I take the oath!"

"It won't give you the oath until you prove yourself," said the older brother, Matias, his golden sun necklace glinting. "Until then, Rhian and Rafal are still the School Masters."

Pan flared. "Then I'll kill them. Gave 'em the mercy of the dungeons, like a hero's *supposed* to, but I'll cut their throats myself if—"

"The Storian has to *choose* you, Peter," Matias rejected, hazel eyes utterly calm. "Look at the book. It hasn't said your name. It says 'the new one.' Which could mean anyone still. You have to show you're worthy first. Then the Storian will take care of anointing you the new School Master and removing the old, like it has with all the others . . ."

Pan's shadow stretched angrily into a giant over Matias. The elder Sader boy held his ground. "So why did we bring you here, then?" Matias preempted. "We brought you here because the Pen is on your side, Peter. It *wants* to choose you. But only after you've earned it."

"How do you know?" Pan hounded. "How do you know it's on my side?"

Luca stepped out of the shadows and pointed at Peter.

Peter glowered at him. "Where's your necklace—"

But then he saw what Luca was pointing at.

Peter's hand.

Pan raised his palm, the tip of the second finger glowing emerald-green. It flickered for a moment before the glow pulsed stronger, Pan already sensing how to harness his emotion to use it. Curious, he bent down and touched his glow to the book on the table. The edge of the page curled up, funneling into a tiny scroll. Little by little, this scroll softened to supple green, then grew from both ends, leaves sprouting as it rose like a vine, higher, higher, until the tip blossomed into an expansive blue flower that bowed towards Peter and caressed his cheek.

"The Pen has taken the brothers' power . . . and given it to you," said Matias.

Pan looked into the swollen blue bloom like it was his own reflection.

He turned to the Saders in a daze.

"And now? What do I do?" Pan asked.

"What the Storian is testing you to do," Matias replied. *"Rule."*

6.

The next day, Rufius woke up feeling lonely.

Every time he'd tried to make a real friend at this school,

it went poorly. Aladdin, who had ditched him for Kyma and Hephaestus. Hephaestus, who he'd helped make valentines for Aladdin when Heph was under a love spell, and then acted like he didn't know Rufius the second the hex was snapped. And now Midas, who he'd helped escape torture in the Doom Room and had since disappeared, never even bothering to thank him. Tears rose in Rufius' eyes. Why did no one want to be his friend?

Yes, he tended to pick the handsome boys, which made him feel like a warthog chumming up to panthers, but those were the boys he was drawn to, the ones he wanted as friends, and since when was following your heart a bad thing? But Midas had been a wake-up call, a lowly, friendless Reader at the bottom of the social heap, and even so, he'd acted like Rufius was a nuisance rather than a mate who had been there for him again and again.

No more, Rufius resolved.

Time to make new friends.

Ones he chose more wisely.

He hadn't slept well though, with all those booms and crackles outside. He'd stumbled to the window in the middle of the night and thought he'd seen a large ship landing, but he was in one of the highest rooms of the boys' tower and he couldn't find his glasses and struggled to make out more than a few silhouettes arguing in the dark. By the time he'd sussed out his eyewear, the shores of the lake were deserted and that ship he'd seen was now anchored peacefully in the waters near the School Masters' tower. None of it made much sense and certainly wasn't worth losing sleep over, so he flopped back into his fort of pillows and forgot all about it.

Instead, his focus this morning was on a fresh start and finding friends who would value him rather than arrogant boys who made him feel bad about himself. So he spent extra time in the shower, poufed his hair with vanilla cream, and as he strode out of his room, Rufius Renewed, nibbling a homemade beignet and sipping goat milk cappuccino, he vowed to befriend the very first Ever he saw—

He dropped his breakfast in shock.

The walls and floor had been paved over with tangles of vines, a green, flowering tunnel so thick and lush that the halls of Good had become a humid jungle. Lady fairies with golden wings, green bustiers, and crowns made out of pearls fluttered around kissing Everboys on cheeks and sprinkling them with fairy dust, so the hall was filled with handsome lads floating and tumbling through the air, giggling and high-fiving and slurping honeysuckle off ceiling vines. Two beefy, shirtless lads in green sarongs and silver star necklaces stood on either end of the floor, dragging boys down from flight and foisting them with schedules before shoving them on their way.

"Isn't it *awesome*?" a freckly boy named Madigan said, levitating upside down behind Rufius before landing on his feet. "Peter Pan's taken over the school!"

One of the beefy lads stuffed schedules in both of their hands. Rufius blinked at his, wide-eyed:

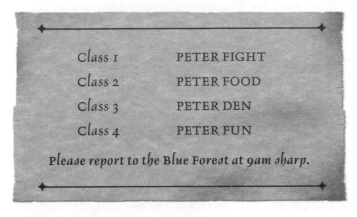

Class 1	PETER FIGHT
Class 2	PETER FOOD
Class 3	PETER DEN
Class 4	PETER FUN

Please report to the Blue Forest at 9am sharp.

"Blue Forest?" Rufius asked. "What's the Blue Forest?"

"Follow the others," the brawny lad grunted back.

For a moment, Rufius considered befriending the chap by asking his name or whether he felt self-conscious wearing so little, but he was dissuaded by the lad's aggressive stare. He'd heard Peter Pan was guarded by an army of Lost Boys, loyal only to the Pan, and this must be one of them. Not exactly the best candidate for a new friend. Besides, he was trying to stay away from handsome types—

Then he noticed a trio of unfamiliar students, two boys and a girl, at the other end of the hall, huddled in whispered conversation. One boy was brown-skinned with far-apart eyes, a crooked nose, and a high forehead. *Strange-looking fellow,* Rufius thought, as if all the bones in his face had been broken and reassembled incorrectly. The girl was even odder, dark-haired, with broad shoulders, stout legs, hooded eyes, and a pointy chin. Her face had a glum, downcast look, definitely Neverish, and yet there was brightness to her gaze and a perk to her posture that didn't match the rest. Only the second lad seemed more like the usual Everboy, with sultry dark eyes, long hair pulled into a ponytail, and pumped-up muscles—on closer inspection, a little *too* pumped up, as if he was made of overinflated balloons. All in all, they looked less like new students and more like runaways from the Ooty Island Circus, Rufius thought.

A smile spread across his face.

What better candidates for new friends?

"Never seen you before," Rufius chimed, interrupting their conversation.

They didn't acknowledge him. The pumped-up boy was whispering to the others: "Saders want us here for a reason. We need to go to class and keep our eyes out for Pan."

"What if we see a chance to get Pan's shadow? To get rid of him once and for all?" the dark boy asked him.

"Then we go for it—" the pumped-up boy started.

Rufius had enough of being ignored. "Helllloooo. Are you all from Neverland? I heard you talking about Peter Pan."

The girl popped her head up like a spooked bird, followed by the two boys.

Rufius flashed a smile and puffed out his chest, trying to look like the kind of boy who made friends. "I'm Rufius. And your names?"

The trio gaped at each other and for a moment, Rufius thought they'd grown up without names at all.

"I'm Laddy," blurted the dark boy.

"I'm Cook," said the muscly one.

"I'm Myma," said the girl.

Rufius pursed his lips. Neverlanders certainly had strange names. He held up his schedule. "Do you know where the Blue Forest is?"

A short while later, Rufius and his new friends were gathered with the rest of the Evers behind the schools at the entrance to the Woods. A portion of the forest had been turned to blue—the same range of hues once seen in Neverland's groves, cobalt, periwinkle, turquoise, indigo, navy, lapis, slate—and enclosed with tall golden gates. Shadowing the forest were the towers of Good, now with the same green coat of vines and leaves that cased the inside of the school, as if the whole of the glass castle had sprouted into wildwood. Meanwhile, Evers jostled against the locked gates for a better look at the school's mysterious new backyard and its blue fernfields, babbling blue brook, blue caves, and blue pumpkin patch. A group of Lost Boys in green sarongs stood guard inside the gates, stone-faced and arms crossed.

Rufius tugged at Laddy, Cook, and Myma before rushing into the jostling mob. "Come on, let's go see!"

The trio didn't follow, standing off from the rest of the Evers.

"Did you have to move every bone in my face!" Aladdin hissed at Hook. "Caught a glimpse of myself in a hall mirror and I look like a leprechaun! Coulda done the same to you, but I made you look like a Camelot prince!"

"Impossible to make me look bad, I'd say," Hook surmised, his eyes on Kyma, who was assessing the Blue Forest. "What are you thinking, princess?"

"Takes serious magic to turn a forest blue," Kyma noted.

"Indeed," Hook replied. "More magic than any ordinary student or teacher has."

"Then how'd he do it?" Aladdin asked. "Pan doesn't have magical powers, does he?"

"Neverland is a mirror of Pan's soul, remember," said Hook. "The geography, the colors, the terrain. The land shifts and changes to reflect his deepest desires. Which means if he's able to change the face of this school . . . then the school has given him the very same permission."

Kyma met James' eyes. "Or the *Storian* has."

"Well, he already has the students' permission, looks like," said Aladdin.

At the gates, the Evers were chanting *"Pan, Pan, Pan!"* while a few of the boys played lutes and girls danced about, fairies lighting up the fun and painting PETER BOY and PETER GIRL in scrawls of glow on students' shirts and blouses.

Rufius came bounding back, stretching his shirt to show off his own PETER BOY. "Never seen our school so happy," he gushed to the disguised threesome. "After the Circus, when Evil beat us, we all got very low. But now everyone's smiling and laughing and showing school spirit, and not in their usual cliques. Only took a new School Master to make everything better! All hail Peter Pan!"

"Hail Peter Pan!" an Everboy nearby echoed, swinging an arm around Rufius.

"Hail Peter Pan!" more Everboys cheered back, and Rufius danced with them to sprightly lutes as fairies detonated colored light in the sky like fireworks.

"Is *this* what it's like in Neverland with all those Lost Boys around?" Rufius called out, hot-stepping amidst princely lads who'd once dismissed him. "If so, I hope Peter Pan takes over more than the school! I hope he conquers the whole *Woods*!"

"Hear, hear!" Everboys concurred.

Meanwhile, Aladdin whispered to Kyma: "Remember when you said the School for Good had gone all wrong? This is wronger than wrong."

"No way the Nevers are okay with this," Kyma ventured.

"Sure about that, princess?" said Hook.

They followed James' eyes to Evil's castle, Nevers busting out the doors and onto the bridge, their black uniforms turned to emerald-colored union suits, the same one-piece button-flap shirts and long johns that Peter's minions had worn in Neverland, the words PETER BOY and PETER GIRL glistening on green. At the fore was Peter Pan himself, leading the Nevers like the Pied Piper, four Lost Boys flanking him like bodyguards. He was dressed in his green vines, a crown of white-and-black feathers on his sun-dyed curls, an impish, no-teeth smile across his face. He swayed his finger in the air like a conductor, its tip glowing green with magic, and the once fearsome students of Evil sang to his count.

> *Good King Peter!*
> *Let us serve you well!*
> *Let us be your wards!*
> *Let us show our love!*

> *Bold King Peter!*
> *Let us tout your brawn!*
> *Let us be your flock!*
> *Let us kiss your feet!*

"How'd he get school magic?" Aladdin whispered.

"Storian must be siding with him as School Master over the twins," said Hook grimly. "Rafal and Rhian had better survive to challenge him. If they die and the Pen swears Pan in as School Master, Peter won't just have sorcerer powers . . . He'll be immortal too."

"If he's immortal, killing his shadow won't work! *Nothing* will work!" Aladdin said. "We need to act fast!"

Hook shook his head. "With a whole *school* protecting him?"

"This is bad," Kyma said as Peter arrived with the Nevers.

"Very, very bad—"

Pan thrust out his glowing finger and cast a cloud of glow over the Evers, turning all their ruffly, decadent Good uniforms to the same green long johns as the Nevers. Hook looked down at his favorite shirt, morphed to servile green pajamas, and he spat into the dirt. As Evil kids flooded into the clearing, joining the Evers, the students of Good hesitated, both sides unable to tell each other apart, a hundred PETER BOYS and PETER GIRLS, united under Pan.

Rufius let out a giddy yelp: "Look at all our new *friends*!"

Neither Good nor Evil moved, trying to hold on to their old divisions.

Then one of the Evers shrugged.

"Huzzah!" she said.

"Huzzah!" said the rest.

All the students joined the singing and dancing, Evers playing their winsome chimes, Nevers drumming on the Blue Forest gates with sticks and stones, a Welcoming for a school renewed.

Rufius accosted the only three students who hadn't cheered. "Laddy! Cook! Myma! Come meet the Nevers!" he gushed, vibrating with giddiness, before he sidled up to a few intriguing Neverboys. "I hope the old School Masters never come back . . ."

THE NAME OF THE ONE

All the while, Aladdin and Kyma had their eyes on Hook, who was chewing his lip, a harsh glower darkening, as he watched Peter Pan ascend to a wooden stump the fairies had laid for him in front of the Blue Forest gates, Pan's fingertip still glowing.

"Welcome, welcome, Evers and Nevers," Peter proclaimed, his shadow doing a playful twirl. "I come to you from far across the sea, a world called Neverland where Pan is King."

"Pan! Pan! Pan!" the Lost Boys hollered, and the Evers and Nevers quickly picked up the chant—

Peter drew his fingers together and the chanting stopped. The sky was a flat gray, the air slick and heavy. Framed against the Blue Forest, the young boy with floppy ears and far-apart eyes looked less like a School Master and more like a mischievous wood sprite. "This is your new home. Not the one you're used to, no no. That was too divided to work. Your old School Masters a failing pair. Yes, that old school made some heroes and villains. Yes, it gave us a few stories we still tell today. But it pit all of you against each other. It left you lost and searching for a leader. But I can help lost souls! In Neverland, everyone unites under the flag of Pan to live out a dream. That's what Neverland is: a land of dreams. *My* dream for all of you. For all the Woods! You're not lost anymore. You're Peter Boys and Peter

Girls. Because this is no longer a school for Good and Evil. Welcome to . . ." He raised his arms. ". . . *Neverland South*."

Behind the students there was a sharp crackling sound and they spun to see the towers of the School for Evil grow the same green vines and leaves and flowers as the School for Good, the wild jungle overtaking the castle, until Evil and Good looked one and the same, dressed in the same emerald foliage as Neverland's forests. On each side of the bridge, a gold statue of Pan rose out of the ground, a crown of feathers on his head. The statues faced each other, twin sentinels lording over the schools.

The students drew breaths in collective awe.

Hook's fists curled at his sides, his rearranged face burning a hot shade of crimson. Kyma gave him worried looks as if he might implode, while Aladdin shot Kyma his own fretful peeks since she'd seemed a little too focused on James ever since they left Neverland.

"You've seen your schedules. All of you will be trained in how to best serve the Pan," Peter crowed, his shadow saluting him. "Lessons you will take into the Woods and teach others how to serve the Pan too. Your first class? *Peter Fight*. Because the old School Masters are out there. The ones who failed you. Until they're gone, the Storian will not swear me in as your new leader. Meaning we cannot rest. Mark my words, they will be coming for us. *All* our enemies will be coming for us."

Disguised under muscles, Hook leveled Peter with a glare.

We're already here.

Pan continued: "This morning, you'll compete in a trial. I'm looking for my best knights. The five Evers and Nevers who will join my Lost Boys. Five of you, who will use your magical skills to defend your king against the old School Masters and those who fight for them. This is your chance to be my King's Guard. My inner circle. In a moment, I'll free you into this Blue Forest. Five fairies are hidden within. Whoever of you manages to capture a fairy will win a place at my side. But rest assured, just like our enemies . . . they will *resist*."

The new school of Peter Boys and Peter Girls buzzed eagerly as Pan's Lost Boys pulled open the gates to the Blue Forest.

"Oh my God, oh my God," Rufius yipped, hopping from foot to foot. "This is my chance!"

"On three," Pan proclaimed. "One . . . two . . . three!"

Evers and Nevers stormed the blue jungle, the trial begun.

Rufius waddled through the pack, pulling up green long johns over his rump, calling back to his friends: "Laddy! Cook! Myma! Let's find fairies!"

Aladdin, Hook, and Kyma watched him vanish into a thicket, the trio slow-walking after the mob.

Behind them, the Lost Boys slammed the gates with a loud jangle and the group swiveled to see Peter Pan flying back to the School Masters' tower in a cloud of fairy dust.

"This all went wrong quickly," Aladdin muttered, itching at his drop-flap pajamas. "What do we do now—"

Hook's focus was back through the gates. "Who's that?"

Aladdin and Kyma followed his gaze.

A boy was coming towards them in a green uniform, PETER BOY scrawled across his chest. He was tall and handsome with dark bronze skin, loose, coppery curls, and gray eyes pinned on the Blue Forest, undeterred by the locked gates.

"Don't know. Never seen him . . . ," Aladdin started.

But now he saw there was another PETER BOY behind him, limping slightly, lanky and hunched, with a hooked nose, black eyes, and a hideous bowl of brown hair.

This one he knew.

This one they *all* knew.

Kyma choked. "That's . . . that's . . ."

"*Fala,*" said Hook.

7.

Rhian startled awake, bumping his head against the cell wall. His arms were still suspended from chains, tingling with nerves deprived of blood. A further reminder that he'd lost his immortality, his body no longer immune to unpleasant sensations. He must have shouted himself to sleep, he surmised, his throat raw from raging after his brother made off with Midas and left him here alone.

But now he heard the sounds of what had woken him. Footsteps, tramping down the tunnel, two heavy pairs, closer, closer, until out of the shadows a figure appeared, bald, dark, muscular, poking at the gold statue that blocked his path into the dungeon cell.

"Is that Dean Humburg?" the figure said, almost to himself. "That can't be good."

"Hephaestus! That's you, isn't it?" Rhian cried, bright with hope. "You came back . . . You can help me!"

The Everboy turned, staring at the Good School Master quizzically through the open door, before he was flanked by a sturdy young man in a wide-brimmed hat, who Rhian instantly thought looked familiar.

"Where's your brother?" growled the man in the hat, who Rhian now recognized as the Pirate Captain, who'd come to school and conspired with Hook to kidnap students to Neverland—Hephaestus included.

"Rafal's not here," Rhian said, turning cold. "Come to steal more students, have you?"

The Pirate Captain shoved past Humburg, giving the gold-turned Dean a disturbed glance, before he stepped into the cell, casting shadows over the prisoner. "Hook and I have come to save your school from that ass-headed Neverland twit who believes he is the one true School Master."

Rhian hesitated. "James is here too?"

"Here to kill our mortal enemy and restore you and your brother to power before Peter Pan kills you both and turns your Woods into a forest of slaves," said the Pirate Captain.

In a split second, Rhian did what he did best: assess the situation with a hawk's speed and find his advantage. His face softened, his tone warming up. "You mean restore *me* to power. I'm afraid that my brother Rafal is in league with the Pan now. That is why he is free and I am chained up here. Like Pan, my twin also believes in the prophecy of the One. And he believes if the Storian doesn't choose him, then it will name Peter the new School Master. So he's cozying up to your mortal enemy to hedge his bets."

"Your brother is working *with* Pan?" Hephaestus said, surprised, stepping next to the Pirate Captain.

"Predictably Evil, as you might expect," Rhian sighed.

The Captain peered down at Rhian. "And you're saying that you don't believe in this prophecy of the One?"

"I believe in the balance between Good and Evil. I believe in the bond of love between my brother and me that has kept this school thriving for hundreds of years," Rhian answered decisively. "But until I can make my brother see reason, I am the only School Master you or anyone in the Woods can trust."

Hephaestus and the Captain glanced at each other.

"Forgive us for being skeptical, School Master," the Captain said, warily. "We did steal your students. Surely you have revenge on your mind."

"Good doesn't believe in revenge," Rhian replied, his focus shifting to his former student. "Besides, Hephaestus went with you willingly, didn't he? As did the others? Why would I resent their freedom to choose?"

Hephaestus stood taller. "So what do you propose, then? That we free you and let you mosey on your way?"

"That we go to the Kingdom Council," Rhian offered, the blue of his eyes reflecting the torchlight. "In ordinary times, they have no jurisdiction over the school. But they are responsible for peace in the Endless Woods and Pan's invasion of the school threatens that peace, does it not? I'll insist they support us with an army of realms, Good and Evil. Then we invade the school, defeat Pan, elevate *me* as the One, and only then, perhaps, might my brother come to his senses and rejoin me to balance."

The Pirate Captain snorted. "Invade your own school with an army of the Woods and begin a *war*? I thought the Good didn't attack."

"You not only have Pan against you. You have all the students of both schools, who Peter has brainwashed into submission, as well as my brother, who despite his weakening powers is still formidable," Rhian said, suddenly hard and sharp. "This isn't about revenge. You and your crew of amateurs will not succeed in defeating the forces that oppose you. Not without help. The sooner we meet with the Kingdom Council, the sooner Peter Pan is dealt with. Until then, you are wasting precious time and increasing the likelihood that *all* of us will die."

His audience fell silent.

Drip, drip, drip went the sewers.

The Pirate Captain nodded at Hephaestus.

The Everboy drew his sword and slashed through Rhian's chains in one blow.

Together, School Master, Captain, and student hustled out of the dungeons, weaving past a gold-cast statue as if it were a common rock or boulder in their way.

A statue that might not be able to move or smile or blink,

but unbeknownst to those that had left it behind . . . could certainly still hear.

8.

Fala?

Inside the Blue Forest, Hook felt his breath lock up as he watched the crooked-nosed boy with the bowl cut limp towards the locked gates, dressed in Pan's assigned uniform, PETER BOY scrawled across his chest.

Hook hadn't seen the boy since he'd plotted with Rhian to murder him.

He hadn't *actually* wanted Fala dead, of course. The boy had singlehandedly beaten the Evers to win the Circus and been the one soul that James most wanted for his crew to take on Pan. Convincing the Good School Master to let him kill the boy was just Hook's ruse to extract Rhian's magic and sneak into the school to steal the best students, Fala most of all . . .

. . . before Fala had mysteriously disappeared.

But now here he was, approaching the gates and Hook inside them with Aladdin and Kyma, Fala accompanied by a second lad with dark skin and red-bronze curls, also in the PETER BOY uniform.

This darker boy moved in front of Fala, reached out a hand, and gently grazed the gates with his palm. Suddenly the gold bars shuddered, as if they recognized the boy's touch, before he pulled the gold apart like it was curtain fabric and stepped his way through, Fala following close on his heels.

James backed up, but Fala gave no recognition of Hook or Aladdin or Kyma, and James remembered that the three of them were in disguise, with different faces and bodies than Fala would have remembered. Though from the looks on Kyma and Aladdin's faces, James could tell that they too were unsure how to play this.

"What is the game?" Fala asked, approaching Hook and his friends. "I see Pan lock students into forest of wrong color. Why?"

"He's set five fairies free," said Aladdin tentatively. "Whoever captures them will become Pan's inner circle. His trusted guards who will fight the old School Masters and help Peter prove he's the One who should rule the school."

Fala and his companion gave each other loaded looks.

"Why aren't you playing, then?" the companion asked the three. "And who are you? I haven't seen you at school."

"We could say the same," Kyma replied.

"I'm Midas," said the stranger.

"I'm Laddy," said Aladdin. "This is Cook. And Myma."

Fala stared at them and Hook saw his eyes flare subtly, as if it was all obvious now. But he only patted James on the shoulder and smiled. "Hello, *Cook*. Fala is my name. We are all in agreement that we do not want Peter as master of school? Yes?"

Hook, Aladdin, and Kyma traded glances, deliberating how to respond, but Fala was already walking ahead. "Come. Midas. And you three with bad names. We find fairies."

Hook followed with sure feet, hearing Kyma and Aladdin patter after him. If Fala wanted Pan gone, then they were on the same side, James thought, regardless of what the young Neverboy was plotting.

Still, James had questions: Where had Fala been all this time? Where had he gotten his limp? Where did he meet this Midas, given that Hook had been attuned to all the students at this school when he'd come hunting for crew—and this boy who'd just bent bars of gold certainly wasn't among them? And yet, Hook found himself putting the questions aside for now, a strange trust for Fala seeded inside him, like he *knew* the boy beyond their limited interaction. Maybe it was Fala's deep calm that reassured him, as if the lad could handle any situation, even the dangerous game they were playing now. For the first time, Hook felt himself let go of the reins and join others in following the leader.

Together, they moved through the Blue Forest, Fala's eyes

roaming the sky-colored fernfields and cerulean canopies, sun slicing through the dense treetops like sabers, lighting up other Peter Boys and Peter Girls who were scampering by, on the hunt for fairies. All the while, James had a pit of dread in his stomach, the same wary darkness he felt in Neverland whenever he crossed into Peter's territory. It didn't matter how clever or thought-out his plans were; this Blue Forest was Peterland, and in Peterland, nothing ever went right for Hook, as if there was an invisible hand always tipping the scales in Pan's favor. The Storian had never told his and Peter's tale, not yet at least, but if the Pen did, who would the Woods root for? Hook, no doubt. Who could ever root for Peter Pan? And yet, Peter had an island of flunkies and now a school mob of followers, and what did Hook have except a ragtag group with their own ulterior motives?

He heard Midas and Fala whispering in front of him.

"You sure you trust them?" Midas was asking.

"Keep gold fingers handy," said Fala. "The rest you leave to me."

Aladdin must have heard this too because he sidled up to them. "How did you bend those gates back there?"

Midas gave him a close look. "Laddy, you said your name was? Which school were you in? Good or Evil? I don't remember you at all . . ."

"Uhhh, girlfriend troubles. Been keeping to myself," said

Aladdin in disguise, eyeing frumpy, Neverish Kyma, who gave a pointed look back, causing Aladdin to trip on blue weeds and knock into Midas. "Seriously, how did you do that with the gold?"

Midas ignored him.

Nearby, Fala flicked at his own finger, the glow weak, before he turned to Midas sternly. "Five fairies. Five of us. We win game, become Pan's inner circle. Beat Pan from inside and get rid of him. Then old School Master can get power back. This is what Midas wants, yes? For that, we need to be team. Tell the boy who you are."

Midas stared at Fala as if he and Fala had a deeper under-standing. Then Midas traipsed ahead, tossing a glance at Aladdin. "I'm a *Reader*, all right? That's what they call me, at least. Not from your world. From a place called Gavaldon, beyond the Woods. And I ate a bunch of Wish Fish eggs. Gave me a golden touch."

"You're from beyond the Woods?" Kyma said, confused. "What's beyond the Woods?"

Hook broke out of his thoughts. "Hold on. You literally can turn anything you touch into gold?"

Midas glided his hand across a hanging blue frond, which crisped to gold, just in time to whack Aladdin in the head.

"Ow." Aladdin rubbed his skull, then saw his palm glittering with gold flakes. "Oh my god. Imagine how rich you can make us . . ."

"Wait a second. Wish Fish eggs? Those don't come for free," Kyma pointed out. "Every time you eat a Wish Fish egg, something bad happens in return. How many did you *eat*?"

"Being stuck in your world is as bad as it gets. Nothing worse could happen," Midas scoffed.

"You don't get it," Kyma pushed. "If you ate that many eggs, then it's only a matter of time before—"

"Fairies not so easy to catch," Fala interrupted, his boots crunching baby-blue grass as they moved into a blue pumpkin patch. The sun fell behind tentacles of gray, giving the pumpkins a more ominous hue. "Fairies are pure instinct. Very small capacity to reason or think. The way like dog or cat loves owner, this is how fairy thinks of its master, in this case Peter Pan. They will be loyal to Pan and expect good treatment in return. Most even fall in love with master and want kisses from him. All this to say if Pan has left them here . . . they will not be happy. And they will fight anyone who tries to catch them."

Screams flew beyond the pumpkin patch, and a moment later, two boys lurched out of the trees, faces specked with blood, eyes shimmering with fear, as they stumbled between rows of vine-grown pumpkins, peeking back in terror, before they disappeared into a turquoise grove from where Hook and his friends had come.

James noticed that even Midas looked unsettled. "How are we supposed to catch them, then?" the boy with the gold touch asked.

"By giving them what Peter has forsaken," said Fala.

He put his hand to his lips, kissed it, and blew the kiss towards Midas. He seized hold of Midas' sleeve and swept the boy's palm through the air where Fala had just blown the kiss—

Gold lacquered the outlines of Fala's lips, the kiss suspended in air like an enchanted bauble, waiting for someone to claim it.

Silence followed. Fala calmly took off his shoe.

Aladdin scrunched his nose. "I honestly don't get what's happen—"

Out of the trees burst a fairy girl with diaphanous wings, untamed black hair, bright red lipstick, and a hugging green dress, buzzing straight for Fala's kiss. She reached out with long-nailed hands to claim it, but Fala plucked her out of the air and before she could jerk or bite, he dropped her into his shoe and clamped the leather opening to seal her in.

Fala leaned against a tree and set his eyes on his teammates.

"I have my fairy," he said. "Where are yours?"

Four pairs of eyes blinked back.

Instantly, they began blowing kisses, Midas slapping and swiping at them wildly like a bear clawing a beehive, turning all the kisses to gold.

"Over here, Midas, over here!" Aladdin said.

"You're blowing kisses in every possible direction except the one where I am," Midas griped, focused on James' and Kyma's kisses, which he cast in gold and sprayed into the air, Kyma's mouth distinctive for its thick round shape while Hook's kisses were long with a thin lower lip. Aladdin progressively grew stiffer, aggrieved by the sight of Hook's and his girlfriend's kisses brushing and caressing each other, until he had enough. He rammed into Midas from behind, manically blowing his own kisses between James' and Kyma's while trying to puppet Midas to turn them into gold. Midas kicked at Aladdin with his feet, Aladdin flapped at Midas' arms, the pair looking less like fairy catchers and more like incompetent mimes.

"That's your boyfriend, huh?" Hook baited Kyma, in a cloud of their own kisses.

"Aren't you Aladdin's *friend*?" Kyma countered, batting a few of Hook's kisses away. "And I don't know what he is to me right now, boyfriend or otherwise. Have *you* ever had a girlfriend?"

"Too busy. Too focused on my goals. Girls derail all that."

"That isn't just sexist. It's stupid. At the Maidenvale school, any time a boy had a girlfriend, his marks went up, while her marks went down."

"Probably because he was studying to get away from her."

"Or she was helping him with his work and doing none of her own."

They watched Aladdin simultaneously blow useless kisses and snatch at Midas' arms, while Midas bucked and flailed, so all Aladdin got was a fistful of buttocks.

Hook smirked. "All I know, princess, is that between you and your boyfriend . . . he looks like the losing party."

Midas broke free, about to shove Aladdin away with his hands, his palms grazing Aladdin's neck, when a voice roared— *"NO!"*

They all froze still and turned to Fala, standing by the tree.

Fala angrily waggled his hands and now James understood. Midas' *touch*.

Aladdin reached up and felt his own neck. The hairs on the back of it snapped off, little stems of gold. Aladdin goggled at Midas. "You almost turned me into a figurine!"

Midas' cool facade cracked as if this wasn't the first time this had happened. "S-s-sorry . . ."

"Still happy you ate all those Wish Fish eggs?" Kyma hounded. "You can't touch anyone again. *Ever.*"

"Look, I just want to go home, all right?" Midas rasped, with a quick sniffle. The boy looked like he might cry, Hook thought. Then Midas raised baleful eyes to Fala at the tree. "And only the *School Master* can fly me home."

Fala glowered at Midas. "Only School Master right now is Pan. You want old School Master back? You want to go home? Then we get on Pan's guard and make him disappear."

"In other words . . ." Hook clapped Midas on the shoulder. "Time to catch some fairies."

They waited in the clearing, a flock of kisses floating around them, the forest a little too quiet. No sound of fairies. No sound of the hundred Evers and Nevers in pursuit.

"Where are they?" said Aladdin.

Even Fala seemed uneasy, moving off his tree and scanning the circle of blue thicket enclosing the pumpkin patch. Harsh sun spilled from behind the clouds, heating up the grass like a spotlight.

Then they heard it: high-pitched whistles, like a burst of alarms—

Three fairies smashed out of the trees like spinning glitter bombs. They beat their wings with violent force, scudding straight for the gold kisses, their shrieking screams hungry and desperate, as if they knew they were headed towards their doom but couldn't help it, the promise of a holy kiss there for the taking.

Hook rushed forward, yanking off his shoe to catch the first one. But Aladdin lunged in front of him and batted the fairy into the top of his boot before whirling to Kyma with a triumphant smile. In that split second, the fairy ripped out of Aladdin's shoe, slashed him with long nails, and sank jagged teeth into the meat of his nose.

"AAAAHHHH!" Aladdin yelped.

Kyma thrust out a lit fingertip, stunning the fairy with a spell, just long enough for it to bounce off Aladdin's cheek. Before it could recover its senses, James volleyed the fairy with his open palm to Kyma, who caught it in her shoe.

"That was mine!" said Aladdin.

"Didn't see your name on it," James clipped, before holding up his own boot, something trapped inside screeching and bashing against the leather. "Or on this one."

"Got mine!" Midas crowed behind them, brandishing his shoe.

"One left," called Fala, eyes on Aladdin.

A dark rumbling came through the clearing. Slowly James looked up at the trees, the blue branches swaying. He exchanged glances with Aladdin. Under their feet, blue grass shuddered,

the pumpkins rolling off their vines. Aladdin snapped his chin up—

A lone fairy blitzed out of the forest, wings tinted red and gold, like a little ball of fire.

Aladdin spread his legs in a ready stance, letting James' and Kyma's kisses bump his head and sift his hair, because this fairy was *his* and no one was going to take it from him—

A hundred students exploded out of the forest, Peter Boys and Peter Girls bellowing in their green union suits, all of them chasing the fairy.

Aladdin's eyes bulged.

"Focus!" Hook demanded. "It's coming for you!"

But the students were gaining, on a collision course with Aladdin.

"Oh my god, oh my god," Aladdin croaked.

"All five of us have to make it on Peter's guard," Kyma pressed. "If someone else gets in, they could blow our whole plan!"

Aladdin gulped. "No pressure."

He took off, sprinting towards the fairy, the fairy angling towards a kiss, a whole school of students closing in on them both. Aladdin dove forward with his palm out, swatting the fairy out of the air, towards the trap of his open shoe . . .

A pink, fleshy palm intercepted it, pulling it in like a goal scored.

"*Yessssssss!*" cried Rufius.

"Oh, HECK NO," Aladdin slung back.

He clobbered the boy, the two tug-of-warring over the fairy, Rufius shouting—"You're supposed to be my friend!"—and Aladdin smacking and clawing at him, before a mob of other students flying-tackled into the melee, blue pumpkins squashing and detonating, raining sticky blue pulp through the sky that torpedoed the rest of the kisses . . .

"*ENOUGH!*"

The fighting stopped.

Slowly eyes lifted to Peter Pan, marching through the trees, his crown of swan feathers gilded in the sun.

"Get up," he commanded.

Peter Boys and Peter Girls rose shamefully, one by one, blue pumpkin-stained grass revealed, until there were only two bodies left on it.

Aladdin.

Rufius.

Each with a hand on the thrashing fairy.

"Looks like we'll have one extra," Peter Pan murmured. "And the others?"

He turned to the rest of the fairy catchers, displaying their shoe traps.

"Tell me your names," said Pan.

"Fala."

"Cook."

"Myma."

Peter inspected the contents of the shoes, the fairies inside flinging angry gibberish at their master.

"You three, plus those two in the grass, are my King's Guard," said Peter. He looked up at the last boy. "And you? What's your name?"

"Midas."

Peter peered in the lad's shoe.

But there was only silence and stillness within.

Pan tipped the boot and a fairy slid out, dropping into the grass with a clink.

He reached down and pinched it between his fingers.

A dead fairy, made of gold.

The whole forest fell quiet, a hundred breaths held.

Peter studied the brilliant corpse.

His eyes went to Midas.

"You're my Captain," said Pan.

9.

Rhian sat tall in the saddle.

He was out of the dungeons and free from danger for now.

More importantly, he had a plan to win back the Storian's favor. To take his place as the true School Master. The One who would rule for centuries to come . . .

"How long until we reach Maidenvale?"

Hephaestus' voice cut into his thoughts.

Rhian glanced over at his former student and the Pirate Captain riding with him, the three horses cantering downhill into a sunflower field.

"We'll be there by nightfall," said Rhian.

Both student and pirate seemed comfortable on their steeds, while his own rump was sore and he was starting to get nauseous. There was something pitiful about a School Master having to ride a horse, since his sorcerer powers once enabled more impressive forms of travel: magical carriages, flying carpets, secret portals, superspeed swims, and more modes of transport off-limits to him now that he couldn't even summon a first-year's fingerglow. Even the Flowerground would have been more agreeable than this, but the Woodswide train system only allowed those with Good souls to ride, and a Pirate Captain from Blackpool would surely be detained as Evil. So they'd taken a chance and broken into Maxime's barn off the side of the lake, where the centaur who taught Animal Communication kept his horses that trained Evers in proper riding and care. They'd snuck out the rear door with their steeds, just as they glimpsed two Lost Boys marshaling Maxime back down the lawn to the barn.

"Either you serve Pan like the other teachers chose to or you're no longer welcome here," he'd heard a boy say, the name STILTON inked on his lower back.

"Centaurs serve no one," Maxime rejected. "I'll take my leave."

"By 'not welcome here,' we mean 'spend the rest of your life in the dungeons,'" said the other boy, tattooed RIMPY. "Your choice."

Rhian hadn't heard anything further, he and his new accomplices already pulling their stolen horses into the nearby Woods.

"And they know we're coming?" the Pirate Captain asked now, their horses making tracks in the sunflowers, light fading out of the afternoon.

"The Doom Room man-wolf spoke of rumors that all was not well amongst the School Masters," said Rhian. "The King of Maidenvale might have heard that my brother is siding with an invader against me."

"I thought we were marshaling the whole of the Kingdom Council to help us against Pan, not just a single king," Hephaestus pointed out.

Rhian arched a brow. "We start with one king . . . and hope the rest will follow."

His fellow riders eyed him as if they didn't fully trust him, even though he was the Good one here, forced into the company of a turncoat student and lawless pirate.

"If anyone should have their guard up, it's me. You're the one who deserted my school," Rhian accused Hephaestus. "From Runyon Mills, aren't you? Some of the best Evers come from the mountain villages there. Hearty, diligent stock. Quite sure they'd be surprised to learn that one of their own abandoned Good."

The Everboy stiffened slightly, his hands tight on his reins. "You cheated to make us win the Circus. And we still lost. That didn't seem Good at all. It felt like we'd become the Evil ones. That's why I left school. To find what *real* Good meant."

"And yet here you are, returned to my side, helping me take back the school from Evil," said Rhian.

Hephaestus looked at him.

"To be fair, it was wrong for me to cheat," Rhian admitted. "Not only did I lose the Circus, but I lost my best students too.

I only hope that in reclaiming my place as School Master, I can restore both your trust and your desire to return to school."

"Keep on hoping," the Pirate Captain jabbed. "Lad's better than any Blackpool boy I got. Ain't giving up my best pirate without a fight."

"No Ever I choose for school will end up a pirate," Rhian said starkly.

"That's up to the boy, isn't it?" the Captain countered.

Hephaestus blushed at the prospect of being fought over. He questioned Rhian: "And what of your brother? There is no School for Good and Evil without balance. That is why both of you rule."

"Well, if the prophecy of the One is true, there will be a single School Master capable of ruling *both* schools," said Rhian.

"If that's you, it means your brother will be dead," the Pirate Captain observed. "Doesn't seem you're shedding a tear about it."

Rhian's face sharpened, suddenly hard as marble. "My brother doesn't trust me and I don't trust him. So we have to make a choice. All of us." He honed in on the Captain. "Good or Evil?"

The Captain stared back, struck by the intensity of the School Master's gaze. Then he snapped out of his trance. "Best thing about a pirate is we don't play for Good or Evil. We play for ourselves. Nor are headmasters at Blackpool given immortality or the right to indefinite rule, which is why no wars are fought over our post."

"And why no Blackpool headmasters are remembered," Rhian replied.

They rode on, past the sacred orchards of Glass Mountain, filled with praying congregations, and the coastline villages of Bahim, aglow with white lambskin tents and firepits stoked for supper as a blue night yawned overhead. Rhian felt himself slipping into the cozy lull of Good kingdoms at peace, none of these realms having the slightest idea that the home of the Storian that kept their world alive was now in the hands of a usurper.

"How long do Blackpool headmasters serve?" Hephaestus was asking the Captain, as they ascended a hill.

"Each of us has a three-year stay at Blackpool. Brought in at seventeen and ushered out at twenty, during which we're erased of our old name and bestowed the title of Pirate Captain. The best years of our youth given to shepherding those who want to follow in our footsteps. Next year, I'll take a pirate name of my own choosing and set off on the Savage Sea. Not so different from the School for Good and Evil, where after three years, Evers and Nevers pursue their quests for glory. Only, a pirate chases more than glory—he seeks to leave a legacy so fearsome, so infamous that forever after people will shudder when they hear his name."

"What's your name going to be?" Hephaestus asked.

His companion snorted. "Think I'll tell that to a boy who might desert me for Hoity-Toity School?"

Hephaestus just smiled.

They both turned to Rhian—

But the Good School Master had his eyes ahead as he slowed his horse atop the crest, overlooking a valley.

"Maidenvale," Hephaestus said.

They surveyed the realm's signature crisscrossing rivers, ten in all, villages packed onto the small banks where the streams met, moonlit ribbons flowing towards the palace that rose at waters' end, a silver castle in the shape of a trident.

But it wasn't the palace that had Rhian's focus.

It was the dozens of royal boats and ships surging down the rivers towards it, each bearing the ornate flag or sigil of a distinct kingdom, Good and Evil.

Rhian grinned to himself.

There was only one reason that the Kingdom Council would be meeting without sending word to the School Masters.

He turned to his fellow riders.

"Word of my troubles has spread further than I thought."

10.

At night, the five members of Peter Guard, as they were named, waited in the School Masters' tower, dressed in orange sarongs and orange shirts with tie-dyed yellow rings, so that together they looked like worshippers of the sun.

The other students had given them envious, admiring looks during the rest of the day's classes—PETER FOOD, where they learned to cook Pan's favorite meals; PETER DEN, where they began renovating two floors of Good's castle into Pan's private palace; PETER FUN, where they wrote anthems in Pan's honor, all under the supervision of teachers once loyal to the School Masters and now coerced to work for Pan. It was a deft move, Fala thought, for Pan to elevate an inner circle of students from the school he'd just infiltrated. Competition for status would distract the Evers and Nevers from the Neverland invasion and make them loyal to their new leader in the hopes they might be elevated too.

Fala stifled a wry smile. Back when he thought he was Evil, he might have employed a similar scheme himself.

But was he really *Good*? The Storian chose him and his twin because they had pure and opposing souls. If Rhian was the Evil one, then he himself must be the Good one. And yet, he didn't *feel* Good, as if all those years of believing he was born Evil had corrupted what he might have been. Indeed, what he'd assumed about himself had guided his actions, and because of his actions, his true nature had irrevocably changed. He was Evil to the core now. As wicked as his brother was born. Proof that it doesn't matter what you are, but what you *do*. That force of soul he'd once breathed into Hook, nothing but a soul decayed.

Near him, the other five fairy catchers silently watched the Lost Boy tattooed ABEL chewing on a reed while he sat in the window, framed by the evening moon, his knees to his chest.

The staring got to him.

"Peter's comin'," Abel grunted. "Investigatin' a disturbance in the dungeo—"

Hands shoved him out of the window and Peter Pan flew into the tower, his skin shining with fairy dust, as he stepped over Abel and glowered at his Peter Guard.

"They've escaped. Both Rhian and Rafal. And that's not all."

Behind him, a massive shadowy object floated through the window in a cloud of fairy dust and landed in front of them. Pan lit it up with green glow.

"I've been told it's Evil's Dean. Or was. Now he's made of *gold*."

He shined his glow on Midas like a spotlight.

"And seeing you just turned one of my fairies into gold, my new captain, I'm assuming you have something to do with this?"

Fala noticed his fellow guards, two lads, a girl, and that plump useless chap, all swing to Midas.

"Told you about those Wish Fish eggs . . . ," the girl mumbled under her breath.

"It was an accident!" Midas defended.

Peter loomed closer. "Well, if you can turn someone into gold, you can turn him back, can't you?"

Midas paused as if he hadn't considered this. With intense concentration, he raised a hand and touched it to Humburg's statue.

Nothing happened.

Then, in the corner, they heard a scratching sound: the Storian at work on its latest tale.

Everyone gathered round, the Pen having kept up with the action and painting the scene as it was now, the ring of Peter and his guards, Humburg's statue behind them.

Only, in the painting, Humburg *wasn't* a statue anymore, but living, breathing flesh.

"Look," said Abel, noticing another detail. "Your finger."

On the page, Peter Pan's finger was pointed at Evil's Dean, spraying a smoky green spell.

Fala tensed. The Storian had given Pan more than a

fingerglow, then. Now the Pen was telling Pan what to do, as if *leading* the story instead of letting it unfold. It had never done that with the old School Masters. Which meant the Pen was fully on Pan's side—

Peter thrust out his finger and green smoke shot out of it at the Dean's statue.

In a flash, the gold melted away, revealing Humburg in the flesh, with his haggard gray skin, salt-and-pepper hair, and bushy black eyebrows.

"Thank you, Peter Pan," said the Dean, stretching his skeletal limbs. He turned to Fala. "Look who it is. The Duckling of Dark Arts. Care to tell us where you've been since the Circus?"

Fala bit down. Threats everywhere now. But the biggest one was the Pen. He needed a plan to get the Storian back on his side.

"Forget him," Peter growled at Humburg. "We found you outside the dungeon cell. You must have seen Rhian and Rafal escape."

"Oh, I saw more than that," said Humburg.

By the time the Dean was done telling his tale, Peter's teeth were clenched and his nostrils flaring. "So let me get this right. The Good School Master is headed to the Kingdom Council to recruit an army to attack *my* school—even though the Storian has stripped his magic and given it to *me*, even though the students support *me*, even though there is no doubt the Pen will swear *me* in as new School Master once Rhian and Rafal are dead and gone." Peter gave Humburg another look. "Speaking of Rafal . . . where is he?"

Humburg's beady eyes flicked to Midas. "Last I saw, Rafal was leaving with *him*. The *Reader*."

Fala caught that pumped-up lad Cook peering at Midas, confused . . . before Cook slowly turned to Fala, his eyes widening as if he'd figured something out.

Pan circled Midas like a shark. "What were you doing with Evil's School Master, Midas? The School Master you are supposed to be leading my guard to *kill*?"

Fala spotted sweat dripping down Midas' forehead. "Dean must have seen wrong, sir," said the Reader.

"Oh no. I heard every word," Humburg insisted. "Rafal promised to send Midas home once Pan was dead. Midas freed him and they fled the dungeons together."

Now it was Fala who was sweating. *Humburg. Dastardly, double-crossing Humburg.*

Pan leered at Midas. "See, the problem is, Midas, I think you're lying to me."

"N-n-no . . . no sir . . . ," the boy appealed.

"You know how we get the truth out of liars in Neverland?"

said Pan, his shadow rubbing its hands eagerly. "We leave them with the fairies. Fairies who will know how to make you tell us where Rafal has gone. And, seeing that you just killed one of their own . . . I'm sure they'll be very *gentle* with you." Pan whistled—

A swarm of fairies stormed through the window, glittering with menace, before they inhaled Midas like flies devouring a carcass and dragged him out by the shirt, Midas' screams trailing back towards the tower.

Fala and the other four guards stood shellshocked.

Soon the boy's shouts faded and the chamber was silent once more, save the Storian, dancing across its book, spilling more ink to tell the tale of the School Masters. Pan eyed the new painting, Midas whisked off by fairies, and the Pen's words:

> *The boy would be punished until he revealed where Rafal had gone. But little did they know . . . Rafal hadn't gone anywhere at all.*

Peter's pupils lit up with pinpricks of red, his eyes trapped on the page.

Fala's heart slid up into his throat. He could feel the heat off his fellow guardsmen, Cook's gaze lifting to his.

"Fala!" Peter said, like a thundercrack.

"Yes, sir," Fala choked out.

THE NAME OF THE ONE

"Rafal must be somewhere in this school. Take the guard and bring him back alive," Peter ordered. "Abel, tell those Sader boys to find where the Kingdom Council is meeting. If Rhian is headed there, I'll be there to meet him. One dead School Master is a start."

Icy stabs went up Fala's spine as Pan studied his Peter Guard.

"I want Rafal found by the time I return. You hear me?" Pan ripped a dagger off his belt and held it to Fala's throat. "Or I'll do to all of you what I do to Lost Boys who no longer have use to me. Come, Abel. Come, Humburg."

He jumped out the window, his henchmen following and flying into the night.

Five shadows remained in the School Masters' tower, while the Storian rushed to keep up with all that had happened.

Rufius quivered. "How do we find Rafal? He could be anywh— Cook, why are you smiling?"

The pumped-up boy had his eyes on Fala. "Easy to find Rafal when he's already *here*."

Fala sighed. He lit his weak fingerglow and reverted back to his snowy, sculpted cheeks, his spikes of silver hair catching the torchlight.

Aladdin and Kyma jolted stiff. *"Rafal?"* Aladdin croaked.

"Didn't take much magic, thankfully," said Rafal. "Body remembered the spell without coaxing. That accent, though . . .

a far bigger challenge."

Rufius gasped. "B-b-but, but you're—"

Rafal targeted the three guards next to him. "While we're revealing ourselves, let's *all* be honest, shall we?"

Cook, Laddy, and Myma peeked at each other.

Three fingerglows were lit and a moment later, Hook, Aladdin, and Kyma faced off opposite Rafal.

Rufius blanched. "You . . . all . . ." He let out a wail. "I thought you were my new friends!"

Rafal glared through him like the Evil School Master of old. "It's supposed to be five guards, not six. You shouldn't be here, whoever you are, no doubt one of my brother's failed whelps. Meaning if you make so much as another peep out of turn, you won't be here or *anywhere*. Understood?"

Rufius ate his own cries.

"Fala . . . was Rafal all along?" Aladdin said, still baffled.

"So it wasn't just Good cheating at the Circus," Kyma realized. "It was *Evil* too."

Rafal ignored them, focused entirely on Hook. The two of them reunited in their own bodies at long last, the tension of shared history waiting for one of them to break it.

"Hello, James," said Rafal. "Last I saw, you were convening with my brother about killing me."

Hook rolled up his sleeves. "We'll have to dispense with the small talk, Rafal. Your brother is about to be hunted by my nemesis, who seeks to replace you and who the Storian seems to be siding with. And we've been ordered to deliver you to that same enemy or risk our own deaths. We don't have weapons. We don't have a ship. We don't have any useful magic. Is there a plan?"

"There is always a plan, James." Rafal smiled at his old friend. "And in this case, the plan is to take back my *school*."

11.

A film of water coated the hallways of the Maidenvale palace, shimmering beneath Rhian's footsteps like a carpet rolled out for him. Two guards in dolphin-head helmets and carrying tridents marched in front, Hephaestus and the Pirate Captain behind, the moon casting sparkles off the rivers outside, lighting up the floor-to-ceiling windows with dancing stars.

At the end of the hall, two more guards held the doors open, carved with the seal of intertwined dolphins, and Rhian didn't break stride, entering the Great Hall, where the King of Maidenvale sat on an elevated throne, divided from the rest of the room by a sunken pool that reflected three white balls of light suspended near the ceiling. On either side of the pool was a riser of chairs, the right side occupied by the kings and queens of the Good kingdoms, the left side taken by those from Evil.

"For thousands of years, the Kingdom Council has invited the School Masters to every meeting as a courtesy, even if you have no jurisdiction over *my* school," Rhian announced, approaching the edge of the white-lit pool. "Since when has that courtesy been abandoned?"

The King of Maidenvale peered down, a fit, upright man in silver robes with almond-shaped eyes, a beakish nose, and a trident-point crown on graying hair. "Since your school has turned into such a disgrace that even my own daughter deserted it."

This hit Rhian like a slap.

The king's focus went to Hephaestus, behind the Good School Master. "Though I see the boy that I'd hoped Kyma would wed has returned to your side. Hephaestus, last I heard from your father, you'd left the school with Kyma and that useless Aladdin boy to join a pirate crew."

"To rid Neverland of the dictator Peter Pan," Hephaestus clarified, stepping forward. "Peter Pan, who now has taken over the School for Good and Evil."

"And intends to do the same to your kingdoms," spoke the Pirate Captain, joining Hephaestus.

"So we hear," the King of Maidenvale replied. "Hence me summoning the Kingdom Council to meet."

Rhian stood taller. "A meeting that should end with the Council supporting me as the one true School Master and using its armies to rid the school of a usurper."

"And yet you just pointed out that we have no jurisdiction over the school," the king reminded.

Rhian bit his tongue.

"Even so, any leader has the right to summon the Kingdom Council to meet, given evidence of a Woodswide concern," the king continued. "And I've kept a close eye on the school in recent months, ever since my daughter wrote me, off-handedly mentioning a rogue love spell in Good's castle that had afflicted two boys. Sounded like nonsense more fitting the School for Evil, frankly. Or at least something a competent Good School Master would have put an end to. So I kept the Kingdom Council on notice and sent my spies to suss out the goings-on at your school. All of which I've presented to the Council today. And what is clear to us now, Rhian, is that you are the author of your own misfortune. Not only that. All proof suggests that it is your brother who is destined to rule as School Master *alone*."

Rhian lost his breath. "My *brother*? My brother the *One*? There is no such proof—"

The king snapped his fingers twice.

The doors opened and into the hall marched three figures: a middle-aged woman with silvery blond hair, a man of the same age, and an elder, frail woman who looked like one of their mothers.

"Adela Sader, Jannik Sader, and Estrella Sader," the King of Maidenvale announced. "Three seers who've sworn an oath to the Kingdom Council that a single School Master will rise, who will rid the school of its instability and bring centuries of peace and balance to come. The one true School Master. The One named . . . *Rafal*."

Rhian gnashed his teeth. He held a finger at the Saders. *"Liars."*

"Then present your own proof," the king said calmly. "Who supports *your* claim to the school?"

"NOT. ME."

The singsong voice came from behind the Saders, and everyone in the room spun to see Peter Pan strut down the aisle, in his swan-feather crown, flanked by Matias and Luca Sader. Pan pushed Rhian out of the way and posed in front of the king. "While you have Mommy, Daddy, and Granny Sader telling you one thing, I have younger, smarter Saders telling me another. Speak now, boys. Won't *I* be the One?"

THE NAME OF THE ONE

Matias and Luca didn't answer. Instead, they just faced the king from behind Pan and said nothing. All the while, their mother, father, and grandmother gazed upon the younger members of their family with inscrutable stares.

Pan reddened. "Matias. Luca. I said to tell the king—"

"Seers won't answer direct questions about the future without aging ten years as punishment," the king reminded. "So what we have is two sides of the same family, each naming a different School Master as the One. The elders name Rafal. The young boys name Pan. And yet, presumably no one is able to affirm this support right here, right now, because they don't want to give up a decade of life—"

"Or because they're lying," lashed a female's voice, and into the hall stormed Marialena Sader, no longer a green-faced fairy, but back in human form, dressed in a black leather pantsuit, her dark hair knotted in a high bun, her big eyes veiled behind tinted glasses. She sideswiped in front of Pan and addressed the king. "Sorry I'm late, Your Highness, but my journey here is a story for another time. The fact is: only *I* know who will be the One."

"I'm sorry," said the king, bewildered. "Who are you?"

"My daughter," Adela Sader replied, staring grimly at the girl.

"And our sister, who doesn't even *have* seer powers," Matias Sader added with a growl. "She was chosen to be a student at the School for Evil because of her false prophecies."

"And you're not a student at either school because you have accomplished nothing in your life and are jealous and resentful that a girl has outdone you," Marialena fired.

Startled, Rhian glanced between Marialena, her brothers, and her parents. So did Pan. So did the Good and Evil leaders, before all eyes went back to Maidenvale's king.

"Not just two sides of the same family, claiming to know who will be the One, but now a third. The Rule of Threes rears its head once more," the king reckoned.

"For all we know, the One could be a *pirate*!" chimed the Pirate Captain.

Chuckles came from both sides of the Council.

"Didn't mean it to be funny," the Captain murmured.

The king didn't laugh either. "Perhaps it would all be amusing if the future of the Woods wasn't at stake. Whoever rules the school protects the Storian that keeps our world alive with its tales. Further, the Pen reflects the heart of its School Master, its stories only as balanced as the soul who presides over it. It is up to the Pen to choose that soul. Not the Kingdom Council. And yet, the Kingdom Council is responsible for peace in these Woods and the Pen's delay in naming the One is threatening that peace. A seer who truthfully names the One can move this story along and ensure the Pen's will is done before things get further out of hand. Only it appears that none of the seers standing before us are willing to prove the truth of *who* that School Master will be—"

"I am."

Everyone looked at Marialena.

"Don't be ridiculous," her father scoffed.

"Ask me who will be the One," Marialena said, her eyes searing into the king's. "If what I say is true, I'll age ten years right now and you'll have your answer."

"And if you stay as you are, we'll know you're lying," the king warned. "Do you know what the penalty is for lying to the Kingdom Council?" He leaned forward on his throne. "*Death.*"

"Ask me the question," Marialena snapped so harshly that Rhian's stomach jumped.

What does she know? he thought.

Marialena gave him a piercing glance, as if she could read his mind, then turned back to the king. "Ask me."

"Stop her, Mom!" Luca Sader cried.

"Marialena, *no*," Adela Sader hissed.

Marialena never took her eyes off the throne. *"Ask me."*

The King of Maidenvale observed the rest of the Council and saw no objection. "As you wish," he said to the girl. "Who will be the one true School Master?"

Adela Sader surged for her daughter—a guard grabbed her back.

Marialena leveled with the king. "It will be . . ."

Rhian's heart jumpstarted. He whirled to Pan, who also looked shaken, the whole of the Council drawing a sharp intake of breath—

Marialena's tongue flicked through her teeth.

"*. . . Rhian.*"

Silence filled the Great Hall like the inside of a tomb, bodies frozen by the echo of a name. Then the Maidenvale king leapt to his feet—

Because Marialena was changing.

Her hair darkened and thickened with a wild luster, now a voluminous black mane around her face, which had itself matured, suppler, tauter, with a sprinkle of freckles. Her neck lengthened, her chin lost its fullness, her limbs gained proportion and grace, the clumsiness and softness of adolescence tailored away. She pulled off her glasses, revealing deep, settled eyes, which danced around the hall, taking in kings and queens, her mother and father and grandmother and brothers, and finally Rhian himself, who she beheld with the sly grin of a woman ten years older than the girl who'd spoken his name.

"The truth," the King of Maidenvale gasped. "She tells the truth."

"No!" Peter Pan roared—

The king stabbed a finger at Pan. "Arrest him! Arrest those false seers too!"

Before Pan could run, guards had snatched hold of his arms and were dragging him from the hall, Matias and Luca along with him, as well as the elder Saders. "You'll die for this!" Pan cried, his crown knocked off him. "All of you! The fire of Neverland is coming!" His shouts reverberated as he thrashed and kicked, the Saders hoisted quietly behind, until the doors slammed, snuffing out Peter's cries.

Marialena smoothed her dress and curtsied to the king. "Your Highness."

She gave Rhian a last nod and sashayed out of the hall.

Hephaestus whispered to the Pirate Captain. "Chose the right School Master to back, didn't we?"

But the Pirate Captain said nothing, watching Marialena go.

The King of Maidenvale's eyes lowered to Rhian.

"You've gotten your wish, School Master Rhian," said the king. "The usurper disposed of. The school returned to your control. Your path as the One paved to peace and prosperity. You have the full support of the Kingdom Council for the rest of your reign."

"We still have a problem," Rhian flicked back.

"Oh?" said the king, off-balance. "What's that?"

The School Master stepped forth. White light spilled off the pool, casting him in milky glow.

"My *brother*," he said.

PART 3

FAITHFUL SOLDIERS

1.

So it had been decided.

Rhian would stay with the Kingdom Council and marshal a force of the best soldiers from the Woods, Good *and* Evil, to invade the school and force Rafal to accept him as the one true School Master. Rhian's Evil twin would have a choice: submit to his brother's command or be put to death.

Meanwhile, Hephaestus and the Pirate Captain were ordered back to school to keep their eye on Rafal and send word to Rhian and his army as to the Evil School Master's plans.

"You can't believe a word Rafal says," Rhian reminded them before they departed at dawn. "You heard the seer. I am the one who can be trusted. The *only* one."

So when Hephaestus mounted his horse and followed the

Pirate Captain out of the stables and away from Maidenvale's castle, he assumed they were headed towards the rivers, along the crisscrossing banks and up the hills that would return them to the School for Good and Evil. But instead, the Pirate Captain simply looped around to the *other* side of Maidenvale's castle, where a kitchen maid had propped open the door and was pouring out slops to a pack of the king's well-groomed dogs.

"Where are you going?" Hephaestus asked, watching the Captain slide off his horse.

"Follow me," the Pirate Captain said, sneaking behind the maid and through the open door.

Hephaestus hotfooted after him, just before the maid turned back around. Now he was inside the palace kitchens, hustling after the Captain, who hid in clouds of steam off the breakfast eggs, then nimbly wove between bustling cooks and butlers until he made a turn into a stairwell and spiraled down the steps. Hephaestus tried to keep up, the two of them circling to the lowest floor of Maidenvale's castle, no longer glowing with the kingdom's blue-and-silver hues, but instead a poorly lit tunnel of iron and brick.

"What's happening!" Hephaestus hissed. "We're supposed to be going to school!"

"Stay back," the Pirate Captain demanded as they approached a corner.

"Excuse me?" Hephaestus snapped, turning with him—

"Oy!" barked a Maidenvale guard. He snatched for his sword, but the Pirate Captain slung back his fist, elbowing Hephaestus's face in the process, and smashed it into the guard's forehead, knocking him out cold.

Hephaestus grabbed his own welted cheek. "What the hell!"

"Told you to stay back," the Captain reminded.

"How'd you even know he was there!"

"His shadow on the floor. Pirates are observant. Pampered Everboys are not. One more ahead."

Hephaestus looked up to see a hulking guard stiffen in front of a grated door, a ring of keys on his belt.

"Halt!" the guard ordered.

The Pirate Captain walked faster. "Good morning. You're the dungeon master, aren't you? Keeper of the keys?"

"Yeah? Who are you?" the guard said, confused.

The Captain punched him between the eyes and took his keys as he fell.

"Just need these for a bit," he said.

He turned to Hephaestus and held up a hundred keys. "Which one of these do you think opens the door? Hmm, this one's a bit worn, isn't it . . ."

Hephaestus' bald head was sweating. "Oh my God. I'm breaking into an Ever kingdom. When *I'm* an Ever."

"Should have thought of that before you started hanging out with pirates," said the Captain. The lock clicked. "Oh, look. First try."

Dungeon row was small like most palace jails, a short corridor of cells lit by trident-shaped torches, reserved for those who had made an ass of themselves in front of the king. They could hear Peter Pan's snarls down the end. "You can't keep me here! I'm the Pan! All of Neverland will come for me!"

"Yeah, yeah, save it for your diary," the Pirate Captain heckled.

"Who's there!" Pan cried, shoving his eye to the bars. "Let me out!"

"Not you we've come to see," the Pirate Captain said.

He unlocked the cell next to Pan's and dragged Hephaestus in.

Five Saders looked back at them, sitting and standing at lengths from each other. Mother, father, grandmother, two teenaged sons.

"You knew she was telling the truth," the Captain addressed them, stern and commanding. "That's why you tried to *stop* her from saying Rhian's name. And yet the oldest of you named Rafal as the One. And the younger named Pan. Why? Why name School Masters who aren't the One? Why come here telling lies?"

"Unless they *aren't* lies at all," Adela Sader replied.

Hephaestus scratched his brow. "I don't understand."

"For a while, the future was uncertain. We knew one would reign. But we could not *see* who the One would be," her husband, Jannik Sader, explained. "But then we all reunited as a family. Marialena, too. After she returned from Gavaldon. And there, with all of us together, we each finally received a vision of who would rule. As if our powers only worked when we were joined as a family. But then a twist. Each of us saw *differently*. Adela, Estrella, and I saw Rafal. My two boys saw Pan. Marialena saw Rhian."

"Seers don't diverge in visions like this. Not without good reason," said Adela. "Even stranger, we foresaw us coming to the Council and presenting our competing sights. Which means this divergence is *part* of the story. By following our sight, by vouching for our individual visions, we would each play our part in the rise of the One. Whoever that One will be."

"Except Marialena didn't agree," Matias groused. "She thought only she saw right and the rest of us saw wrong. So she didn't just name Rhian to the Council, she answered the king's question with Rhian's name and aged ten years, making them think that it's the one and only truth. When each of us saw a different truth, the One not yet clear."

"That's Marialena. Selfish like always," Luca piled on.

"Thinks she's better than us. Second time we've ended up in jail while she goes free."

Matias nodded. "She's thrown things totally off course. Now the Council thinks she told the truth and the rest of us are liars . . . School Master got it right picking her for Evil."

"So if things are off course, who will be the One now?" Hephaestus pressed. "Who do you see?"

"Can't answer questions," Adela reminded. "But the question is wrong, regardless. It's not 'who' we see. It's 'what.'"

"A school paralyzed," said Matias.

"Frozen in chaos," said Luca.

"Instead of the rise of the One . . . the fall of a school," said Jannik.

Hephaestus and the Captain exchanged glances.

"Marialena uttering a name has shortcut the future. A future that was paved with peace and balance," Adela spoke. "But that future relied on three in contention. The way our visions kept three School Masters still in play. Three with an equal chance at the One. But now, the hope for peace and balance is gone. This time we all see the same thing. Rhian will attack his brother with the might of the Woods and this will lead to the fall."

Grim silence overtook the cell.

But young Luca was peering at something. "Unless . . ."

His family tracked the boy's eyes to the dungeon keys in the Pirate Captain's hand.

Slowly their faces changed, a collective dawning.

"Unless . . . ," said Adela.

Hephaestus straightened. "Unless?"

"Unless three School Masters *stay* in play," a prisoner called.

A prisoner in the next cell over.

A prisoner who'd been listening all this time.

"Which means the third needs to be *free*," Peter Pan's voice piped.

"You got a School Master's magic, don't ya? Free yourself!" the Pirate Captain shouted back.

"It stopped working! Moment that witch said Rhian's name!" Pan protested. "You heard those seers. Free me or the school will fall!"

"You'll be free when you kiss my bloomin' arse!" the Pirate Captain bellowed.

Pan's voice went mum.

"The school *can't* fall, Captain," said Hephaestus urgently. "You don't think I want Pan to stay locked up? But I also want the school back the way it was. Balanced. Peaceful. The way we all learn about as children. The way everyone knows it, from here to Pasha Dunes. And if letting Pan war with the School

245

Masters brings us that end, it's worth any cost."

The Pirate Captain boomed a laugh. "Blackpool Headmaster, educator of pirates, teacher of every Hook of Neverland . . . freeing Peter Pan? Toss off!"

Then he saw the Saders.

Five pairs of hazel-green eyes, cutting into him, as if Pan had hit on a truth.

"Oh, please." The Pirate Captain fluttered a hand. "Fall of a school. Doesn't affect me, does it? I'll be the world's most fearsome pirate, sailing the Savage Seas . . ."

"You'll be dead," said Luca.

The Pirate Captain snorted. "Very funny."

Luca's stare hardened.

So did all the other seers'.

The Captain cleared his throat. "You're serious?"

No response.

He shifted from foot to foot.

"God help us," the Captain growled, and flung Hephaestus the keys. "Free that damn, dirty imp."

2.

Midas was owed a lot of Bad Things.

That was the price of Wish Fish eggs, of which he'd eaten

many. But truth be told, he'd been so taken with the power of his golden touch that he'd forgotten there was a price at all. Now the Piper came to be paid.

Because an angry fairy was a very, very Bad Thing.

But *twenty* angry fairies?

That was enough to make him wish he'd never eaten those Wish Fish eggs at all.

The swarm of Peter's fairies had flown him down to the Blue Forest, binding his hands with twine before dropping him from a great height into the Blue Brook, his body slamming belly first into navy-colored water. Searing with pain, he launched to the surface, choking for breath, but the fairies were there, dunking him back in again, again, again to the edge of drowning, and shrieking gibberish, which he presumed to be Fairy for: *"Where is Rafal?"*

He wanted to tell them—Rafal is Fala and Fala is Rafal—but how would that help? Admitting that he, the chosen leader of Peter Guard, was in league with the School Master rival that Pan wanted to kill and replace? That wouldn't save him. Pan said he cut the throats of Lost Boys who failed him. What would he do to *traitors*?

But he had another reason to stay silent.

There was something about Rafal.

Something that drew him to the young School Master and

made him care about helping him win back his place atop the school. Not just so he'd regain his powers and take Midas home. Something else. The same thrill that went through his skin when Rafal held him by the throat and stared into his eyes. The same stirring that pulled Midas across the bridge from Good to Evil to see him—

Again his head went into water, liquid exploding through his nasal cavity, his ears crackling and popping. Fairy shrieks echoed and amplified underwater, demanding he confess.

His thoughts slowed as if his brain had flooded . . .

In storybooks he read back in Gavaldon, fairies were dainty little things in flowy dresses that hid flowers in your hair and whispered secrets and danced in fountains whenever it rained. The kind little children kissed on the nose because they were made of love. Peter's fairies were nothing like those. They wore hip-hugging bodices and slashes of lipstick and horrible perfume and were angry and vengeful and they seemed to take glee in killing a boy as revenge for all the kisses they never got. They reminded him of Evergirls: sweet on the surface, psychotic underneath. But he was delirious now, his head flinging through washes of sunshine and back into the brook, gasps then glugging, over and over, until the life wrung out of him. He'd give up his golden touch for this to end. He'd give up everything. He just wanted to be where there was no magic, no wishing fish, and *no fairies*. And go where? He had no friends. No family he cared about. He had nothing except his pet snake, his empty cove, and . . . Rafal.

And yet, Rafal wasn't here to save him.

There, in that fog between life and death, came clarity.

No one would save him. Because no one cared about him.

He would die alone.

Fairies dunked him harder, angrier, giving up on an answer, his lungs a ravaged ocean, the blue storm blackening to a cold, quiet grave—

Then the pressure released.

Wild shrieks rippled underwater and he turned to see fairies scooped in a net and dragged out of the brook, into the blinding sun. For a half second, he thought he was dreaming. Then he saw a face break through the light, magnified and distorted by the water, two hands breaching the surface to cradle his neck.

A hero, he thought. *An angel.*

Midas' mouth hit air and he gasped violently, surrendering to his rescuer's hold.

This is what it felt like.

To have someone care about you.

To be vulnerable to another soul.

He could feel himself smiling, his eyes so raw he left them closed, the euphoria of his own breath returning.

Maybe home wasn't where he belonged.

Maybe it was here.

With the only friend he'd ever had.

A fairy-tale ending.

Like he was an Ever after all.

"Hurry up," a voice snapped.

He opened his eyes to see his rescuer tramp off, dressed in black, toting the net of fairies.

"Where we going?" Midas asked, dazed.

Rafal flicked back an Evil look.

"To see how much you're worth," he said.

3.

"This . . . is . . . *horsecrap*," Botic panted, crawling out of waves onto Neverland's beach.

Two Lost Boys lurched after him, one tattooed TOOBI, the other BAUHAUS, sunburnt and bruised in green sarongs, peeling their way onto the sand and collapsing on their backs.

Botic was angrily flushed, violet eyes glowing like two seeds in a red fruit. "Tossed from cliffs by pirates and left to die. No

Pan to save us. We bring him Hook and what do we get? No reward, no nothing."

"And now we got no Hook either," Toobi pointed out. "Peter's gonna beat us all when he comes back."

"Let him try," Botic seethed. "All these years he makes us think Hook is the prize. That catching Hook will make us more than a Lost Boy. That it'll make us *special*. Then we find Hook and instead of rewarding us, he flies off on some top-secret mission as if he's found something more important. What could be more important than *Hook*?" He gritted his teeth. "It was those two boys. The snooty-looking ones with dust-colored hair and sun necklaces. They told him to abandon us. They convinced him of something. But what?"

"Suppose Peter doesn't come back?" Bauhaus added. "Then what happens?"

Botic sat up, purple eyes glittering. "Then Neverland will need a new king. That wouldn't be so bad, would it?"

"Unless Peter finds out," said Toobi. "That new king would be very, very dead."

Botic chewed this over. "We need to know where Pan's gone. And if he's coming back."

"No way to know, is there?" said Toobi. "Only ones who know are Pan and those two boys he took with them."

"And the mermaids," Bauhaus yawned, eyes closed in the sand. "They know everything."

"Because they're *monsters*," said Toobi. "There's a reason Pan never messed with them or tried to seize their territory. Remember that boy Cormick who put a finger in the lagoon? They reached up and tried to pull him in before we grabbed him back—"

A shadow cast over him and he looked up to see Botic walking between the cliffs. "Where you going!"

Alone, Botic continued on the path that led back into Neverland's jungle, dreamy colors inflamed by the sun. Wind blew the sand out of his hair and cooled his pink, tender chest. It was an odd feeling to be on his own, without duties to fulfill or orders to obey. He remembered when he didn't have a name. Just a Peter Boy, like all the others. Only when he'd risen in the ranks to Pan's inner circle, his six-some of Lost Boys, was his name plucked out of ashes and inked on his back. He'd remembered catching its reflection in a pond once. He should have been proud. But in that moment, seeing his name branded in his skin—BOTIC LESSO—he only felt resentment towards the one who'd taken it from him in the first place.

He's come to Neverland for a new life. His old one was untenable. A dad who'd disappear for months and return with a new wife; a mother who put up with it and numbed herself with wine. There was never food or clean clothes or water for a bath. He raised himself, rummaging swamps for meals, wishing and wishing for Neverland fairies to rescue him, until one day they did. Most his age wished for the School for Good and Evil. The chance to be an Ever or Never. A legend in a fairy tale. But he wanted freedom. No parents. No School Masters. No rules, Good *or* Evil.

Only when he got to Neverland did he realize that runaway boys invest even more in rules and masters. It's why Pan became more than a School Master to them. Pan became *king*.

Silence rippled over the island, Botic's eyes roving free-swaying trees. A sign lay ahead, staked into the dirt: PAN'S GROVE.

Botic kicked it down.

There were eight lagoons, the water bubbling fiery colors of every shade. He'd heard the whispers. That mermaids never aged. That they had teeth of diamonds. That they watched the world from below like birds watch from above and knew all our secrets and stored these secrets like pearls. He didn't know if any of it was true. Peter forbid talk of mermaids because he was scared of mermaids and Peter forbid anything he was scared of. But Peter wasn't here. And whatever secrets the mermaids knew of where he and those sun-chained boys had gone . . . Botic was willing to pay the price to find out.

He stepped to the edge of a pink pool and sucked in air.

Then he jumped feet-first and plunged in.

He didn't get far. The lagoon resisted him, like it sensed an intruder, buffeting him in place, the water smoky and pink everywhere he turned. It smelled strange too, like burning sage, which stung his nose and addled his head. He was running out of air . . . Then came a loud, rushing sound, like an animal grunting or a land mass collapsing. Something grabbed him from below, a current, a wave, a force. Down he went—

Then he was there.

As if there'd been a cut or a severance in time. Some part of his memory blacked out.

He was underwater at the base of the lagoon, seated in a chair of white coral, his arms and legs bound to it with golden cuffs. The water was no longer pink, but ruthlessly clear, the way things look in the cleanest mirror. Breath flowed in and out of him, as if he was still on land, the puffs of air from his mouth and nose turned to soapy little bubbles.

But who put him here?

Slowly Botic lifted his head.

Hundreds of mermaids treaded water in front of him, an

army of sleek, muscular bodies and diaphanous fishtails in hues of pink, purple, and blue, the females with starfish brassieres, the males strapped in sea-vines like harnesses. All of their bodies were young and strong, their nails long and curved like talons. No sign of elders at all. But it was their faces that quickened Botic's pulse—each in a gold mask that covered every inch, except their eyes, saturated with alien hues, pink and orange and lime green, like the colors of the lagoons themselves.

One mermaid was different, though. His chest bigger, brawnier than the rest. His mask wasn't gold but brilliant white like the coral Botic was trapped in. He wore a crown made of a shark's jawbone. When he glided towards Botic, three mermen in gold masks flanked him like sentinels. He peered closely at the prisoner and his voice echoed with easy power.

"You seek where Pan is," spoke the Mer King.

"H-h-how did you know?" Botic asked.

The Mer King circled him. "It is why you're here. To see if you can replace Pan. To see if *you* can be Neverland's king in his stead."

Botic stiffened as the Mer King's tail caressed the nape of his neck.

"The truth is I can't reveal the secrets of Pan's affairs," said the king, "the same way Peter cannot breach our lands and claim them like he does everything else in Neverland. A pact that stretches back eons between Pans and Mer Kings. As long as mermaids serve me as king, we will not interfere in Pan's politics or attack him. Violate this pact and our own tribe is at risk." He curled around Botic's side and put his mask to the boy's face, his crimson eyes shining. "But if the mermaids were to serve another . . . if they were to declare loyalty to a *new* king . . . then they could interfere all they like. You might even get an answer to Pan's whereabouts."

"I don't understand," said Botic, at a loss. "What king?"

The Mer King plucked the crown from his head and put it on the boy. *"You."*

All the mermaids bowed to Botic.

"Hail, King Botic!" the Mer King proclaimed.

"Hail, King Botic!" the mermaids rejoiced.

Botic bolted tall, as they undid his cuffs. "Me? *K-K-King?*"

"As long as *I* was king, mermaids couldn't kill that vile, pillaging Pan and seize the island for ourselves," said the Mer King. "For a hundred years we prepared, waiting for a human boy to fall into our clutches who could take my crown. The way you seek to take Pan's. And now the title is transferred. A technicality, yes. But the pact between mermaids and Pan no longer holds. At last we can kill that boy and make Neverland the way it should be. All because of you, *King* Botic." His red eyes shimmered. "Careful what you wish for."

Botic shook his head, stunned—

A conch call boomed through the water. From behind coral reefs, mermaids pulled shark-tooth javelins, seaglass sabers, urchin maces, kelp whips, and seashell hand blades.

"Prepare for war!" the conchbearer declared.

"War!" the mermaids roared.

The once-king smiled at Botic. "You wanted to know where Pan went, didn't you?" he cooed at his replacement. "Better be a fast swimmer . . ."

Another thunder of conch and the mermaids were off, scudding to the west.

Breathless, Botic glimpsed a last tail flash by and grabbed onto it, just in time to go ripping after them into the sea.

4.

"It defeats the purpose to free me and then leash me like a horse," Pan carped, towed by a rope that bound his two hands.

"It defeats the purpose to be a boy of adequate age and wearing *that*," the Pirate Captain retorted, nodding back at Pan's swirl of green vines.

"You heard the seers. If you hadn't freed me, you'd be on a path to *death*," said Peter.

The Captain gripped his rope leash tighter. "Still don't trust you."

"Surely *you'll* see reason?" Peter appealed to Hephaestus, the three of them on a route through evening forest, fireflies hovering in balls of glow like lanterns. "I'm not the enemy. I'm trying to save the school from those bickering twins. Two School Masters who broke their oath. That's why the Storian welcomed me into this tale. To save the school. To help the Woods. To *replace* them."

"Then why did it take away your magic, huh?" the Pirate Captain taunted, pulling him ahead. "Maybe it's not on your side after all."

Pan thought about this. "The seers said that without me, Rhian will attack his brother and the school will fall. Magic or no magic, the Storian has a plan for me. The Pen wants a new soul to be the spirit of its tales. *One* soul that can bring us into the future. Can't you see? I'm the *hero*!"

The Captain spun. "What you are is a needy, whiny brat who needs a thrashing!"

"Peter does have a point," Hephaestus admitted. "The seers saw him as the One who could bring peace and balance, just as much as they saw Rhian and Rafal. Each has an equal chance at being the School Master the Woods needs. We have to let the story unfold."

The Pirate Captain chortled. "We came to school to *stop* Pan from being School Master, not enable him! And what do you think Hook will do if he sees us cavorting with his nemesis?"

"*James* is with you?" Pan flared. "Botic was supposed to jail him in Cannibal Cave—"

"Whoever Botic is, he *failed*," the Captain snapped, and turned to Hephaestus. "We can't let Pan roam free. Not with Rafal on the loose. Pan's in league with him! You heard what Rhian said!"

"Rafal in league with *me*?" Peter said, baffled. "That's a bold-faced lie. I sent my men to *capture* Rafal and bring him to me alive."

The Pirate Captain and Hephaestus locked eyes. Slowly the Captain shook his head.

"That filthy snake Rhian," he said.

"Made the whole thing up to get us to free him," Hephaestus growled.

"And now he has an army of Good and Evil kingdoms at his disposal," Peter Pan pointed out. "You freed and trusted him when you should be trusting *me*."

The Captain said nothing, but his grip on Pan's rope loosened, the three moving silently from green woods into the skeletal grove of the Stymph Forest, the nocturnal birds peering down with eyeless sockets from bony nests high in the trees.

"Honest question for you," Hephaestus said finally, with a glance at Pan. "You really believe the Woods would be better off with *you* as School Master?"

Pan considered this. "You know the difference between me and those twins? I'm honest about what I want. Those two cling to illusions of love and balance out of fear of losing their power. But deep down, each wants to rule the school for themselves. They broke the Storian's oath the second they took it because they never truly believed in what they were swearing to. It was only a matter of time before it all went wrong. But me? I know what I want. I want the Woods behind *one* leader. I want everyone to be as happy as the boys in Neverland."

"You think your brainwashed toadies are happy?" the Captain asked. "They're servants. Minions. The opposite of pirates who are bold, courageous, and think for themselves. No wonder Hooks have been fighting Pans since the dawn of time. It's free will versus slavery!"

"Pirates desert their captains all the time. No one in my crew does," Pan crowed back. "None of them leave. None of them revolt. And every day, more lads wish under their bedcovers to come and be a Peter Boy. Maybe free will isn't as valuable as you make it out to be—"

Hephaestus shoved a hand over Peter's mouth. Before Pan could fight, the Everboy snapped his fingers at the Pirate Captain, nodding at the clearing ahead. "*Pssst.* Look!"

The Captain peeked from behind a tree.

Marialena was huddled with an old crone in moonlight, the former Nevergirl dressed in black leather and now ten years older after her confession to Maidenvale's king.

"You promised me a sack of silver coins," the crone was arguing, her small balding head like an ostrich's atop a patchwork cloak. "Two spells deserves a fair price. First, to undo that fairy hex and make you human. And then the second spell you asked for . . ."

"And you'll have your silver after you *undo* that second spell," Marialena reminded.

The old crone grumbled and pulled a vial of brown liquid from her cloak. "The antidote. Bainberry, moonrock, and a touch of foxglove. Hold it under your tongue." She opened the vial and squeezed a few drops into the girl's mouth.

Marialena shuddered at the taste . . . Then her face began to change. Little by little it softened, the fullness of her cheeks returning, a rosiness growing in her skin, until she was ten years younger again, the girl Hephaestus and the Pirate Captain once knew.

The old crone clucked her tongue. "Telling lies in front of a king and masking it with an aging spell. You are a bold child. That is sure."

"I didn't tell a lie. I just didn't tell the *full* truth of what I see," Marialena defended. "When I joined my family, I finally understood why my sight had been unclear. Their visions helped me understand mine. There's a reason we each saw a different School Master. There's a reason why I broke ranks and spoke a name to the king. It's because I can see the whole picture where they only see pieces. Maybe because my soul skews Evil, where theirs are Good. And Evil is the key to how this story unfolds . . ."

"Just give me my silver and I'll be on my way," the crone pushed. "School Masters' affairs are none of my business. And a lying seer can only bring bad luck."

"How do you think I got the silver I'm paying you with?" Marialena pulled a satchel from her jacket and held it to the crone. "Lies earned every single coin."

The crone hesitated, peering at the sack. She smacked her gums and tugged at her scanty hair. "Best you keep it," she puffed finally, hurrying out of the clearing. "Cursed money is worth less than no money at all."

Marialena smiled, watching the crone go. She opened the satchel, emptied a mound of dust and not a lick of silver, and turned to start walking—

A leg swept under her, knocking her to the ground.

Flat on her back, she looked up at the Pirate Captain and Hephaestus standing over her, Peter Pan leashed to a rope behind them.

"Hope you're ready to get those ten years back," the Captain warned. "Because now you're going to tell us what you *really* see."

5.

Rafal kept his eyes on Midas' hands, clutching the laces of Rafal's black shirt. One touch from Midas' fingers onto Rafal's bare skin and the Evil School Master would be turned to gold.

He jostled his shoulders so the boy's hands slipped further down the fabric.

Midas stirred against him, peeling open saintly gray eyes.

"I had the strangest dream . . . ," Midas breathed. He caught clouds in his mouth and for a moment, lost view of Rafal. His eyes shot downwards through open sky and he saw the School for Good and Evil a thousand feet below, his body wrapped in Rafal's arms, both of them glittering with fairy dust.

"Shook it out of Pan's little pests before I locked them in the Evers' horse trough to teach them a lesson," said Rafal, bathed in red-pink sunrise. "Oh, don't make that face at me. They practically drowned you."

"Before you swept in to save me," said Midas, relaxing in his grip, his orange tie-dyed shirt still damp. "I've never had a friend before. Let alone one who punishes fairies for me."

"Evil School Masters don't have friends," Rafal snorted. "Especially first-year *Readers*."

"Mmhmm. You can pretend to be Evil all you want but I know the truth about you. That's why you came to rescue me. Because you can't help who you are."

Rafal glanced down at the boy, who smiled up at him. The same smile James Hook had once given him, searching for the warmth beneath Rafal's chill. Both boys hunted in vain. Whatever Good he was born with had all corrupted to Evil. And he was thankful for it too. He needed that side of himself back now. The side that knew how to take on his brother and win. And yet, inside he could feel his blood roiling, his head and heart at war. He longed for the days when he didn't need to remind himself he was Evil. When it was natural, automatic.

"See, now I got you thinking," Midas said sleepily, nuzzling against his shirt. "We both say we're Evil, but when it comes down to it, you're as Good as me . . ."

Rafal's expression went cold. "When it comes down to it, you're the one turning people into gold. That doesn't seem very Good. And be careful, you fool. You're getting too close to my skin."

"I'm fine," Midas murmured into his chest. "Learned my lesson. First chance I get, I'm wishing my gold touch away and all the bad things." He closed his eyes and yawned. "That's how it goes in fairy tales if you're Good. I wish I may, I wish I might . . ." His voice trailed softer. "Where are we going? To find me a wishing star?"

Rafal gazed down at the boy's peaceful face. "You could say that." Midas didn't hear, already lost in sleep.

Rafal descended towards Good's castle. The joy of flying again was compromised by the irony that it wasn't by his own powers, but those of Pan, his nemesis. He had no real magic anymore, not after the Storian punished him and his brother for breaking the peace, for putting their own rift over the balance between schools. What did the Pen want from him now? For Rafal to rule alone? For he and his brother to restore their bond? For fresh blood to replace them both? He kicked the questions aside. This was *his* destiny to write. Not the Pen's. Just like it was *his* school.

Gliding down, he spied through the glass towers, Evers once dedicated to Good now attending morning classes dedicated to Pan: building his residence . . . preparing his feasts . . . training for his army . . .

How had they fallen so far?

Rhian's fault, Rafal thought. His brother left them weakened as School Master. Honor, valor, purity, and charity had given way to ego and doubts. They were ripe for Pan's takeover.

Over Halfway Bridge, Rafal soared, Midas still slumbering, the Evil School Master flying him up towards the School Masters' tower and peeking in on the Storian at work.

The Pen finished a painting of Rhian leading Good and Evil soldiers, his new Woodswide army training for combat and building weapons, before the Storian inked words below:

A Great War was coming.

Rafal's heart rumbled as he skimmed back out, this time to Evil's castle, where he hid behind a stone gargoyle to watch Humburg on a low balcony with Lost Boys, Rimpy and Stilton.

"Pan's escaped the Maidenvale dungeons," the Dean was

saying. "Had a report from the Kingdom Council. Word is the Pirate Captain and Hephaestus are helping him. Could be on their way back to school, but Maidenvale's king sent men after them."

Rafal flew higher. The Captain and Hephaestus on Pan's side? *Not possible.* Some part of the story had to be missing . . . Even still, Pan was free again. And so was Rhian.

Three rivals vying to be the One.

Pan had the school behind him. Rhian had the Woods.

Who did *he* have?

Rafal landed on the roof of Evil's castle.

Two runty boys in yellow shirts and orange sarongs were waiting for him.

"What took you so long!" Aladdin said.

Rufius eyed Midas slumped over the School Master. "Is he . . . alive?"

Rafal put the Reader down. Midas jolted awake. "Where are we?" he groaned, surveying the Woods from the top of Evil. He spun to Rafal and the two boys. "Where's the other pair on our team? That pale boy and the girl?"

"My thought exactly," Aladdin crabbed, addressing Rafal. "Where'd you send Hook and Kyma?"

Rafal glared at him. "Did you find what I asked for?"

"If only you knew what it took to get it," Aladdin frowned, digging into the band of his sarong and pulling out a small, bronze lamp, shaped like a tea kettle with an elongated tip and carved with an intricate pattern of suns and moons. "Last we heard, Humburg found it after the Snow Ball and locked it in the Evil Dean's office. So we asked Timon and our Never friends to distract Humburg while we sneak in to steal it. Except then Rufius starts poking around in Evil cookbooks and one of the books has an Ever repellent charm on it and chomps his arm and he starts shrieking like a poodle and nearly gets us both caught."

"Excuse me, there was a recipe for Infinitely Rising Cornbread that any person with a reasonable appetite would be curious about," Rufius argued, rubbing his bruised limb. "I didn't even agree with this mission in the first place. That—" He pointed at the bauble in Aladdin's hand. "—is a *bad* lamp. It's the one that cast a love spell on Hephaestus and messed up our whole school. A School Master should have gotten rid of it long ago, not sent us to *find* it." He shot Rafal a stern glance. "If my parents knew I was helping Evil . . . My father is Foxwood's royal baker! I want to be just like him! I follow rules. I do what I'm told. *I'm Good!* All I wanted was to make new friends, be a good Peter Boy and win a place on Pan's guard, because he's

School Master now, not *you*, and instead, I'm stuck with outcasts and pirates and—"

Rafal's eyes slashed into Rufius so lethally the boy clammed up.

"Kyma's my *girlfriend*. You could have put her with me instead of sending her off with James," Aladdin griped.

Rafal replied coolly: "She chose him all by herself."

Aladdin reddened. "Then where'd they go—"

"Give me the *lamp*," the School Master demanded.

Aladdin mumbled under his breath and handed the lamp to Rafal, who inspected its carvings. The School Master raised his brows. "You used this to coerce a girl to love you. You don't think she's forgotten that? Somewhere deep inside her, she still doesn't trust you . . ."

Aladdin bristled. "That thing doesn't even work," he said, but Rafal was already rubbing the lamp and learning this fact for himself, the metal stubbornly cold. "Told you," Aladdin snapped.

Rafal put his eye to the tip of the lamp, then his lips, and spoke softly into it. A language and tone that neither Aladdin nor Rufius had ever heard before. Sharp in its consonants, drawn-out in its vowels, with a hissing lilt on every *s*.

"*Vaahaa massssssiska . . . Duoosssssoominaaa . . .*"

Red smoke spun out of the lamp, unfurling into scaly, shadowy form, a snake blocking out the sun.

"You sssssspeak the wordsssss of dark magic, young ssssssorcerer . . . ," hissed the genie. "You sssssssay you have the power to free me?"

"I will soon enough. Once my sorcery is restored," spoke Rafal. "And when I do, I'll set you free. My promise to you. Provided you grant me a wish."

The snake sneered. "How can I—"

"—trust me?" Rafal preempted. "You can't. But you have nothing to lose other than another thousand years in that wretched lamp."

The genie considered this. "I have no power to grant real wishes. I am a—"

"—Demimagus, I know," said Rafal. "You have only the power to interfere in a wish. But it's not my wish that you're to interfere with. It's *his*."

He pointed at Midas.

"Tell him your wish, Reader," Rafal ordered.

Off-guard, Midas cleared his throat. "To be rid of my gold touch."

The School Master smiled, then beckoned the genie closer and whispered into his ear.

The snake squinted thoughtfully and reared its head. "Honor your promise to me, young sorcerer. Or there will be a price." It shot back into the lamp, leaving an ash of red smoke behind.

"Did he do it? Did he grant my wish?" Midas pressed Rafal.

"In a sense," said the School Master.

Midas looked down at his finger, the tip still luminous with gold. His eyes narrowed, lifting to Rafal's. "What did you say to him?"

"You trust me, don't you?" the School Master said archly. "Aren't I your *friend*?"

"I don't like this at all," said Rufius, glancing between them. "Using dark magic lamps. Making deals with a Demimagus. I don't want to be here. I'd rather be in class, like other Peter Boys, making *real* friends . . ."

The roof door opened and Hook and Kyma came through—or rather Cook and Myma—snickering and smiling, Hook back in a pirate's shirt, Kyma wearing one of James' black cloaks.

"You didn't actually do that in a Siren's den," Kyma was saying.

"Best way to escape Sirens alive," Hook boasted.

"But what did you do without *clothes*?" Kyma asked.

She turned and saw three boys glowering at them, her boyfriend included.

"Yeah, what did you do without clothes, James?" Aladdin grumped.

Kyma lit her finger and reverted both she and James to their usual appearance.

"Where are they?" Rafal demanded. "You were supposed to bring them here."

"No 'thank you' or 'nice to see you've made it back alive,'" James replied. "You leave me on a dangerous mission and show little gratitude in return. Some things never change, Rafal. Left me to die with the Night Crawlers. Left me to die in Monrovia. And now you leave me and Kyma to die with—"

"*You* chose this mission," said the School Master. "I suggested you handle finding Midas and you preferred to jolly off with the girl."

"I didn't think it wise sending a girl alone into a beast den," said Hook.

"What beast? Whose den?" Aladdin hounded, whipping to Kyma. "And why'd you leave me with this doughnut?" He pointed at Rufius, who gasped in offense.

"Hold on, I thought *you* wanted to rescue me," Midas said to Rafal, the Reader looking hurt. "That you were my . . . friend."

The School Master gave him a vacant look.

Meanwhile, Kyma was after James: "You didn't think a girl could do the job? Well, who did all the talking between us? Who actually got the job *done*?"

Aladdin barked: "WILL SOMEONE PLEASE TELL ME WHAT'S HAPPENING—"

Kyma and Hook both pointed in the same direction, off the roof.

Rafal took a few steps forward, craning over the edge of the tower.

In the forest just beyond school, a pack of twenty giant, hairy man-wolves waited, peering up at Evil's School Master, led by a familiar black-furred leader. The Doom Room man-wolf who'd abandoned Rafal for two armfuls of gold.

"They're skeptical of your offer to pay them their weight in gold, given your previous failures," Kyma said to Rafal. "They won't come any further until you prove it to them."

"Kingdom Council already offered them plenty to fight for Rhian," Hook advised. "They aren't inclined to come and fight for who they believe will be the *losing* brother."

"I see," said Rafal, pausing. He looked at Midas. "You wish to be rid of your golden touch, dear Reader. That's what you told me and the genie. So you want to know what *I* told the genie? I told him to grant your wish by doing precisely what a Demimagus does. By interfering in it. By giving control over that gold touch . . . to *me*."

Midas squinted blankly, not understanding. At least until Rafal lifted his finger. Because as did the School Master, so did Midas, the boy's finger raising like he was Rafal's puppet, the gold touch glowing at the edge of his fingertip . . .

. . . before Rafal directed it at Rufius.

"Sorry, lad," Rafal sighed to Rufius, "but you really are a pest."

Rafal stabbed his finger like a wand. Under Rafal's control, Midas lunged forward and thrust his finger into Rufius' neck.

"No!" Midas and Rufius screamed together.

But Rufius was already hardening, his round, rosy cheeks sealing in gold, his body cased in rock-hard metal, his hand outstretched in horror, the accidental member of their inner circle now a silent statue atop Evil's rooftop.

Midas cried out, while Hook, Kyma, and Aladdin spun to Rafal in shock.

Rafal ignored them and shoved Rufius' statue over the edge of the roof.

Down it flew, plummeting towards the man-wolves. They scattered and dove out of the way—

Rufius crashed into the earth with a deafening *boom*!, punching a crater in the forest.

All around, students of both schools raced to balconies and windows at the sound.

Man-wolves gathered over the pit, looking down at a boy's weight in gold . . . then slowly back up at Rafal.

Rafal raised his brows at the leader.

The man-wolf raised his brows back.

"So, Midas . . ." Rafal turned to the Reader. "What was that about me being *Good*?"

6.

It was only a matter of time before Evil turned a suspicious eye on the Good brother.

At first the preparations for war had gone smoothly. The Kingdom Council had pledged fifty soldiers each from four Ever and four Never kingdoms, giving him two hundred Good soldiers and two hundred Evil ones. It would be more than enough to accomplish the mission: invade the school, capture Rafal, and give the Evil School Master a choice—swear loyalty to Rhian as the one and only School Master or spend the rest of his life in Monrovia Prison. Since Rafal had neither magic nor immortality nor the Storian on his side and four hundred armed soldiers ready to dispose of him if he rejected either choice, the Kingdom Council assumed there'd be little struggle or resistance. As the Council saw it, their commitment to war would ensure there'd be no war at all.

They pushed for a quick invasion a few days from now.

Rhian resisted.

As the leader of an Ever Never Army, he'd gotten a taste of absolute control. To have both sides loyal to him alone. Now that he had a seer's backing as the One, he pushed the Council to accede to his every request: use of the vast grasslands between Maidenvale and Akgul to build a sprawling training camp, full dominion over the pledged soldiers until the mission was done, access to the best weapons, whether Gillikin's invisible fairies, Drupathi's spike-tusked elephants, Akgul's lava-filled battering rams, or Maidenvale's catapults that hurled destructive waterspouts.

Even so, Rhian felt little peace. Marialena had foretold he'd be the One. That his victory was guaranteed. But this victory was surely dependent on his *action*, Rhian fretted. By night, he lay in his sheepskin tent anticipating every way his brother might thwart him. By day, he trained the soldiers for a thousand scenarios. Would his brother set traps in the forest surrounding the school? Would he fortify the School Masters' tower to repel invaders? What of the students, who were loyal to Pan? With their former School Masters at war with one another, would they split to their old sides—or stay loyal to Pan and go to battle against *both* brothers?

Speaking of Pan, that slithery fiend was a wild card of his own, given he'd escaped from Maidenvale's dungeons, with Hephaestus and the Pirate Captain helping him. The king's men were on the hunt, but it had been days and they'd yet to be caught. Rhian wasn't worried about Peter Pan himself. The boy was as serious a threat as a termite. Pan didn't have what it took to run the school. The Storian would never choose him. Instead, Rhian suspected that the Pen brought Pan as a wedge between the two twins. To force them to either fight Pan together or ally with Pan against their own blood. The Rule of Threes . . . Rhian's hackles went up. What if Pan made it back to school and teamed up with Rafal? The thought made Rhian's skin crawl. Each new day, then, he presented more plans—nighttime Giant ambushes, daytime Harpy raids, underground troll tunnels, attacks by flying carpet—until it was a manic mishmash, the soldiers rankling under a leader who conjured a thousand questions about the impending battle and addressed them all, except the only one they cared about . . . *When?*

But Rhian couldn't commit. They'd attack when they'd prepared for every situation. When he knew victory was as true as a seer's prophecy. At night, more worries came, a trickle bursting into a deluge. What if Rafal found black magic? Didn't he have Midas on his side? What would he do with the boy's golden talent? What of James Hook? Didn't the Pirate Captain say James was at school to fight Pan? Whose side would Hook be on if the brothers went to war? What if Rafal refused to surrender? Would Rhian have to kill him?

He lay there, in the big, black silence.

Could Rhian kill him?

He searched his soul for the answer, a soul he'd once breathed into Hook, a soul whose essence was the only force the Storian had left him with . . . but inside he found no clarity or truth, only the same fire and yearning that had grown hotter and hotter with each passing year . . . a soul no longer under his control but blazing with a full life of its own. And it was because of this soul, that he did not know or understand, that at night he lay awake, the future fractured from sure triumph to a million possibilities, Rhian too scared to trust himself or let his future unfold, pushing the war out further, further, until the soldiers' question was no longer *When?* but . . . *Why?*

A scream tore through the night.

FAITHFUL SOLDIERS

Rhian jolted from sleep.

Firelight painted red and orange shadows on his tent, the jagged outline of flames.

He surged out of his tent to find a pack of Foxwood soldiers brawling with a motley crew of Evil ones, punches and kicks flying, while a tent burned behind them. Other soldiers rushed in with buckets of water to put out the blaze and separate the fighters.

"Who did this!" Rhian shouted.

"Stole our rations, they did!" an Evil soldier accused, a finger pointed at the Foxwood men. He was dressed in the red-and-black colors of Akgul and had the kingdom's silvery-pale, pearlescent skin. "Been stealing from us for days! Let 'em try stealing from our side now!"

Rhian fumed, "We're all on the same side, you fools!"

"No, we aren't!" a Foxwood lad fired back. "Can't be on the same side as Evil! All a bunch of dirty thugs that can't be trusted!"

A Drupathi fighter got in his face. "Callin' us dirty, you do-gooding cream puff? We'll show you dirty!" He punched the boy in the throat. Instantly, the rumpus rekindled, more soldiers rushing out of tents to join, the fighting spilling into the embers of the dying fire, sparks flying past warring shadows,

Good and Evil, Evil and Good, until the whole army had split into the sides they were supposed to go to war to unite. Swords were grabbed from Ever tents, spikes and flails from Never ones, the clash about to turn deadly—

A waterspout crash-landed into the fray, grabbing hold of soldiers like a wet tornado and spraying them apart. Shaken and soaked, they looked up to see the leader of their army standing by one of Maidenvale's catapults, dripping with the remnants of the water bomb.

"You selfish, ass-brained idiots," Rhian seethed. "You're lucky your kings and queens are sleeping soundly in Council's quarters at Maidenvale's castle or a good lot of you would be suffering the punishments of traitors. Get back to your barracks at once."

"Or *what?*" growled the Drupathi soldier who'd punched the boy. He stepped forward, his grizzly beard dripping, his thick brows united. "You're the Good School Master. You have no power over Evil."

Rhian scoffed. "Your leaders pledged your service—"

"We don't work for *Good*, no matter what our leaders pledge," said a hulking Ravenbow one, bare-chested, his bronze-colored hair knotted in a bun. He stepped next to the Drupathi fighter. "Gave you a chance 'cause they said you're the One who'll help

Evil win. The One who cares about balance, instead of Good just winning again and again. But you're too chicken-livered to actually go to war. You ain't the One. You're nothing but a *coward*. Wasting our time and making fools of us. Let the Good tarts fight for you. We'll fight for your *brother*!"

Never soldiers roared agreement and the Ravenbow hulk led them in chant—*"Rafal! Rafal! Rafal!"*—so bold and loud that the sound vibrated through the forest, rattling in Rhian's chest. At first, the School Master looked shaken, listening to the Evil half of his army spit his brother's name in his face. The Ever soldiers also looked cowed, as if Evil's questioning of Rhian's mettle had made them question it too.

"Rafal! Rafal! Rafal!"

More and more, his brother's name came, taunting him, heckling him, a reminder not of the love he and his twin once shared, but of the fact he had a twin at all, holding him back from his destiny. A chill came into his blue eyes, his soul jolted awake, dispelling all his nighttime terrors, as if he'd misunderstood his fate from the beginning.

There could be no negotiating with Rafal.

No offers of banishment or prison. No forcing of his twin to accept his place.

Because he wasn't meant to be the Good to Rafal's Evil. He

wasn't meant to be half to a whole. His brother's existence . . . Rafal's place at the school . . . It was *all* an obstacle. A test to overcome.

To save the school, Rhian had to erase Rafal.

He had to kill his own twin.

This was why he couldn't sleep, circling an answer he was afraid to find.

An act of Evil for the greater peace.

One must fall for the One to rise.

Good and Evil, balanced in a single leader.

Slowly, Rhian's whole face chiseled to ice. He glared the hulk down, the School Master's eyes like blue fire, until the Ravenbow soldier trailed off chanting Rafal's name, followed by the rest of the Nevers, sensing something in their leader had changed.

Rhian prowled towards the barechested giant. "You don't think I can lead Evil? That I'm too Good to fight for?" He asked the question so gently that it sang with menace.

The soldier stood taller. "I . . . I . . ."

Rhian clasped him by his cheeks. "How about you look inside and see for yourself?"

Before the soldier could react, Rhian put his mouth to his and breathed the force of his soul into him, a golden blaze that flashed beneath the lad's skin.

The soldier withdrew in shock, pushing the School Master away. For a moment the fighter's face retained the warm glow of Rhian's soul. But then the glow cooled, moving down, illuminating the skin of his neck with icy blue color.

The lad's eyes flared with warning.

A sense of what was about to happen.

He grabbed at his throat.

Blue chill spread from his neck to his face and down his chest, a paralyzing cold that lit up the veins and vessels of his body with winter frost, Rhian's soul going colder, colder inside of him, until every last shred of the lad froze over.

The soldier forced out a crackling scream. *"Noooo!"*

His face shattered, slivers of ice fraying everywhere. His frigid, headless body faded gray and thudded into the dirt.

A hundreds-wide army repelled in horror.

Wide, wild eyes shot to Rhian from every corner.

The School Master wiped his lips.

"Anyone else have something to say?" he asked.

The forest resounded with silence.

7.

"You said Rhian would be the One, but that wasn't the full truth, was it?" the Pirate Captain sneered. "So tell us, Marialena

Sader. What is the *full* truth?"

Marialena squinted at him, her cuffed hands unable to shield the rising sun from her eyes. She was tied to a tree next to Peter Pan with the rope of Pan's leash, her bottom seated in dirt, her legs stretched out in front of her, two sharp-heeled boots on her feet. Pan was dwarfed by his own shadow and struggling to get free, but his shadow wasn't following his lead. Instead, Pan's shadow was turned towards Marialena, as if it too was interested in the young seer's answer to the Pirate Captain's question.

"Well?" Hephaestus hounded Marialena, standing over her with the Captain.

"Asking the same question again and again isn't going to make me answer it any more than I already have," Marialena sighed. "I saw Rhian as the One. My parents saw Rafal. My brothers saw Pan. That's all the truth you need."

"Then why did you fake an aging spell? Why did you tell that crone there was more?" Hephaestus challenged.

"Why is it so important to you?" Marialena asked curiously. "You act as if you or the Captain might end up as School Master. I assure you. Neither of you will."

The Captain tightened his jaw. "Listen, you fraudulent clown. We need to know who the School Master will be so we don't fight for the *wrong* one and end up dead. Three can't be the One. They can't all be School Master."

"Or can they?" said Marialena.

The Captain and Hephaestus peered at her, confused. Even Pan was attentive now, he and his shadow united, their focus pinned on the girl.

"Last chance," the Captain groused. "Tell us what you really see."

Marialena tossed her hair. "No, thank you. I like my youth."

The Captain drew a knife and lunged in a single move, holding it to her throat. *"Tell me."*

"Or what?" Marialena threw back at him. "You'll kill me like you plan to kill Pan? Separate him from his shadow and do the boy in? I see exactly what you're going to do." She turned to Pan. "They only freed you to murder you. To curry favor with whichever twin wins."

The Captain pulled back in surprise.

"Lies!" Hephaestus cried.

But Pan had already turned pale. "How do they know about my shadow? How do they know how to kill me?" He swiveled to Hephaestus and the Captain. "It's true, isn't it? You want to murder me! I don't want to die!" His shadow peeled away from him, bolting forward to escape—

Marialena thrust out the heel of her boot and stabbed Pan's shadow to the ground by its throat.

Bound to the tree, Pan clutched his own throat, any suffering to the shadow also his own to bear.

"Oh dear. Must have made a mistake," Marialena drawled, looking up at Hephaestus and the Captain. "It wasn't you that got his shadow. It's *me*."

The two lads surged for her—

"Move another inch and I kill him," she said, her heel digging into the shadow's neck, Pan gurgling and choking in response.

"Go ahead," the Pirate Captain dared. "Can't kill a shadow without magic."

"A seer *is* magic," Marialena boasted.

She pierced deeper into the shadow, Peter wheezing faded breaths—

"STOP!" Hephaestus yelled.

Marialena let up on her heel just a touch, Pan gasping for air.

"Free me or he's dead," the Sader girl demanded.

Hephaestus didn't hesitate, moving straight for her.

"She's lying, Hephaestus," the Captain warned.

"Pan is a *child*. And I won't let a child die, no matter how dangerous he is," Hephaestus retorted, undoing Marialena's cuffs.

"She's our only hope to know the future!" the Captain barked. "Stay back!"

He snatched at Hephaestus, but his charge elbowed him in the groin, doubling him over. Hephaestus pulled the girl's last knot free—

The second she was loose, Marialena rammed his chest with both hands, Hephaestus toppling hard as the young Sader girl cast off her ropes and sprinted into the forest, howling back, *"Fools! Fools! Fools!"*

Flat on his rump, Hephaestus lifted his eyes and saw the Captain glaring daggers.

"Disobeying orders. Betraying a captain. Sparing enemies instead of saving yourself and your friends. There's nothing of a pirate in you," the Captain thrashed. "You're a spineless sop. A faithless tweety bird. You're no crew of mine."

He strode into the forest, Hephaestus left behind, stunned in silence.

Too much silence. He whirled around—

But Pan and his shadow were gone too.

8.

When the man-wolves came at dawn, the students ran for their lives.

Rafal had given the beasts the order to bring down Pan's school, and they did it with relish. They burst into classrooms, snarling and salivating, smashing desks and chairs while the PETER FUN group prepared their musical tribute to Pan. They tore up the kitchens and devoured the banquet the PETER FOOD team was finishing for Pan's return, truffle pies, lobster risottos, king melons with caviar, strawberry budinos, until there was nothing but crumbs and sauce-stained footprints where students had fled. They raised hairy fists and pulverized the marble floor of the hall in which PETER FIGHT trained, sending them crashing into sewers below. As for PETER DEN, in charge of building Pan's new palace atop a Good tower, the last they heard as they fled screaming was the sound of all their work shattered and the roars of brutes drunk on their own rage.

Midas watched this from the window of the School Masters' tower, while Rafal inspected the Storian, painting scenes of students fleeing from both castles into the safety of the Blue Forest. "I had you all wrong," Midas said to the School Master. He

wore one of Rafal's dark shirts, his gray eyes glassy and defeated. "I thought you had a Good heart."

"Maybe once upon a time, before I took my soul for Evil," Rafal murmured, not looking at him, huddled over the Pen in a black cloak. "Now there's nothing left of Good in me."

"You don't need to be Good to protect your own students," Midas retorted. "I thought that you cared about them. That you cared about *me*."

"I care about staying alive, as should you if you want to get home," said the School Master. "And to stay alive, I need these students to be my army."

"You think *this* will breed an army? Destroying your own school? Terrorizing students? Turning one of your own to gold?" said Midas, snarls and shrieks echoing from across the bay. "You have no one loyal to you. No friend to call your own. Not even me, who once believed in you. Instead, you betray and puppet me, like you do every student at this school."

Rafal spun to him and raised a hand; reflexively, Midas' own hand went up, swiping across a lock of his hair, which instantly froze to gold. "And I will happily puppet you into a figurine that will stand silently in my chambers," the Evil School Master lashed.

Midas held his tongue.

Rafal moved past him to the window and watched the last of the students evacuating the castles. His eyes tracked deeper into the Blue Forest, where Hook, Aladdin, and Kyma waited, the three youths looking up warily at the School Master.

"Come, Reader," Rafal flicked back, his cloak sweeping behind him as he hustled down the stairs.

Midas didn't move. "Now I'm not even worth a name?"

Midas' own finger suddenly thrust out, turning a lane of stone floor to slick gold, and he slipped and fell, pulled face-first towards the stairs by an invisible hand. "I'm coming, I'm coming!" the boy growled.

Meanwhile, the students had presumed they were herding to safety, but instead they'd run right into a trap well-planned. By the time Rafal arrived in the Blue Forest, the morning heavy with a damp breeze, a hundred Peter Boys and Girls, disheveled and scared, were cornered—on one side, by Timon and the eight Nevers, who'd cast off their green pajamas for Evil's black and blocked the students from escaping the way they'd come; and on the other side by Aladdin, Kyma, and Hook, who barred the rear gate to the wider Woods with a big, gold statue.

"That's Rufius!" an Evergirl cried.

"Rufius? Wasn't he a student?" Timon said, his single eye widening.

"An Everboy!" someone shouted. "He turned an Everboy to gold!"

Timon backed away from the School Master. So did his Evil crew mates.

"That's not Evil. That's . . . *barbaric*!" a Never yelled. "What have you done to him!"

"The same thing that will happen to anyone else who isn't loyal to me," said the School Master coolly.

All eyes went to Rafal.

"Pan is not your School Master. My brother Rhian is not

your School Master. I am," he dictated. "You follow me now. Understood?"

He expected them to bow their heads in respect, to be his loyal troops from here on out. But instead of submission, he only saw fear, as if the School Master they once trusted to be fair and just—even if he wasn't on their side—had revealed himself to be a selfish, hard-hearted monster. Behind them, he glimpsed Midas slouching into the forest, wearing the same grim mask. All Rafal's prisoners now, instead of his students.

Guilt stung at his heart and the School Master shoved it down. Guilt was the tool of the Good. He had to hold fast to Evil. He had to make them understand what was at stake.

"War is coming! War is coming *here*!" he rallied, breathlessness overtaking his cold tone. "A war for the soul of our school and the future of these Woods. The Storian reflects the heart of its School Master. If the wrong School Master wins, do you know what will become of you? Do you know what will happen to this school? I know you doubt whether I am the right School Master. For good reasons. I've made my mistakes. But you know the others are *wrong*. My brother, whose vanity leads him astray and will lead you with him. Pan, who leads only to serve himself. Neither will be honest with you. Neither puts the balance between Good and Evil before their own aims. Neither puts you or this school first."

He could see an alertness in the eyes of those watching him, as if this struck a chord somewhere inside them.

"Because once the balance between Good and Evil is lost, once the wrong soul has power over our stories . . . our whole Woods is at risk. I took an oath to protect this balance. An oath I still stand by, even if my soul calls to Evil. Because there is no Evil without Good or Good without Evil. They are two sides of the same coin." He stared directly at Midas. "If I act barbaric, if I have gone too far in my wickedness, it is because I'm trying to keep you safe. To defend you against those who will destroy this school forever. That is why I ask you to be my soldiers. To wear my armor and fight for me. Just as I will fight for you and your future."

He turned back to the students. His eyes landed on Rufius, cased in gold. Guilt rose once more, now studded with shame. Once upon a time, he knew how to be Evil to get a job done. But something had cracked within him. The Evil no longer as easy to find.

"This can't be done with threats," he confessed, his voice as heartfelt and earnest as his brother's was once upon a time. "So I ask you now. Your choice. Step forward if you will join my army. Or else . . . you are free to leave."

No one moved. A school of students paused like a hundred statues.

Then Princess Kyma stepped forward—

"If what you say is true, then turn him back."

She leveled a finger at Rufius.

"Aye," said Aladdin, stepping next to her. "Fix your Evil!"

"Aye!" said an Evergirl.

"Aye!" said Timon.

"Aye! Aye! Aye!" the forest echoed.

Rafal shook his head, downcast. "Only a School Master can undo an Evil curse. And I no longer have a School Master's magic. But Rhian . . . He ruled Good for generations. That Good force. That Good essence. It must still be inside him." His eyes flashed. "Wait. James!" The Evil School Master spun to Hook, who was standing apart, watching Rafal leerily. "Rhian breathed that Good force inside of you, James. When you were the Dean of Good. *You* can reverse the curse. Just breathe Rhian's goodness into him," he said, pointing at Rufius.

All the attention on the Evil School Master veered to Hook.

James grimaced. "Hanging me out to dry again, Rafal?"

"Just try—" Rafal started.

"I have no control over your brother's soul. It's not like yours, which felt warm and welcome. Rhian's scares me. It has a mind of its own," James corrected. "And if I did have control of it, believe me, I'd turn *you* into a statue at the gates, with no one asking to turn you back."

"Please, James," Rafal asked of him. "Goodness can fix this. Without it, nothing can be set right."

James scanned the slumping students behind the School Master, Evers and Nevers who'd had their school thrown into upheaval for months—School Masters at war, invaders playing them as pawns, beasts laying waste to their new home. Rafal was trying to wake them to the threat at hand. But they were all asleep, beaten down by betrayals, Good and Evil both. They'd given up on balance, because they no longer believed in the righteousness of either side. That's why they'd followed Pan. A stranger. That's why they'd surrendered without a fight. Because they'd lost trust in the power of this school. All of them appealed to Hook now with plaintive stares, as if with one breath, he could revive not just Rufius but their faith too. But it was Kyma's encouraging smile that finally made James move from his spot, a girl who once scorned him, like every boy at Blackpool, like most people he'd met in his life, before she'd grown into his loyal teammate, because unlike the rest, she'd taken the time to know him. Hook's first true crew member, urging him on. Aladdin noticed this too, the honest, deepening bond between them, and for the first time, he didn't revolt or react. Instead, he stood by as James drew in a breath, stepped up to Rufius' statue, his lips rising to gold and blowing the force of his lungs inside. For a half second, James lit with a burnished glow that streamed into Rufius' face, absorbing the hot light as Hook pulled his mouth away, like a wind of magic passed between them—

Then nothing.

Rufius stayed locked in metal.

A chill blew through the garden, blue roses shuddering.

Rafal couldn't understand. "I saw it . . . my brother's soul moved into him . . . To reverse an Evil curse, you need—"

Good.

But Rhian's soul was never Good.

That's why Hook was scared of it.

It's not like your magic, James had said.

Rafal's heart surged against his ribs.

Was it possible?

After all this time? After all this Evil?

That his soul's nature was still Good?

That deep down, he was still as he was born?

He moved towards the statue, his black cape snaking behind

him. James saw the intention in Rafal's eyes and stepped aside. The Evil School Master inhaled, his chest filling up, before he put his lips to the statue and blew all his force into it. Instantly, a cold blue gleam cut beneath Rufius' skin, crackling through his veins and vessels like a winter frost. Rafal's stomach sank, the truth of his soul confirmed . . . Until all at once, the gleam warmed and smoldered, like a freeze overtaken by sun, sparkles of glow rippling around the statue and ricocheting like comets. The gold tomb shattered open, fraying and falling in glittery flakes, revealing baby-pink, sweat-soaked skin—

"I'm alive!" Rufius gasped, stumbling into blue grass, waving his arms wildly. "Gosh almighty! A School Master just kissed me . . . but I'm alive!"

A hundred cheers sang out in the forest. *"Rafal! Rafal! Rafal!"*

A tear rose to Rafal's eye, emotions he once reviled, now embraced. He was still Good. Pure and powerfully Good, underneath all his Evil. At last he had proof. *He* was the One who could bring peace to this school. Who could bring this tale to a happy ending. He was honor and valor against his brother's wickedness and sin.

"Who will fight for me? Who will wear my armor?" he challenged. "Step forward and show yourselves!"

Every soul took a step.

Kyma, Aladdin, Hook, Rufius, Timon.

Every Ever and Never, one and all.

Every soul . . . except Midas.

Rafal raised a hand. Midas instantly flung forward on the School Master's command, Midas' own fingers rising to sweep across the students' uniforms, erasing Peter Boys and Peter Girls, and morphing their green to gold-plated armor. Midas let out an aggrieved cry, but Rafal swished his finger and puppeted Midas to the next body, and the next, until Good and Evil were both lined up in gold, ready to fight.

"Ever Never Army! *Rise!*" Rafal bellowed.

A collective roar blew him back.

Then he saw Midas, his eyes screwed upon Rafal, glowering with vengeance, the only student not on the School Master's side.

Rafal flicked his finger, forcing Midas' to do the same, only this time at the School Master himself, turning his black cape to resplendent gold, his chest gilded and glowing in armor.

A Good School Master, reborn.

He raised his brow at Midas, asking the question, inviting him into the fold.

Midas spat at him and dashed out of the forest.

Rafal let him go.

The boy had served his purpose.

The story bigger than a Reader now.

A soul sacrificed for the One to rise, his true face finally revealed, shining back at him in the gold of a hundred faithful soldiers.

9.

In the forest primeval, a School for Good and Evil.

And beyond that school, a Woods untamed and endless, with paths serpentine to a Reader who had no clue how to find home.

Rain lashed down, soaking a wild lemon grove. Midas sat hunched in the dirt against a tree, still clad in Rafal's shirt, his face pressed to his knees. These weren't tears, he told himself. Boys don't cry. Not real ones. The rivers from his eyes were rain.

"I want to go home . . . I've had enough bad things . . . Someone help me. *Please.* I won't steal . . . I'll be nice to my dad . . . I'll make friends . . . I'll be a Good boy . . ."

His wishes went unanswered.

Acid burned in his heart, fear scorching to fury.

"Those no good, dirty twins . . . I hope they *die* . . ." he snapped—

"*That's* more like it," said a voice.

Midas jerked to his feet. "Who's there!"

A shadow slid out from behind the trees, a shadow with a life of its own, prowling towards the boy, before a body came with it, green vines roping a whip-thin body, cupid curls buoyant despite the rain.

"It's brother against brother for the school," said Peter Pan. "But there's a third side in this fight. And seems like you and I are on it."

His dazzling green eyes locked on Midas, who couldn't look away.

A siren of horns in the distance—

Trumpet blasts followed by the thunder of hooves, the forest rattling with impact, the sound of earth moving upon itself.

Midas eyed wet saplings, quaking in the dirt.

"What's happening?" he breathed.

Pan knew the sound well.

"War," he crowed.

10.

King of the Mermaids, runt of the pack.

His knuckles were white around a fishtail, desperately hanging on as mermaids romped through the Savage Sea, armed with weapons. Botic's head rolled with dizziness, his freshly magical lungs pumping water in and out, his stomach lurching with every swerve and change in direction, twisted in knots like a magician's balloon. All he'd wanted was to find out where Peter Pan had gone and if he was ever returning to Neverland. That's why he'd taken a chance and approached the mermaids—in the hopes that Pan was away for good and Botic could slip into his place. The new King of Neverland.

How naive and stupid he'd been.

Instead, the mermaids had used him as a pawn, anointing him king of their kind, so they could break a truce with Pan and declare war, and that's where they were taking him: straight towards a death match with the boy he'd served loyally for years. He didn't even know whose side he was on. Pan's? The mermaids'? Whoever won would lord over Neverland forever. Neverland that was Botic's one and only home.

The mermaids' shark-tooth crown pierced into his temples. *Wait,* he thought. *I'm the mermaids' king. Meaning if they kill Pan and rule Neverland . . . I'm King of Neverland.*

Naturally, the mermaids would try to dispense with him when the time came. He was nothing to them. But one thing at a time, he told himself, his blood pumping faster. Make the right moves and this could end with Botic as the new Pan. The ruler of island paradise.

At last, the pack slowed, pulling out of the open ocean through a dark, narrow passageway, the water thicker, sludgier, moldy bedrock hemming them into a single-file line. Botic's breathing shallowed, his lungs struggling to churn through, and he could hear the mermaids wheezing, as if they too couldn't find air, until the rock dropped off and clean water flushed all around, immersing them back in open bay. Sun cast sparkles through the surface, gilding the undulating silhouette of two castles linked by a bridge.

The School for Good and Evil? This is where Pan went? Botic wondered. Peter's Boys had always pooh-poohed the place. The whole point of Neverland was to be free of Good and Evil and find your own story, away from rules and teachers and . . . *school.* Why would Pan come here?

Shadows drew over him and he turned to see the army of mermaids gathered in a tight cluster, like petals in a living bloom, all staring at him through gold masks with unusually colored eyes, their long nails curled around blades, whips, and sabers. The former king was at the center, his mask white, his irises the color of blood.

"You are to find Peter Pan up there and bring him to us, King Botic," he spoke. "Succeed and you'll continue to wear that crown. Betray us to Pan and you'll be hunted until you're dead."

"And here I thought *I* would be the one giving orders, seeing I am your king," Botic pointed out.

The mermaids persisted with strange, blank gazes.

"How do I know you won't kill me the second I bring you Pan?" Botic asked. "How do I know you're not using me as a mule up on land only to get what you want? Like you used me to break the truce?"

More eerie stares without answers.

A worming chill went up his spine. A silent alarm of danger.

"Uhh . . . I best get going then," Botic said, kicking towards the surface, feeling the heat of their stares, even without looking back.

He'd made a mistake going to these mermaids.

He'd erred in thinking he deserved to be more than a Peter Boy.

Forget helping these monsters. Forget being king.

He had to find Pan and tell him everything.

Peter would save him.

Peter would know exactly what to do.

11.

There is a myth that war sparks with two armies roaring and raging across a field, each committed to the cause, before they smash into each other like colliding ships, the noble first battle begun.

But most don't begin like that at all.

Most great wars begin with misunderstandings.

Rhian led his army through the Woods, lit pink and red by a sinking slash of sun. The air was thick, an ominous fog rising, coating the skin beneath their uniforms in sweat, two hundred soldiers from Ever kingdoms with bright sigils and armor, two hundred from Never ones smeared in eyeblack and wearing dark chainmail and leather. Through the trees, Rhian glimpsed the School for Good and Evil, hidden behind the smoky mist, which in the smoldering tones of sunset made the whole of the Woods feel like it was on fire. The closer they drew to the school, the more Rhian expected baited snares and booby traps and the first signs that his Evil brother was as cocked and ready for war as he was, which is why he pulled back and let his front line of soldiers advance on the gates to the school, swords and crossbows out, their eyes darting all around for a certain ambush.

His troops showed no hesitation to put lives on the line for their captain—not just because they feared Rhian's powers after he'd so brutally disposed of one of their own, but also because there was no love lost amongst them for the famed school, which once upon a time had passed them over for candidates worthier of a Storian's tale.

Closer and closer they came to the spiked, golden gates, carved with the warning: "TRESPASSERS WILL BE KILLED." Boots crackled between white-blossomed trees, tension caught in choked breaths. But there was no attack. No traps. No surprises. Not even the inkling that their presence was known, even when the first guard leapt the gates and others followed, Rhian included, who swallowed the indignity of breaking into a realm that he once ruled.

But it was only when he landed on the other side of the gates and looked up at the school, the fog thinning around the two castles, that he saw how far it had fallen. Pan's lush jungle of vines, which had coated the towers, were dead, rotting and ripped to shreds, hanging like putrid tinsel. A rancid smell stung Rhian's nose, flies and moths feasting on decaying blooms. Windows were smashed, classrooms destroyed, shrapnel and debris tumbled out on balconies, as if the school had imploded from the inside. As if the school hadn't fallen prey to a rogue School Master . . . but to the chaos of no School Master at all. Tears filled Rhian's eyes. He looked up at the School Masters' tower and through the window, the Storian was writing peacefully, as if this was all part of its plan. The Pen that had taken away his and his brother's powers. That had brought in an invader to threaten their reign. That, if the prophecy held true, would surely end this tale with only one of them alive.

Rhian's heart steeled and he drew his sword. It would be him that lived. Because in the war between Good and Evil, Good always wins.

He stormed forward, leading his army around the bay, but suddenly from the School for Evil, the doors flung open and a pack of man-wolves marched out towards them, twenty or so, well-fitted with cudgels and hammers, their hairy chests armored in pure gold.

The two sides faced off, separated by a hill of dead grass.

"Go back from where you came, Brother Traitor," the leader of the man-wolves snarled. "Rafal is the one true School Master now. Take your men and stay banished from this place."

Rhian laughed. "Nice armor. Did he pay you in Midas gold, fair-weather friends? Is that why you side with Evil's loser? I have an army of four hundred. The Woods on Good's side. You fight for a coward too scared to show his face."

FAITHFUL SOLDIERS

Sounds flooded above him, metal and footsteps in sync, and Rhian raised his eyes to see the balconies of both towers fill with armed students, Evers and Nevers, dressed in the same gold breastplates as the wolves. Rafal stepped out onto the highest balcony of Good, flanked by Kyma and Aladdin on one side, Hook and Timon on the other.

"And the coward appears," Rafal said, looking down at his brother.

The first thing he noticed was Rhian's countenance, paler than it once was, his once full cheeks now hollow and pulled tight, the gold waviness of his hair sharper. Rhian, too, saw that Rafal had changed: his skin warmer, his silver, spiked hair now tussled, a rosiness to his cheeks where there had once only been chill.

"You don't have to do this," Rafal cautioned. His green eyes were vibrant, urgent. "There is still a way back, brother."

"Back to what?" Rhian replied. "Even the Storian knows. The bond between us is broken."

"The bond was broken the moment you decided I wasn't enough for you," said Rafal.

"No." Rhian shook his head, fixing his twin with a cold blue glare. "The bond was broken the moment you were born."

The sun plunged between the castles with a last flare of

light. As darkness spread, so did a building silence, each brother waiting for the other to make his move.

"The first rule of fairy tales. Evil attacks, Good defends," Rhian touted. "Go ahead, *Evil* brother. Do what you've always wanted to do. *Attack* me."

"You know the truth as much as I. Even if you can't admit it to yourself," said Rafal. "I'm not the Evil one. I never was."

Rhian's eyes flared as if he'd been struck by a blow. He sneered, trying to find a laugh. But the conviction in his brother's eyes knotted his throat. He waited for his soul to fight back. To tell him this was all lies. That he was Goodness and Rafal was pure Evil. An obvious law. A law as clear and undisputed as the first rule of fairy tales. Instead, Rhian's lip quivered, his hands went to sweat, a blaze of dragonfire scorching through him. He thought of the Ravenbow boy that he'd killed . . . the warmth he'd breathed into him . . . how easily it'd swerved to deadly frost and eviscerated a life young and strong . . . How natural it felt to turn Evil. How much easier than to *be* Good. Slowly, his gaze met his brother's, Rafal's hair catching the last shreds of sun. This was why it had all gone wrong. This was why no matter how many times they'd tried to reconcile, he and his other half kept growing apart. This was why the Storian had taken away their powers, weakening them, more, more, until all they had left was the souls they were born with. Because only with souls bared could they see the mistake, now reflected in each other's eyes. Good become Evil, Evil become Good. Perhaps Rhian had known it all along, for the revelation came not with shock or pain, but a curious kind of relief. For the first time in his life, he didn't feel unsure of himself or strain to find his conscience or chase a phantom of who he should be. Now, he could act from his heart. And yet, Rhian knew better than to fall into his brother's trap. Even if he *was* Evil. To attack Rafal now would play right into Good's hands—

A golden arrow skimmed over his head, rifling towards Rafal's balcony.

It missed the School Master and impaled through Timon's chest.

The Neverboy cried out in shock, then fell forward dead, collapsing over the balcony.

Rafal's face swelled red. His body heaved with rage. He stabbed a finger at his brother. "*Monster!* You did this! Evil *started* this! And now . . . now we *defend*!"

Students roared with vengeance and leapt off balconies, dashing down the hill towards Rhian's army.

And yet, Rhian didn't move, still palpitating with shock.

His brother had been attacked.

The war between School Masters started by an arrow from his side.

Only it wasn't his side that had shot it.

As far as Rhian knew . . .

It wasn't *either* side at all.

12.

A short while before sunset, Pan and Midas had been walking through the Endless Woods, Midas' tears gone and dried, because Peter had offered him a way home.

"You'll really fly me back to where I come from?" Midas asked, stumbling through vines off trees big as giants.

"Soon as we get some fairy dust, Gold Touch Boy," said Peter, nimbly maneuvering through the tangles with jumps and skips, the Reader struggling to keep up. "Lickety-split, you'll be safe and sound in . . . what's the name of your place again? Grammarnun?"

"Gavaldon—"

"In Neverland, things are easier. It's all named after me."

"We need fairy dust? Rafal hid your fairies in the Evers' horse trough! Trapped them there after he rescued me. So we just need to free them, get their dust, and you can take me home!"

"Not so easy, Gold Touch Boy," said Pan, his shadow wagging a finger in Midas' face. "You tried to infiltrate my inner circle . . . plotted with my enemies against me . . . sided with Rafal as School Master . . . and now after he betrays you and you are alone, you think I'll suddenly forget all you've done to me? That I'll help you for *free*? Is that how it's done in Grammarnun?"

Midas had no response.

"I thought not," said Peter, barreling ahead into a foggy grove of white-blossomed trees.

"What do you want, then?" Midas asked.

Pan had already vanished into mist.

By the time Midas plunged into the fog to find him, Peter was nowhere to be seen. Midas spun round, spotting nothing but white billowing waves, glowing brighter and brighter, the sun lost to encroaching darkness. He hacked his arms through the mist, trying to clear it away, until he caught a glimpse of gold gates, flashing a familiar warning to trespassers . . . Except the school gate wasn't locked as always, but cracked open, the ground leading up to it worn with a thousand bootprints. Far ahead, Midas heard the thunder of competing voices, and despite the fog and fading light, he made out a mob beyond Halfway Bay, gathered in front of the schools, with a second mob high in the castles, clad in gold armor, two rival armies whose captains were shouting at each other in full-throated argument. But just as Midas slipped past the gate and hustled to investigate, a twiggy arm stabbed out of a bush and dragged him down.

Peter Pan had a gash under his eye, his chest covered in scratches and welts like he'd been ambushed. Breathlessly, Pan pointed to a young soldier, dressed in bright colors, gagged and lashed to the bush with some of Peter's green vines, the soldier writhing to get free, his crossbow just out of his reach.

"Hurry! Do it!" Peter berated Midas.

"Do what?" Midas said, boggled.

"Turn him to gold! Before he kills us both!" Peter hissed.

The guard thrashed harder, practically ripping the bush out by its roots.

"I don't do that anymore!" Midas protested. "I made a mistake ever wishing for a gold touch. Why do you think I left Rafal! He only wanted me for—"

The soldier tore off the bush, lunging straight at Midas.

Midas choked in shock and thrust out both hands, smothering the guard's face and instantly turning him to gold.

"N-n-no . . . not again . . . ," Midas rasped.

He clawed his own neck in horror, tears clogging his throat, furious at himself, furious at Peter. He whirled to Pan—

But Peter was twenty feet ahead now, crouched by a tree near Halfway Bay, wielding the soldier's crossbow, and aiming an arrow past the collected mobs, towards one of the towers.

Midas squinted in that direction, confused what Pan was targeting, until moonlight broke through the fog, casting glow on the highest balcony of Good's tower and a figure hurling words down, flanked by student guards . . .

Rafal.

Pan was about to kill him.

Without thinking, Midas was streaking towards Pan, hearing the taut stretch of Peter's bow and Pan's murmur as he aimed—*"one down, one to go"*—before Midas threw himself forward, hand out for the arrow. But his fingers only grazed it, the arrow morphing to Midas gold as it sprung off Pan's bow, slashing high through the air, over soldiers on land, over students on balconies, before the arrow sank, not in Rafal . . .

. . . but in a tall, hulking boy beside him.

Midas froze still.

So did the rest of the forest.

A child killed in cold blood.

Rafal stabbed a finger down at his enemies.

Students charged at soldiers.

Soldiers raised their weapons.

A Great War begun.

Slowly Midas looked at Peter Pan.

For a moment, Peter had the same dazed expression, his plan to kill a School Master undone.

Then he considered the clashing armies . . . the bloody chaos . . . both brothers baited into a fight to the death . . .

Pan shrugged. "Good enough!"

He seized Midas by the arm and dragged him towards the bay.

13.

Good to Evil. Evil to Good.

To Rafal, it was clear at last that they were on the right sides.

Because Rafal wanted to save his brother.

And Rhian wouldn't be happy until Rafal was dead.

Even knowing this, Rafal believed a happy ending was possible.

Yes, Rhian had started this. His side had killed a *student*. But still, Rafal didn't want him hurt. There had to be a way to beat the prophecy. To capture Rhian and stop this war until his brother came to his senses.

FAITHFUL SOLDIERS

First things first. He needed to find his twin.

Darkness had turned the battle into muddled chaos. Rafal hid around the side of Good's castle, surveying the field. Rhian's soldiers launched flaming arrows and fiery catapult bombs that lit up the night, while Rafal's students cast first-year spells from a rainbow of fingerglows—flimsy shields, weak stun spells, storms of hot rain—all in blasts of incandescent color that rose like fireworks and quickly ebbed, so that again and again, there was nothing but pitch black and frantic cries of "Find Rafal!" and "Find Rhian!" The soldiers presumed they'd extract fast surrender from Rafal's wards, bashing them into the mud with relish and binding young Ever and Never prisoners to a chain which they'd threaded through the doors of the students' own castle. But they'd forgotten about the man-wolves, who could see in the dark, and were watching and waiting, climbed up on the underside of balconies like spiders, poised for the moment to attack.

"Now!" cried their leader.

The wolves plummeted like cannonballs, smashing soldiers with fists and instantly regaining control of the battle. Seeing his chance, Rafal surged into the brawl behind the wolves, hearing the crush of soldier bones against the hairy beasts' armor, the School Master ranging further astray, towards the shores of the bay, his eyes darting left and right across school grounds for any sign of his brother—

"It's him! It's Rafal!" a soldier cried, trapping him in a head-lock from behind.

Rafal tried to wrench free, but now other soldiers were onto him, grappling him in the darkness by the shore, away from the heart of battle.

"Let's kill him!" one cried, with a punch to Rafal's neck. "Our kingdoms will reward us!"

An ogreish voice retorted: "How 'bout *I* do it and get the glory me'self?"

Rafal saw a flash of sword. He kicked out his leg, connect-ing with someone's face, but then rough arms grabbed his knee, swinging him off the ground so his head was trapped under a soldier's arm and his whole body swarmed by six others, like a pig about to be skewered. More swords came out of sheaths, Rafal unable to delay his death with futile flails and slaps—

"Put him down," snapped a cold voice.

The soldiers turned.

James Hook had a sword tucked under his arm as he pulled his hair into a knot.

"Or *what*?" a Never soldier taunted.

"Or . . . hold on . . ." Hook finished meticulously tying his bun. He regripped his sword. "Or this."

He knifed the soldier in the thigh, then ran up his buckling body like a launchpad, backflipped, and stabbed the other men, two in the flank, two in the shoulder, one in the buttocks, before landing in front of Rafal, just in time to watch all six soldiers on the School Master crash to knees and faceplant into mud.

Rafal gazed at the once whiny, soft boy he'd kidnapped from Blackpool, now a bold, strapping captain.

"You and me, School Master," said Hook. "Just like old times."

A scream erupted behind them—*"Help!"*

Princess Kyma, dangled from a balcony by two Good soldiers.

Hook's face darkened.

"Not *quite* like old times," Rafal winked. "Go."

He watched James charge to rescue her, past man-wolves pinning a soldier to the ground . . .

Rafal's eyes flared.

Not a soldier.

Rhian.

Rafal ran towards him.

Meanwhile, Hook was marching towards the castle, teeth

clenched, knuckles cracking, as those two Good soldiers on the balcony tossed Kyma to two Evil ones below who heaved her back up in a demented game. Again the Evil soldiers caught her—

James flying-kicked both in the head, catching Kyma as they fell. Instantly, the Good soldiers on the balcony drew arrows at Hook and his princess, about to spear them through. Hook leveled them with a glare, a familiar dark heat stoking inside him. Only this time he wasn't scared of Rhian's magic. This time it fed into his rage, as if like recognized like, as if Rhian's spirit could only make sense to one lost in vengeance and wrath. Hook pinned his eyes on the soldiers and roared the soul inside of him, a cold blue fire that exploded towards the balcony and devoured them all, immolating their bodies whole and leaving crumbling heaps of ash. Hook gnashed his teeth as if he wanted more death, more savagery. When a hand touched his shoulder, he spun around to blast fresh fire and punishment . . .

"It's me," a girl breathed.

But Hook wasn't himself anymore. He was possessed by Rhian's soul. And Rhian's soul had no use for a girl.

Hook grabbed her by the throat, squeezing hard—

A punch hit his jaw.

Hook reeled, just in time to get another bash to his nose, spraying blue blood in his once best friend's face.

"Touch her again!" Aladdin bellowed. "I dare you!"

James clocked him in the eye, the two boys going down. Aladdin kneed Hook in the groin: "You're going to treat a girl like that! *My* girl!" Hook snarled and smashed Aladdin's head into the dirt, again and again, still in the throes of Evil's soul. Aladdin tried to fight back, but he was losing consciousness, his mind fogging, his tongue lolling out of his mouth—

A kick landed in James' throat and he spun off his friend.

Before he could stand, a boot heel slammed his chest, flattening him to the ground.

"Look at me," said the girl.

Hook jerked and struggled, foaming at the mouth.

"*Look* at me," the girl repeated.

James thrashed and grunted, but she didn't relent.

Slowly the fight went out of him, his unfocused eyes losing heat, his breaths deepening. The color came back to his cheeks. His lips softened, no longer retracted over his teeth. At last he could see.

"Kyma," he whispered.

"Hi, James," said his princess.

Hook looked at Aladdin, specked in James' blue blood.

"Rhian's magic . . . ," James rasped. "It's Evil . . ."

"Give it to me," Kyma ordered.

For a moment, James didn't understand. Then he saw the clarity in his princess's eyes.

"No! That's madness!" Aladdin cried, going for her—

But Kyma shot him a glower that stayed him in place.

In the shadows of Good's castle, she lowered to her knees in the grass, bent over James, under the faintest halo of moonlight.

Hook shook his head, as if he couldn't dare do what she was asking.

"Give it to me," Kyma repeated, softly, sternly.

"No . . . ," James begged.

Kyma put her lips to his. For as long as he could, he resisted, holding on to the demon inside him. But Kyma waited patiently, her mouth on his, until James knew he had no choice. He breathed Rhian's soul into her, a cold-fire fury surrendered fully to his princess. She pulled off Hook, letting the School Master's spirit rise and roil inside her, a wild, destructive beast . . .

But Rhian's Evil thrived only in the hearts of those vulnerable to it.

Little by little, it cooled and diminished inside the princess, until it was nothing but an empty wind rattling around her bones. Kyma raised her neck and breathed out a weak tuft of smoke that sputtered into the night and trailed away.

FAITHFUL SOLDIERS

Aladdin sighed.

Kyma helped James up, the two arm in arm—

Shouts resounded from the field ahead.

Rafal was throwing man-wolves off his brother, but instead of thanking Rafal, Rhian clobbered him, his soldiers following suit and assaulting the man-wolves before Rafal's students came bounding into the fray. Reduced to their fists, brother and brother traded punches, then head-butted and clawed at each other, Rafal wrestling Rhian under him, trying to plead reason into his twin, Rhian lashing out and flipping him over, pounding his face into mud. Brothers exchanged useless blows. So did their armies. All around, the field was slippery muck, tripping both Good and Evil off their feet, foiling the battle, until the Great War for the school was nothing but pointless stalemate.

Hook assessed all this, lost for words.

"Fools everywhere you look," cracked a deep voice. "Maybe I am the One after all."

Hook turned to see the Pirate Captain, green eyes twinkling beneath his wide hat, the Blackpool headmaster dressed in black. He'd grown the beginnings of a black beard too, suddenly looking more man than boy.

James nearly jumped out of his skin. "Where you bee—"

"Pan's here somewhere," the Captain relayed, Kyma and Aladdin sidling in to hear. "Found his green vines around a young soldier who'd been turned to gold by the school gates. He must be with Midas."

"Let's find the rat," Hook resolved. "Laddy, come with us. Kyma, stay here and keep an eye out!"

Aladdin joined Hook and the Captain, heading off towards the School Masters' tower.

Kyma watched them go, a tribe of boys without her.

Some things never change, she thought.

Out of the corner of her vision, movement drew her attention across Halfway Bay.

Two shadows waded into the water, due west, a fair distance from the fighting.

She stepped closer, squinting through fog for a closer view . . .

Then a cloud came across the moon and all she saw was darkness.

14.

"Where'd you get those Wish Fish eggs?" Peter Pan demanded of Midas, jabbing him in the rib with a heavy broken stick as they waded into the bay. "Show me!"

"What Wish Fish eggs?" Midas said, feigning cluelessness. He hesitated, peering across the water at shadows of warring armies. He needed to find Rafal. At least the School Master had a soul. He'd made a mistake abandoning him for a murderer—

Peter slapped him. Midas fell backwards onto the bank. "Don't *lie*," Pan hissed. "I heard the girl say it in the tower. That you used Wish Fish eggs to get that gold touch. Now show me where you *found* them."

Midas crawled back onto the shore. "I'm done with all that—"

Peter pressed the lethal end of the stick against his heart. "Take me to the Wish Fish nest or I kill you."

But Midas didn't know where the Wish Fish eggs came from. Rufius had gifted them to him when Midas needed to spin straw into gold and Rufius had said nothing about where he found the eggs. *Or had he?* Midas recalled his rambling . . . something about a black-leafed tree . . . near Evil . . .

Slowly Midas raised his eyes to a twisted oak down the shore, its squiggly leaves the color of coal.

"There," Midas breathed, pointing to the water in front of it.

"What you waiting for, Gold Touch Boy?" Pan said. "Go *get* them for me."

Midas stared at him, confused. "Me? But—"

"First law of Neverland. Pans stay outta water in case there's mermaids." Peter drove Midas with the stick, towards the water near the tree. "Bring the eggs back. Every last one. And don't think about eating them yourself."

FALL OF THE SCHOOL FOR GOOD AND EVIL

Give him what he wants, Midas told himself. *Stay alive and find a way to Rafal—*

He jumped into the bay.

Beneath the water, night's ink left nothing to see. He focused his mind and, little by little, his gold touch glowed through his fingertip like a torch. He scanned the water: balls of kelp tumbling by, crabs burrowing into the sandy floor, a beaver breaststroking . . . Suddenly, a fluorescing cyclone of silver spun past. For a second, he thought it was a giant fish, then realized it was a *thousand* fish, ducking and weaving, a school on the move. Midas pointed his finger from where they'd come and there it was. A spongy, round nest packed with thousands of sky-blue bubbles, each the size of a beetle, glowing by their own light. If only he could stuff his face with them and wish his way home. But he knew better. All the Bad Things happening to him now were punishment for eating those eggs the first time. A golden touch balanced by Evil after Evil. How many eggs had he swallowed? Hundreds. Thousands. This was only the beginning, then. The beginning of the Bad Things . . . And how many *more* Bad Things had he accumulated with the wickedness of his actions? Betraying friends. Lying. Cheating. Turning people to gold. Guilt and shame consumed him, with no way to atone. What he would give to be free. To find a way out of this dead end and start over. But instead, he had only one route. Give Pan the eggs or die. He was losing breath. He had to make a choice . . .

He dove and grabbed the nest. *Let Pan have them*, he thought. *Bad Things would come.* Quickly, he launched towards the surface, afraid what Wish Fish would do if they caught him—

Midas choked a scream.

A pack of creatures were rushing in his direction.

Gold masks . . . human torsos . . . tails of . . . *fish* . . .

Mermaids!

They fanned into formation, a wall of monsters, weapons strapped across chests, long nails out to snare him—

Midas flung out of the lake and collapsed onto dry land with a shriek. He curled his feet to him in fetal position, away from the water, the nest of eggs still tucked under his arm.

"I'm alive . . . ," Midas wheezed. "I'm still alive . . ."

A shadow draped over him, wielding something long and sharp.

Slowly he lifted his eyes and didn't see anyone there.

"When a Lost Boy serves his purpose, it's time for him to grow up," spoke a voice.

Midas spun.

Peter gave him a sad smile. "Only there is no growing up in my world."

He stabbed Midas through the heart with the stick.

Shock and awe flooded Midas' veins. The Reader's gray eyes clouded, watching his killer back away. But instead of pain, there was warmth. And in this warmth, an understanding: This is why he'd been brought to this world. To be more than just a boy in Gavaldon. To have an awfully big adventure, even if this is how it came to an end. Good Things and Bad Things in balance. But this wasn't The End, Midas knew. Death was just another adventure. And one day, he would be brought back here, in another time, in another life, by the School Master who would surely win this war. The One who deserved to win. The One who would rule Good and Evil to balance. With a last breath, Midas spoke his name . . .

"Rafal."

His body went limp, rolling off the bank, into shallow water.

Peter waded in and snatched the nest of Wish Fish eggs from under his arm. With a crow of victory, he tipped the eggs towards his mouth.

I wish to be the One—

Two hands threw Pan to the shore, the eggs flying into the lake.

"Stay away from the water!" a voice cried. "Mermaids in there! They came to kill you!"

Dazed, Pan watched a thousand blue orbs sink into the lake. His eyes raised to Botic Lesso, once his favorite Lost Boy, standing over him, a crown of white coral on his head.

Slowly Pan stood, his shadow unfurling over Botic, taller, taller, until Botic was subsumed in it. The two boys were alone, the sounds of war echoing from the other side of the lake.

"Mermaids, huh?" Pan nodded down at Midas' body. "Midas was down there a long time and didn't make a peep about mermaids. Yet here you are, wearing the mermaids' *crown.* Strange . . . Even stranger is that you're far from Neverland, when I gave you strict orders to stay in Neverland and protect Hook and the prisoners. Prisoners who have all since *escaped.*"

Botic held out his hands. "Listen, I'm on your side. The mermaids gave me this crown because they think I'm on theirs—"

"You know what I think? I think you're lying to me," Pan sneered. "I think the Lost Boys put you up to this because they want me back. I think they sent you with your phony tale of mermaids and that fake crown to thwart me from being the One. The lot of you fawning, incompetent twits can't live without me! You all hope I'll fail and come slinking back to Neverland. Do you really think I'm meant to be nothing but a master of peons? That I'm meant to spend my life *bored*?"

"I came on my own—" Botic defended.

"Funny, all of a sudden I can't remember your name. Because I don't remember the names of *peons*. That's right. You're not my Lost Boy anymore. You're a nobody. In fact, you have no right to a name at all," Pan lashed. "So here's what's going to happen. I'm going to go in that water and get my Wish Fish eggs back. And if there's no mermaids, like you and I both know, then I'm going to take my time cutting your throat with that crown you're wearing. So if you are lying to me, now's your chance to beg for mercy . . . *Peter Boy*."

He spat the last words, flecking Botic's face.

The tension went out of Botic's spine. Instead, a cold calm glazed his violet eyes. He stared deep into Pan's.

"Go and see for yourself," he said.

Pan gnashed his teeth at him and leapt in the water.

He couldn't see a thing, his field of view blacked out. Then he noticed light from the lake floor and spotted the Wish Fish eggs, glowing underwater like luminescent pearls, bunched up against the overturned nest. Peter scooped them back into the nest, careful not to squish the blue balls or miss a single one, because who knew how many he'd need to make a wish as big as his come true? He swiped the last few, ready to spring towards the surface and deal with that traitorous, no-name scab—

A storm of silver slammed into him and he crashed back, only to be bludgeoned from the other side by swirling phosphorescent scales. Pan clung to the nest, kicking at a light storm of Wish Fish, yanking himself free with his remaining air, just long enough to surge upwards . . .

. . . right into a mermaid's claws.

Peter's scream was snuffed out, the female mermaid crushing him by the throat. Pan threw out a fist, hitting her in the stomach, knocking her off him. But now there were more mermaids coming, ten, twenty, thirty, armed with weapons. He couldn't breathe, his lungs run out. And now the Wish Fish were coming round too, spotlighting their prey, about to attack him once more. *Botic!* he cried uselessly into water. *Botic, save me!*

But the boy wasn't coming. And there was no way to save himself, this far outnumbered. Not unless . . . With a last gasp, Peter swung the nest up and dumped the eggs down his throat, hundreds, thousands, swallowing and swallowing until there were none left, even as mermaids seized hold of him, spears and sabers raised. He had to make a wish. Not a wish for power this time. A wish to save himself. But in that wish . . . there would *be* power. Pan leered triumphantly at the mermaids. *Poor Midas.* The boy hadn't wished big enough.

Pan thrust out his hand—

Gold exploded from his palm, a titanic wave, turning every mermaid and Wish Fish to metal. But more than that: the lake clotted to gold too, every last drop of water become precious stone, so that all things living were fossilized and gilded in place. Only Pan could move within it, the stone liquefying at his touch, his body lifting effortlessly through solid gold, until he bunted his head through the surface and saw that his powers extended far beyond the bay. Indeed, all of the School for Good and Evil had turned to gold, both castles paved into aurous monuments, towers cased in flaxen smoothness, students and soldiers warring on balconies petrified to ore. So too were the armies gilded and immobilized, teeth bared and weapons raised, all circling Rafal and Rhian, stalled midair as they flew at each other, two School Masters who once reigned, frozen in perpetual war.

Pan looked out at his land of toy soldiers.

No one could contest his place as master now.

His twin rivals included.

Maybe the whole Woods should be like this, Pan grinned.

But there was still one force higher than him.

A force that had given him magic and then taken it away.

A force that must be dealt with, once and for all.

Pan stepped over Midas' gold-embalmed body and headed for the School Masters' tower.

15.

Two brothers, eternal once more.

Trapped in a golden pose of war.

Still, they can see, hear, sense.

Instead of a leader's rise . . .

A school fallen.

They languish together in moonlight.

Once upon a time, they were this shiny and new, only flesh and bone, standing before the Storian which had summoned them over all others.

It gave them the oath.

School Masters, put to the test.

But there was someone else in the tower that day.

A dying old man, dark red curls, scanty and thin, freckles clumped across his leathery face.

Hunched in the shadows, like a warning.

Something terrible had happened to him.

Because he'd failed his test.

Just as something terrible has happened to the brothers.

If only they'd asked who he was.

If only they'd learned his name.

Two might be on their way to the tower now.

Instead of a Pan.

16.

The Pen is the only thing he cannot turn to gold.

Pan discovers this after he finds his way into the Storian's den. It isn't as easy as before. The fairies, wherever they are, have been cast to metal, so there is no magic dust to fly him; instead, he walks across the gilded lake, the water solid under his feet. When he reaches the gold-turned tower, he touches his hands along the base until he finds the outlines of a door. The door glows and opens on its own, recognizing his touch, as if the Storian expects him. He walks up the staircase, every step, every wall, every bookcase that lines the chamber, paved to gold. Then, as he nears the top of the stairs . . . he stops.

There are people in his way.

James Hook.

The Pirate Captain of Blackpool.

And a third boy, scrawny and brown, who he faintly recognizes as Hook's companion.

FAITHFUL SOLDIERS

All three are statues, stopped mid-stride as they'd ascended the steps, no doubt come looking for him. Pan smiles and runs his hand over Hook's gold face. If only James had learned the lesson that a thousand Hooks had learned before . . . Pan always *wins*.

He'll find a good place to put James' statue, Peter thinks.

A warning to those who dare take him on.

When he reaches the chamber, nothing is moving except the Pen, still a slash of silver steel, flitting over an open book, neither Pen nor pages touched by Pan's magic. Peter leans in, watching the Storian paint a picture of him as he is now, wheatish curls and far-apart eyes, bound in his tangle of vines, green the only dose of color in a tower full of gold. Words ink beneath.

Pan had come to be School Master.
Demanding the Pen give him the oath.
He wasn't the first Pan to do so, of course.

Pan stares at the page.

"Huh?" he says, out loud.

The Pen writes nothing more.

Then something hits the ground behind Peter.

A book, tumbled off a bookcase.

It is a solid gold brick, but when he picks it up, it melts to his touch, back to a wood-bound tome of parchment, the title carved in the cover:

THE TALE OF PAN AND PEN

Peter opens the book.

It is a familiar story. Every hundred years, the North Star descends to earth, slipping into graveyards, combing through boys who never grew up. In these souls, she finds the best one. The boy who deserves a second chance at life. A hundred years in the prime of youth. *This is how the first Pan was born and all the ones after,* the Storian writes.

Pan is bored by a tale he already knows.

Then there is a single line, all alone on the next page.

But do you know how Pans die?

Pan's heart thrums faster.

He'd never considered the question.

A hundred years of youth is a long time. Long enough to not have to think about death. He assumes that when death comes, it is gentle and loving, the same way the North Star births a Pan into the world.

He keeps reading.

The first Pan ruled Neverland for years and years, lording over his Lost Boys, terrorizing pirates, dominating the island and claiming every inch of it in his name. Pan, the king. Pan, the conquistador. Every new pirate challenge dismissed, each Captain Hook sent to a watery grave.

And yet, little by little the thrill wore away, the Storian says. *Pan grew bored, longing to be more than a master of peons.*

Reading this, Peter's palms are cold and clammy. He turns the page, leaving little wet fingerprints.

Yes, he was King of Neverland.
But now he wanted to know . . .
Who made Neverland?

This is how the first Pan comes to know of the Storian.

The Pen with powers bigger than a Pan. The Pen protected by a school with the loyalty and respect of the Woods. It was only a matter of time before Pan learned that the world is bigger than his island. That he is not god of his realm.

He knows he should leave it be. That he should be happy

with his lot. With his second chance at life and his island of dreams. This is what his soul tells him.

But there is also his shadow, the Storian points out.

The shadow of his first life. The shadow that never grew up. The shadow that is bitterness and anger and Evil to all of his soul's Good.

All along, Pan kept his soul and shadow in balance. The way any child does, effortlessly, without thought. This is how Neverland stays at peace, year after year.

But now, the first seeds of the adult that never was take root.

The shadow rises.

It wants the Storian.

Pan sails across the ocean, shadow at the helm, scheming and plundering until he conquers the school the way he once did Neverland. When he stands before the Pen, it does not fight. Instead, it lays down a challenge.

> *In exchange for immortality*
> *In exchange for eternal youth*
> *I choose you.*
> *A soul that is as Good as it is Evil.*
> *But every School Master faces a test.*
> *Yours is balance.*

FAITHFUL SOLDIERS

Between the Goodness of your soul
And the Evil of its shadow.
Neither side must win out.
Tip the balance and the test is failed.
You will wither and die.
You will be replaced.
Raise your hand to seal this oath.

Pan obeys and the Storian seals his oath in blood.

But the oath does not last long.

The first Pan fails his test. He is dead within the year. And the same with the next Pan and the next, for it is a Pan's nature to see how far he can fly. Not all Pans make it before the Pen, some foiled along the way. But those that do repeat the story. Each takes the oath of soul and shadow. Each tips towards Evil. Yet, no warnings are passed down in Neverland. No memories of the mistake. This is what happens when children don't grow up. Present and Past never meet. Nor does the Woods remember, for a hundred years is a long time, each Pan that finds his way to school an aberration between reigns of peace. So it goes, round and round again, until the last Pan comes usurping, a young lad with dark red curls and a dusting of freckles.

He, too, stands before the Storian to take the oath. He, too, fails and withers to die, until the new School Masters find him.

Twin brothers who go on to rule a long time.

But far far away, another Pan was rising, the Storian writes.

The last page is a picture of the North Star, clasping a sleeping child in its arms, with sun-dyed curls and far-apart eyes, his nose a tight little button.

Beneath the painting of Peter are the tale's last words.

Maybe this one would be different.

Pan slowly closes the book.

Run away from here, his soul thinks. Run back to Neverland and do not return. Sing a song of warning that all boys in their graves will hear . . .

But his shadow is already peeling away from him, gliding across the chamber and circling the Pen hungrily.

Pan is no match for his own shadow.

The Pen speaks the terms, its voice warm and ageless.

The same vow it's given to every Pan.

"Raise your hand to seal this oath," it ends.

"At last," Pan crows, victorious.

He shows his palm—

The Pen slashes into it, spilling his blood, the promise sealed.

His finger pulses with magic once more, his powers returned

and greater than before. He doesn't just have a golden touch, but an infinite one. Nothing bad can happen to him now. He is invincible, immortal, with the whole of the Woods yet to be conquered. Outside the sun peeks between the castles, crowning a new day. He is not like the other Pans. There is nothing to foil him.

Then a subtle sound echoes, almost imperceptible, like a bird's feathers through air—

He spins and sees the Storian an inch from his eye, its tip pointed at his pupil, watching him, taunting him, a reminder that there is still a power greater than his.

Pan grits his teeth.

He swats it out of the air, blasting a wave of gold—

The Pen gilds instantly and plummets to the floor with a clink.

Quiet fills the tower, nothing else alive.

Pan is suspicious for a moment, that the Storian would surrender so easily. He flicks the Pen on the floor, but it does not move, the gold as solid and impregnable as everything else he's claimed with his touch.

He picks up the pen and slips it behind his ear.

There are no more threats to face.

He is School Master now, oath taken, test passed, powers bestowed and unmatched.

He looks out the window at his domain. All those from

Neverland who came before him were feckless saps. He is warrior, king, lord. Pan of Pans.

And yet . . .

Something disturbs him.

It is too still now.

No Peter Boys to pester him.

No pirates to challenge him.

No School Masters or rivals to vanquish.

Even his shadow sits bored on the floor.

That boredom snakes deeper through his bones, binding him like his green vines. Will the rest of the Woods go down so easy? What will he do with a kingdom of gold? Who will stand to oppose him? Who will make his time worthwhile? He looks out at the world, but there is nothing to see.

It happens without thinking, his steps padding out of the chamber and down the stairs . . .

"Hello, James," he coos, looking Hook in the eye.

There is something comforting about addressing his old nemesis. About standing face-to-face with him and having a battle. He touches James' cheek. Slaps him. "Fight me, coward." He raps his fists against Hook's head with no resistance. "Come on, fight me!" He punches Hook in the stomach, bruising his own hand. Peter slams both palms against him. *Fight me, you loser!*

He jams his glowing finger in Hook's face and casts away the gold, so he can see the fear in James' eyes when he kills him—

Instead James seizes Pan by the throat and smashes him to the stairs.

"What have you done!" Hook cries, scanning the gold tower, the statues of the Pirate Captain and Aladdin, the gilded carnage out the window. He chokes Pan harder. "What have you *done*!"

Pan's shadow laughs on the wall. "You fool . . . I'm School Master now!" Peter crows in Hook's face, rasping out breaths. "Immortal . . . indestructible . . . forever and ever . . . You have no power over me! Nothing does!"

Hook's fingers come off Pan's throat. At first, he's ashen, scared. Then his face changes. He arches a brow. "You sure about that, Panny Boy?"

Because there's a second shadow rising on the wall, long and sharp at both ends—

Pan grasps for the Storian behind his ear.

It's not there anymore.

His eyes lift to the Pen, a golden lance, rising over him.

"Looks like you've already failed your test, School Master," says Hook.

The gold melts off the Storian, restoring the steel, the Pen

341

turning its lethal tip to the shadow on the wall.

Pan's face blanches. "No . . . *no!*"

His shadow flees—

The Pen impales it against the stone.

The shadow jerks and writhes, and as it does, the youth seeps out of Peter Pan's body, his skin shriveling and hanging loose off his bones, his muscles bloating, his blond curls shedding in patches, until he staggers out of James' hands towards the window, teeth rotted, eyes liverish, waving and snapping his fingers, searching uselessly for magic. But the years are flying, the Storian giving him what the North Star held back, Pan aging faster, faster, his shadow fainter, fainter until it's lost in morning light. James stands to see Pan at the window, facing him. Peter twitches one last time, mouthing Hook's name, before he lets out a sigh and slumps over the edge, head and arms hanging out into the sun, a gold-soaked corpse ready to fly.

17.

The gold seeps away like a wave receding, the school returned to its wreckage.

But war does not resume. Instead, soldiers and students peer down at their bodies of flesh and blood, as the last sparkles of gold recede, leaving in their place a second chance at life, as if all have been plucked from the grave by the merciful North Star and renewed with youth.

So too do the School Masters surrender their battle.

Both look at each other, chastened, exchanging an unspoken wish to undo all their mistakes. To bring this tale back to the beginning. Rhian's face warms, regaining its color, his gold hair softly wild once more. Rafal's cheeks cool to a delicate pallor, his hair rising to prickly silver spikes.

"Brother," says Rhian.

"Brother," says Rafal.

They reach for each other, a love renewed—

"He's dead!" a soldier cries. "Pan's *dead*!"

Heads turn to James Hook, holding Peter in his arms, the green vines around Pan's body tarnished brown.

All bow their head, not just in respect to the dead, but because they sense now who's responsible. For the Storian gleams high and sharp in the window of the School Masters' tower, an all-seeing eye. The Pen turns this eye from Pan and fixes it on the other two responsible for this war.

Rafal and Rhian know it is their turn to meet their fate, whatever it will be.

Rafal holds out his hand.

Rhian takes it.

Together, they walk towards the tower along the lake, passing Princess Kyma, who is kneeled by Midas' body, lying peacefully in shallow waters. Both School Masters give the Reader heavy looks, but continue on their march, for it is the Pen that will do the reckoning now, instead of their souls.

Kyma watches the School Masters go.

By the time she looks down, Midas' body is gone, stolen away by shimmering shadows, fishtails kicking him deeper and deeper, further and further, to rest in peace, far from the tyranny of men.

18.

When Rhian walks up the stairs, listening to his brother's steps match his, he is calm and at ease. The blue of his eyes is clear, unblemished. His hair has an unburdened freedom.

Whatever the Pen has to say, he will abide by it. Too much has happened to defend his actions or desire an outcome in his favor. He and his brother have both failed their test. If the Pen punishes them both, it is warranted. If it chooses a single brother to be the One and banishes the other . . . so be it. The

Storian is law of this world, not the School Master. Rhian will respect its word.

And yet, from the way Rafal is holding his hand, tightly, anxiously, Rhian senses they both cling to another hope. That the One is, in fact . . . Two. That they've passed the Pen's test by acknowledging their failings and restoring balance between them. He glances at Rafal's cool green eyes and icicles of hair and for the first time, sees not an opposite or enemy, but the other half of himself. At last they can rule the way they were supposed to. The Pen just has to give them a chance.

At the top of the stairs, it waits over the open storybook, the Storian standing between the seams of the School Master's tale, like a king seated stiffly in a throne.

On a blank page, words are already written.

Two had come.
But One would leave.
This was the only path to balance.

Twin hopes are dashed.

Rhian's skin flushes and he lets out a cry. "It's not true! There is another path!"

But the Pen has begun to draw a face.

The face of the One who will take its oath.

The next and only School Master.

"Whatever happens, brother, we must accept it," says Rafal.

Rhian nods, tears stinging his eyes.

Because he knows who the Pen will draw.

The outlines come first: the chin they both share, the same smooth, high-boned cheeks and pinned-back ears, but it is with the hair that it diverges, pulling lines up in sharp, knife-like slivers—

Rafal comforts his brother. "I will protect you, Rhian. You will always have a place at school. Even if you're no longer its Master."

Rhian says nothing, his eyes fixed on the colorless drawing.

The Pen speaks the oath. *"In exchange for immortality . . . in exchange for eternal youth . . . a test for One to redeem himself . . ."*

But now Rhian is trembling, his neck red with sweat.

"Wait—" Rafal says to the Pen, thrusting a hand out, silencing the vows from proceeding. "Rhian, look at me." He turns to his brother, his breath faster now. "You don't have to be banished. You can stay. You can be a Dean or teacher or anything you want in my school—"

"*Your* school?" Rhian hisses softly.

The fire is rising within him. The cold dragon flame he thought had been snuffed out. Rhian looks at his brother with frost-blue eyes and Rafal's full body tenses, his own green eyes alert.

"Not like that. It's my school in name only—" Rafal presses.

Rhian lashes out like a snake. "What is my name, then? The *Fallen*? The *Failed*?"

"We are two impure hearts. Good and Evil in both," says Rafal. "We are the same, brother."

"We are *not* the same," Rhian strikes. "You said it yourself. *Your* school."

"We were made as one!" Rafal says.

"Then why are *you* the One?" asks Rhian.

"Because I need you like you need me," Rafal pleads. "That's what love is, Rhian. Accepting each of us is as Good as we are Evil. We'll always be together, whatever the Pen says—"

"I can't," Rhian whispers.

The light in Rafal's eyes dims. "You can't what?"

"Be *Good*," says Rhian.

He sweeps the Storian out of the air and stabs his brother in the heart.

Rafal unleashes a cry of sadness, reaching for his twin.

Rhian steps back and lets him fall.

He stands over his brother, his face like a marble mask, watching Rafal breathe his last, his dying brother's hand stretching towards the sky and slowly falling, the Storian lodged in his chest. Whatever betrayal and horror pools in his twin's green eyes, Rhian reflects back without guilt. Rafal thought he could rule without him. That Rhian would go quietly into the night, the loser.

Maybe he is Evil.

100%, natural-born Evil.

But he is not a loser.

He pulls the Storian out of his brother and it rips out of his hand, spinning into the air.

Rhian is not scared. He tears open his shirt and bares his chest, expecting the Pen to kill him for violating its word, to dispense with him like it did Pan.

But instead, the Storian continues to write, spilling color into its painting, the milky-white skin, the stiff, silver hair, all the signatures of Rafal, until it gets to the eyes—

Which are blue.

Rhian blue.

His own color, painted in his brother's face.

A finger on his right hand prickles and he sees the tip flickering with glow, alive with a sorcerer's magic.

Now he understands.

The painting was never Rafal.

It just wasn't *finished*.

He puts his fingerglow to his hair, turning it to silver spikes.

He puts his hand to his skin, draining it of warmth and color.

He's become the Pen's painting. The Storian's tale his mirror.

"*In exchange for immortality,*" the Pen begins. "*In exchange for eternal youth . . .*"

This is why the Saders saw three School Masters instead of one, he realizes.

Because there *were* three School Masters.

Each given the oath.

Pan first.

Then Rafal.

Now the last who would endure.

Only Marialena had seen the full truth of how it would end.

Only she knew how Evil this tale would be.

That two must die for One to rule.

Rhian raises his hand to seal the oath.

Blood sprays across the page.

19.

A year later, the School Master sits in the Theater of Tales.

He wears calming blue robes and a steel mask that covers every inch of his face except for his young, sparkling blue eyes and his silver hair loosely rumpled. To all in his presence, he is the blending of two brothers, Rafal and Rhian both. His high glass chair straddles the crack that runs down the middle of the stone stage.

"Evil hasn't won a single tale in the past year," Professor Humburg addresses him, Evil's Dean slouched in the warped wooden benches on Evil's side of the theater.

"And that's a cause for alarm?" Dean Mayberry responds, a dark, elegant woman perched across the aisle in Good's pink and blue pews. "From what I remember during my *previous* term here . . . Evil was on a long losing streak."

"Evil was on the rise before last year's upheaval. A new School Master was supposed to bring *balance* to this school," Dean Humburg counters. "Evil losing every one of the Pen's tales since suggests otherwise."

"With my return, you can expect that streak to continue," Dean Mayberry touts. "Truth is, I came back as Dean because in the new School Master, I sensed restraint and order and discipline and an attention to Good, where there seemed to be a lack of it before."

Humburg peers up at the School Master onstage and his shiny blue eyes. "I see why you would think that's the case."

The School Master finally speaks. "The Pen elevated a single School Master in the name of unity. It was the Storian's word that felled my brother and brought me here. The death of my own blood is a terrible price to pay for peace and balance. But it's that price that makes this balance sacred and personal. And hasn't there been balance this past year? Haven't I shown equal favor to both schools in my time so far? The Pen reflects the School Master's soul, so if you respect me, then you must also respect the Pen to move our world forward in the way it thinks best. A stretch of Good victories will be balanced by Evil ones soon enough, as it always has before."

"And won't *that* be the day," Humburg mutters, eyeing Mayberry.

"Speaking of imbalances, there is the matter of the stymphs," says Maxime, the centaur who teaches Animal Communication. "They've been agitated of late, snapping at the Nevers who they usually favor. And the stymph that you rode to spread your brother's ashes to sea tried to eat a Nevergirl during Forest Groups—"

"Stymphs are wild creatures that have moods and vagaries of their own," the School Master dismisses. "Anything else?"

"I hesitate to speak up since I'm only a Forest Group leader," says Minerva, a tall nymph with fluorescing hair and electric-yellow lips, "but I overheard the Evergirls whispering that Princess Kyma has a visitor at night. A boy who sneaks in on a flying pirate ship."

"Oh, what nonsense, Minerva, and shame on you for bringing it up here after we already discussed this!" Mayberry sours. "I told you. Kyma is a rule follower. Sneaking in pirates after curfew is beyond her."

"So was running away from school to join said pirates," Humburg notes. (Mayberry purses her lips.)

"Has anyone seen this mysterious boy?" says the School Master. "Or his ship?"

"*No,*" Mayberry moans. "I kept watch last night, depriving myself of sleep, and all I saw was a night's worth of clouds."

The nymph responds: "The girls say the ship *hides* in the clouds—"

"*For heaven's sake*, Minerva!" Mayberry barks.

The School Master taps his chin with his thumb. "Kyma furtive with a boy . . . If it's true, Aladdin would know. Did anyone ask him?"

"He says it's lies," Maxime volunteers.

Mayberry and Minerva swivel to the centaur.

"Boys were teasing him about it during my class," Maxime says briskly.

"Then the matter is settled," the School Master resolves. "If that's all—"

"What about Blackbeard?" Professor Sethi prompts.

"Pirates really are the theme today," the School Master murmurs. "Why should Blackbeard be a concern of ours? Unless he's going to appear in your Physical Training course and menace all your Everboys . . ."

Sethi responds: "The former Pirate Captain of Blackpool has amassed a crew of rebels, taken Neverland for himself, and declared himself king. You and your brother knew the Captain. Surely you can dissuade him from illegally usurping an island of innocent boys."

"If there's one thing I know about the Pirate Captain, it's that he has a heart warmer than Pan's, regardless of what he calls himself," says the School Master. "His weakness is a lust for power, of course. But those who lust for power in Neverland don't fare well in the end. The same will apply to Blackbeard. My intervention isn't required."

A buzz rises overhead along with the rumble of footsteps.

"Ah, seems our time is at an end," says the School Master, standing from his seat with a smile. "A new day of class begins."

He returns to his tower with a firm plan for the morning.

There is the matter of racking through his spell books for something to subdue a rogue stymph . . . then missives to the Kingdom Council to keep their eye on Blackbeard should he begin angling beyond Neverland for power . . . then a trip to Drupathi to see if there's any new young Nevers he should keep his eye on. With Evil's losing streak growing, he needs to improve the quality of the Nevers' next class. He glances at the Storian, in the middle of a tale about a gluttonous boy on the hunt for a golden goose. It does not seem promising for the lad, who only graduated from the School for Evil a few years earlier. The School Master tries to ignore the sounds of the Pen's calm, crisp scrawl. He will turn things around. He just needs the right students. Perhaps even a return to Gavaldon for a bold new Reader . . .

But first, stymphs. He opens a chest of his best spellbooks—

"Whatever spell you're looking for, I hope it's better than what that old hag in the forest gave me," says a familiar voice.

The School Master turns to see a green-faced, black-winged fairy on the edge of the Storian's book.

"Her potion to turn me human was cheap magic. Only

lasted a few weeks," Marialena sighs.

"Pity," says the School Master.

"You could turn me back, you know," the fairy notes. "Evil helping Evil. Right, Rhian?"

"Rhian isn't my name." The School Master bends over the chest and goes back to his books. "I am only the School Master now. I favor neither side."

"Then I suppose it won't matter to you that Evil will never win as long as you're School Master. That your place here means Good is now invincible."

The School Master stops looking for a book.

"It knows what you did," says the fairy. "And it will balance the murder of your brother by making sure your side loses forever after. Unless you do something to correct it."

Slowly, the School Master raises his head.

"How do you know this?" he asks.

"Safe to say I see it the same way I foresaw your victory," she answers.

The School Master speaks nothing for a moment.

He leans against the wall, arms crossed over his blue robes.

"Unless I do something to 'correct it' . . ."

"You killed your twin ruthlessly and without mercy. You broke the bond of blood," Marialena says. "You proved once and for all that Evil can never love. To correct it, you would need to prove it *can*."

The School Master breaks into a grin. "Prove I can love? True love's kiss and an Ever After, you mean? To replace my brother? Oh, I think I've been down that path and am far happier off it—"

"A *different* kind of love," the fairy says intently. She springs off the table and hovers near his face. "A love so Evil, so destructive, so cold and calculated, that it flies in the face of Good's love and their Ever Afters. A love that only two purely Evil souls could sustain."

The School Master's smile dissipates.

"And this is possible?" he asks, color rearing in his cheeks. "That kind of love?"

The fairy glides closer, gazing into his eyes. "I don't know, Rhian. Is it?"

"Tell me." His breath quickens, his heart stoking. "What's his name? The one who I can love like this. Who is he?"

Marialena wags her wings in his face. "You should know better than to ask a seer questions."

The fire licks back into the School Master's eyes. He seals the hunger and yearning in its old cauldron, his manner cool, collected once more.

"Oh, I forgot to mention," he says, turning to his books. "I ordered your family released from Maidenvale. Wasn't that part of the prophecy too? That the new School Master would lift the Sader name to glory? Though I wonder whether they want you with their name at all anymore, seeing you've put them in jail *twice*. So maybe it's them meant for glory and not you. Wouldn't that be a twist?"

The fairy delivers a withering stare.

Spinning midair, she skims out of the tower, her reflection tinting the Storian green for the briefest moment, before she pauses at the window and glances back with the darkest eye.

"It's not a he. It's a '*she*.'"

The fairy dives into the morning.

Silence soaks the chamber where the School Master stands. He looks up at the Pen, which has paused its writing, its tip eyeing him with a wicked twinkle.

"She?" he says softly.

He unleashes a howl of laughter.

She!

He doubles over, laughing too hard to breathe.

That would be Evil's love indeed!

Slowly he stops laughing, thinking of the seriousness in the fairy's eyes.

Impossible.

How far from himself he'd have to be. How lost in his heart. What deviance! What perversion! *She!* That wouldn't be love. That would be something abominable . . . something far twisted and darker and alien to his soul . . . He might as well call himself Rafal . . .

No, he thinks, going to the window, looking out where she had flown. It was just her cruel jibe. A punishment for his own about her family.

His eyes lift to his Good and Evil castles, linked by a bridge.

Things are rebalanced now. He is at peace. He can feel it in his own heart. A heart that the Storian reflects in its tales.

The Pen will reward him soon.

It would forget all about what happened with his brother, just as he had.

He is alone forever and that is enough.

He doesn't need anyone else.

He is the One.

Good things are coming, thinks the School Master.

A golden age of Evil was ahead.

Now it's time to go to school!
Read an excerpt from *The School for Good and Evil*,
Book 1 in Soman Chainani's *New York Times* bestselling series.

3
The Great Mistake

Sophie opened her eyes to find herself floating in a foul-smelling moat, filled to the brim with thick black sludge. A gloomy wall of fog flanked her on all sides. She tried to stand, but her feet couldn't find bottom and she sank; sludge flooded her nose and burnt her throat. Choking for breath, she found something to grasp, and saw it was the carcass of a half-eaten goat. She gasped and tried to swim away but couldn't see an inch in front of her face. Screams echoed above and Sophie looked up. Streaks of motion— then a dozen bony birds crashed through the fog and dropped shrieking children into the moat. When their screams turned to splashes, another wave of birds came, then another, until every inch of sky was filled with falling children. Sophie glimpsed a bird dive straight for her and she swerved, just in time to get a cannonball splash of slime in her face.

She wiped the glop out of her eye and came face-to-face with a boy. The first thing she noticed was he had no shirt. His chest was puny and pale, without the hope of muscle. From his small head jutted a long nose, spiky teeth, and black hair that drooped over beady eyes. He looked like a sinister little weasel.

"The bird ate my shirt," he said. "Can I touch your hair?"

Sophie backed up.

"They don't usually make villains with princess hair," he said, dog-paddling towards her.

Sophie searched desperately for a weapon—a stick, a stone, a dead goat—

"Maybe we could be bunk mates or best mates or some kind of mates," he said, inches from her now. It was like Radley had turned into a rodent and developed courage. He reached out his scrawny hand to touch her and Sophie readied a punch to the eye, when a screaming child dropped between them. Sophie took off in the opposite direction and by the time she glanced back,

THE GREAT MISTAKE

Weasel Boy was gone.

Through the fog, Sophie could see shadows of children treading through floating bags and trunks, hunting for their luggage. Those that managed to find them continued downstream, towards ominous howls in the distance. Sophie followed these floating silhouettes until the fog cleared to reveal the shore, where a pack of wolves, standing on two feet in bloodred soldier jackets and black leather breeches, snapped riding whips to herd students into line.

Sophie grasped the bank to pull herself out but froze when she caught her reflection in the moat. Her dress was buried beneath sludge and yolk, her face shined with stinky black grime, and her hair was home to a family of earthworms. She choked for breath—

"*Help!* I'm in the wrong sch—"

A wolf yanked her out and kicked her into line. She opened her mouth to protest, but saw Weasel Boy swimming towards her, yelping, "Wait for me!"

Quickly, Sophie joined the line of shadowed children, dragging their trunks through the fog. If any dawdled, a wolf delivered a swift crack, so she kept anxious pace, all the while wiping her dress, picking out worms, and mourning her perfectly packed bags far, far away.

The tower gates were made of iron spikes, crisscrossed with barbed wire. Nearing them, she saw it wasn't wire at all but a sea of black vipers that darted and hissed in her direction. With a squeak, Sophie scampered through and looked back at rusted words over the gates, held between two carved black swans:

THE SCHOOL FOR EVIL EDIFICATION AND PROPAGATION OF SIN

Ahead the school tower rose like a winged demon. The main tower, built of pockmarked black stone, unfurled through smoky clouds like a hulking torso. From the sides of the main tower jutted two thick, crooked spires, dripping with veiny red creepers like bleeding wings.

The wolves drove the children towards the mouth of the main tower, a long serrated tunnel shaped like a crocodile snout. Sophie felt chills as the tunnel grew narrower and narrower until she could barely see the child in front of her. She squeezed between two jagged stones and found herself in a leaky foyer that smelled of rotten fish. Demonic gargoyles pitched down from stone rafters, lit torches in their jaws. An iron statue of a bald, toothless hag brandishing an apple smoldered in the menacing firelight. Along the wall, a crumbly column had an enormous black letter *N* painted on it, decorated with wicked-faced imps, trolls, and

Harpies climbing up and down it like a tree. There was a bloodred *E* on the next column, embellished with swinging giants and goblins. Creeping along in the interminable line, Sophie worked out what the columns spelled out—N-E-V-E-R—then suddenly found herself far enough into the room to see the line snake in front of her. For the first time, she had a clear view of the other students and almost fainted.

One girl had a hideous overbite, wispy patches of hair, and one eye instead of two, right in the middle of her forehead. Another boy was like a mound of dough, with his bulging belly, bald head, and swollen limbs. A tall, sneering girl trudged ahead with sickly green skin. The boy in front of her had so much hair all over him he could have been an ape. They all looked about her age, but the similarities ended there. Here was a mass of the miserable, with misshapen bodies, repulsive faces, and the cruelest expressions she'd ever seen, as if looking for something to hate. One by one their eyes fell on Sophie and they found what they were looking for. The petrified princess in glass slippers and golden curls.

The red rose among thorns.

On the other side of the moat, Agatha had nearly killed a fairy.

She had woken under red and yellow lilies that appeared to be having an animated conversation. Agatha was sure she was the subject, for the lilies gestured brusquely at her with their leaves and buds. But then the matter seemed settled and the flowers hunched like fussing grandmothers and wrapped their stems around her wrists. With a tug, they yanked her to her feet and Agatha gazed out at a field of girls, blooming gloriously around a shimmering lake.

She couldn't believe what she was seeing. The girls grew right from the earth. First heads poked through soft dirt, then necks, then chests, then up and up until they stretched their arms into fluffy blue sky and planted delicate slippers upon the ground. But it wasn't the sight of sprouting girls that unnerved Agatha most. It was that these girls looked *nothing* like her.

Their faces, some fair, some dark, were flawless and glowed with health. They had shiny waterfalls of hair, ironed and curled like dolls', and they wore downy dresses of peach, yellow, and white, like a fresh batch of Easter eggs. Some fell on the shorter side, others were willowy and tall, but all flaunted tiny waists, slim legs, and slight shoulders. As the field flourished with new students, a team of three glitter-winged fairies awaited each one. Chiming and chinkling, they dusted the girls of dirt, poured them cups of honeybush tea, and tended to their trunks, which had sprung from the ground with their owners.

Where exactly these beauties were coming from, Agatha

hadn't the faintest idea. All she wanted was a dour or disheveled one to poke through so she wouldn't feel so out of place. But it was an endless bloom of Sophies who had everything she didn't. A familiar shame clawed at her stomach. She needed a hole to climb down, a graveyard to hide in, something to make them all go away—

That's when the fairy bit her.

"What the—"

Agatha tried to shake the jingling thing off her hand, but it flew and bit her neck, then her bottom. Other fairies tried to subdue the rogue as she yowled, but it bit them too and attacked Agatha again. Incensed, she tried to catch the fairy, but it moved lightning quick, so she hopped around uselessly while it bit her over and over until the fairy mistakenly flew into her mouth and she swallowed it. Agatha sighed in relief and looked up.

Sixty beautiful girls gaped at her. The cat in a nightingale's nest.

Agatha felt a pinch in her throat and coughed out the fairy. To her surprise, it was a boy.

In the distance, sweet bells rang out from the spectacular pink and blue glass castle across the lake. The teams of fairies all grabbed their girls by the shoulders, hoisted them into the air, and flew them across the lake towards the towers. Agatha saw her chance to escape, but before she could make a run for it, she felt herself lifted into the air by two girl fairies. As she flew away, she glanced back at the third, the fairy boy that had bitten her, who stayed firmly on the ground. He crossed his arms and shook his head, as if to say in no uncertain terms there'd been a terrible mistake.

When the fairies brought the girls down in front of the glass castle, they let go of their shoulders and let them proceed freely. But Agatha's two fairies held on and dragged her forward like a prisoner. Agatha looked back across the lake. *Where's Sophie?*

The crystal water turned to slimy moat halfway across the lake; gray fog obscured whatever lay on the opposite banks. If Agatha was to rescue her friend, she had to find a way to cross that moat. But first she needed to get away from these winged pests. She needed a diversion.

Mirrored words arched over golden gates ahead:

THE SCHOOL FOR GOOD
ENLIGHTENMENT AND ENCHANTMENT

Agatha caught her reflection in the letters and turned away. She hated mirrors and avoided them at all costs. (*Pigs and dogs don't sit around looking at themselves,* she thought.) Moving forward, Agatha glanced up at the frosted castle doors, emblazoned with two white swans. But as the doors opened and fairies herded the girls into a tight, mirrored corridor, the line came to a halt and a group of girls circled her like sharks.

They stared at her for a moment, as if expecting her to whip off her mask and reveal a princess underneath. Agatha tried to meet their stares, but instead met her own face reflected in the mirrors a thousand times and instantly glued her eyes to the marble floor. A few fairies buzzed to get the mass moving, but most just perched on the girls' shoulders and watched. Finally, one of the girls stepped forward, with waist-length gold hair, succulent lips, and topaz eyes. She was so beautiful she didn't look real.

"Hello, I'm Beatrix," she said sweetly. "I didn't catch your name."

"That's because I never said it," said Agatha, eyes pinned to the ground.

"Are you sure you're in the right place?" Beatrix said, even sweeter now.

Agatha felt a word swim into her mind—a word she needed, but was still too foggy to see.

"Um, I uh—"

"Perhaps you just swam to the wrong school," smiled Beatrix.

The word lit up in Agatha's head. *Diversion.*

Agatha looked up into Beatrix's dazzling eyes. "This is the School for Good, isn't it? The legendary school for beautiful and worthy girls destined to be princesses?"

"Oh," said Beatrix, lips pursed. "So you're not lost?"

"Or confused?" said another with Arabian skin and jet-black hair.

"Or blind?" said a third with deep ruby curls.

"In that case, I'm sure you have your Flowerground Pass," Beatrix said.

Agatha blinked. "My what?"

"Your *ticket* into the Flowerground," said Beatrix. "You know, the way we all got here. Only *officially* accepted students have tickets into the Flowerground."

All the girls held up large golden tickets, flaunting their names in regal calligraphy, stamped with the School Master's black-and-white swan seal.

"Ohhh, *that* Flowerground Pass," Agatha scoffed. She dug her hands in her pockets. "Come close and I'll show you."

The girls gathered suspiciously. Meanwhile Agatha's hands fumbled for a diversion—matches . . . coins . . . dried leaves . . .

"Um, closer."

Murmuring girls huddled in. "It shouldn't be this small,"

Beatrix huffed.

"Shrunk in the wash," said Agatha, scraping through more matches, melted chocolate, a headless bird (Reaper hid them in her clothes). "It's in here somewhere—"

"Perhaps you lost it," said Beatrix.

Mothballs . . . peanut shells . . . another dead bird . . .

"Or misplaced it," said Beatrix.

The bird? The match? Light the bird with the match?

"Or *lied* about having one at all."

"Oh, I feel it now—"

But all Agatha felt was a nervous rash across her neck—

"You know what happens to intruders, don't you," Beatrix said.

"Here it is—" *Do something!*

Girls crowded her ominously.

Do something now!

She did the first thing she thought of and delivered a swift, loud fart.

An effective diversion creates both chaos and panic. Agatha delivered on both counts. Vile fumes ripped through the tight corridor as squealing girls stampeded for cover and fairies swooned at first smell, leaving her a clear path to the door. Only Beatrix stood in her way, too shocked to move. Agatha took a step towards her and leaned in like a wolf.

"*Boo.*"

Beatrix fled for her life.

As Agatha sprinted for the door, she looked back with pride as girls collided into walls and trampled each other to escape. Fixed on rescuing Sophie, she lunged through the frosted doors, ran for the lake, but just as she got to it, the waters rose up in a giant wave and with a tidal crash, slammed her back through the doors, through screeching girls, until she landed on her stomach in a puddle.

She staggered to her feet and froze.

"Welcome, New Princess," said a floating, seven-foot nymph. It moved aside to reveal a foyer so magnificent Agatha lost her breath. "Welcome to the School for Good."

READ THEM ALL.

SCHOOL FOR GOOD AND EVIL: BOOKS 1–6

SCHOOL FOR GOOD AND EVIL: A PREQUEL DUOLOGY

EVER NEVER HANDBOOK

THE OLD FAIRY TALES ARE DEAD.

THE INSTANT *NEW YORK TIMES* BESTSELLER

Beasts
AND
Beauty

DANGEROUS TALES

Bestselling Author of *The School for Good and Evil*

SOMAN CHAINANI